more . . .

"Exciting . . . a classic Patterson page-turner."
—**TheBookHaven.net**

"The most suspenseful hospital drama since *Coma*."
—**FantasticFiction.com**

"Newcomers and devoted fans alike will love the fifth entry in the prolific Patterson's latest detective series . . . Patterson, known for a steady stream of artful thrillers, again delivers the fast-paced action that has won him millions of readers." —*Justice* **magazine**

"Yet another must-read page-turner from Patterson."
—**EdgeBoston.com**

"*The 5th Horseman* is the best—be it in terms of suspense, thrills, adventure, or anything else."
—**RebeccasReads.com**

"Patterson and Paetro do an excellent job, as always . . . This is a must-read book." —**BestsellersWorld.com**

"Patterson and Paetro have delivered a hit."
—*Ottawa Sun* **(Canada)**

"Patterson and Paetro are at their best here, weaving a number of plots together to create a novel that dips and flows across genre lines. *The 5th Horseman* continues the winning ways of a series that shows no signs of fatigue or flagging." —**BookReporter.com**

4TH OF JULY

"Stunning . . . nail-biting . . . a great read."
—**RebeccasReads.com**

"The suspense and plotting are still right on target."
— **MyShelf.com**

"Excellent . . . a fine work." — **BookReporter.com**

"A compelling page-turner that, once you start reading, you can't put down . . . Grab a hold of this one."
— **EdgeBoston.com**

"A fast-paced page-turner guaranteed to keep you up long into the night." — **TheRomanceReadersConnection.com**

"Excellent . . . fast-paced . . . Patterson is such a skilled writer and a master at the art of the mystery. If you want to read a good mystery, one you just don't want to put down, this book is for you . . . Highly recommended."
— **BestsellersWorld.com**

"Compelling . . . exhilarating . . . You just keep turning the pages as fast as possible to reach the resolution, and it's an explosive one." — **FreshFiction.com**

3RD DEGREE

"Buy this one—you will understand why Mr. Patterson is referred to as 'the most addictive writer at work today.'"
— **Bestsellersworld.com**

"Incredible . . . chilling . . . The suspense is never ending and the plot is to die for!" — **Myshelf.com**

"A pulse-pounding race against time . . . Suspense is never in short supply." — **TheBestReviews.com**

more . . .

2ND *CHANCE*

1st TO DIE

"Terrific . . . a great thriller . . . What's not to love about a 'club' formed by four women to catch a psycho killing newlywed couples?" **—Providence Sunday Journal**

"I can't believe how good Patterson is . . . He's always on the mark." **—LARRY KING, USA Today**

"Patterson boils a scene down to the single, telling detail, the element that defines a character or moves a plot along. It's what fires off the movie projector in the reader's mind."
—MICHAEL CONNELLY, author of The Closers

"His clever twists and affecting subplots keep the pages flying." **—People (Page-Turner of the Week)**

"Delivers a sharp punch." **—Chicago Tribune**

"That rapid-fire, in-your-face, you'd-better-keep-reading-or-else format will make you finish 1st to Die in one sitting (barring World War III, a 9.1 earthquake, or the Ebola virus)." **—Denver Rocky Mountain News**

"Patterson knows where our deepest fears are buried . . . There's no stopping his imagination."
—New York Times Book Review

"A clever plot with enough last-minute revelations to keep you guessing." **—Entertainment Weekly**

"A slick, taut thriller . . . Patterson keeps the pace moving at top speed . . . a darn good book."
—Orlando Sentinel

THE WOMEN'S MURDER CLUB

7th Heaven (coauthor Maxine Paetro)

The 6th Target (Maxine Paetro)

The 5th Horseman (Maxine Paetro)

4th of July (Maxine Paetro)

3rd Degree (Andrew Gross)

2nd Chance (Andrew Gross)

1st to Die

A complete list of books by James Patterson is on page 388–389.
For more information about James Patterson, go to
www.jamespatterson.com.

JAMES PATTERSON

AND MAXINE PAETRO

THE **6**TH

TARGET

VISION

NEW YORK   BOSTON

Copyright © 2007 by James Patterson
Excerpt from *Sundays at Tiffany's* copyright © 2008 by James Patterson
All rights reserved. Except as permitted under the U.S. Copyright Act of 1976, no part of this publication may be reproduced, distributed, or transmitted in any form or by any means, or stored in a database or retrieval system, without the prior written permission of the publisher.

Vision
Hachette Book Group
237 Park Avenue
New York, NY 10017
Visit our Web site at www.HachetteBookGroup.com

Grand Central Publishing is an imprint of Grand Central Publishing.
The Vision name and logo is a trademark of Hachette Book Group, Inc.

Printed in the United States of America

Originally published in hardcover by Little, Brown and Company
First International mass market edition: April 2008
First United States mass market edition: December 2008

10 9 8 7 6 5 4 3 2 1

Our thanks and gratitude to these top professionals, who were so generous with their time and expertise: author and psychiatrist Dr. Maria Paige; Dr. Humphrey Germaniuk, forensic pathologist and ME of Trumbull County, Ohio; top cop Captain Richard Conklin, Stamford, Connecticut, PD; Allen Ross, MD, Montague, Massachusetts; and legal experts Philip Hoffman, New York City; Melody Fujimori, San Francisco; and criminal defense attorney extraordinaire Mickey Sherman, Stamford, Connecticut.

And special thanks to our excellent researchers, Don MacBain, Ellie Shurtleff, and Lynn Colomello.

6THE 6TH
TARGET

Prologue

DAY-TRIPPER

Chapter 1

A KILLER IN WAITING, Fred Brinkley slumps in the blue-upholstered banquette on the top deck of the ferry. The November sun glares down like a big white eye as the catamaran plows the San Francisco Bay, and Fred Brinkley glares right back at the sun.

A shadow falls across him, a kid's voice asking, "Mister, could you take our picture?"

Fred shakes his head—*no, no, no*—anger winding him up like a watch spring, like a wire tightening around his head.

He wants to smash the kid like a bug.

Fred averts his eyes, sings inside his head, *Ay, ay, ay, ay, Sau-sa-lito-lindo,* trying to shut down the voices. He puts his hand on Bucky to comfort himself, feeling him through his blue nylon Windbreaker, but still the voices pound in his brain like a jackhammer.

Loser. Dog shit.

Gulls call out, screaming like children. Overhead, the sun burns through the overcast sky and turns him as transparent as glass. *They know what he's done.*

Passengers in shorts and visors line the rails, taking pictures of Angel Island, of Alcatraz, of the Golden Gate Bridge.

A sailboat flies by, mainsail double-reefed, foam flecking the rails, and Fred doubles over as the bad thing whips into his mind. He sees the boom swing. Hears the loud crack. *Oh, God! The sailboat!*

Someone has to pay for this!

Startling him, the ferry's engines grind into reverse and the deck vibrates as the ferry comes into dock.

Fred stands, works his way through the crowd, passing eight white tables, lines of scuffed blue chairs, his fellow ferry riders giving him the eye.

He enters the open compartment at the bow, sees a mother berating her son, a boy of nine or ten with light-brown hair. "You're driving me *crazy!*" the woman shouts.

Fred feels the wire snap. *Someone has to pay.*

His right hand slips into his jacket pocket—finds Bucky.

He slips his finger into the trigger loop.

The ferry lurches as it bumps the mooring. People grab on to one another, laughing. Lines snake out from the boat, bow and aft.

Fred's eyes shoot to the woman who is still belittling her son. She's small, wearing tan clam diggers, her breasts outlined in the soft skin of her white blouse, nipples pointing straight out.

"What's wrong with you, anyway?" she yells over the engines' roar. "You really piss me off, buster."

Bucky is in Fred's hand, the Smith & Wesson Model 10, pulsing with a life of its own.

The voice booms, *Kill her. Kill her. She's out of control!*

Bucky points between the woman's breasts.

BLAM.

Fred feels the jolt of the gun's recoil, sees the woman jump back with a little hurt yelp, a red stain blooming on her white blouse.

Good!

The little boy follows his mother's fall to the deck with his big round eyes, strawberry ice cream plopping out of his cone, pee spreading across the front of his pants.

The boy did a bad thing, too.

BLAM.

Chapter 2

BLINDING WHITE SAILS fill Fred's mind as blood spills onto the deck. Trusty Bucky is hot in his hand. Fred's eyes pan across the deck.

The voice in his head roars, *Run. Get away. You didn't mean to do it.*

Out of the corner of his eye, Fred sees a big man charge him, rage on his face, hell in his eyes. Fred straightens his arm.

BLAM.

Another man, Asian, hard black eyes, a white line for a mouth, makes a grab for Bucky.

BLAM.

A black woman stands nearby, locked in place by the crowd. She turns toward him, round cheeked, wide-eyed. Stares into his face and . . . *reads his mind.*

"Okay, son," she says, reaching out a trembling hand, "that's enough, now. Give me the gun."

She knows what he did. How does she know?

BLAM.

Fred feels relief flood through him as the mind-reading

woman goes down. People in the small forward compartment move in waves, cowering, shifting left, then right as Fred swings his head.

They are afraid of him. Afraid of *him*.

At his feet, the black woman holds a cell phone in her bloody hands. Breath rasping, she presses numbers with her thumb. *No, you don't!* Fred steps on the woman's wrist. Then he bends low to look into her eyes.

"You should have *stopped me*," he says through clenched teeth. "That was your *job*." Bucky screws his muzzle into her temple.

"Don't!" she begs. *"Please."*

Someone yells, *"Mom!"*

A skinny black kid, maybe seventeen, eighteen, comes toward him with a length of pipe over his shoulder. He's holding it like a bat.

Fred pulls the trigger as the ship lurches — BLAM.

The shot goes wide. The metal pipe falls, skitters across the deck, and the kid runs to the woman, throws himself down. *Protecting her?*

People dive under the benches, and their screams rise up around him like licks of fire.

The noise of the engines is joined by the metallic clanking of the gangway locking into place. Bucky stays trained on the crowd as Fred looks over the railing.

He judges the distance.

It's a drop of four feet to the gangway substructure, then a pretty long leap to the dock.

Fred pockets Bucky and puts both hands on the rail. He vaults over and lands on the flats of his Nikes. A cloud crosses the sun, cloaking him, making him invisible.

Move quickly, sailor. Go.

And he does it—makes the leap to the dock and runs toward the farmer's market, where he dissolves into the throng filling the parking lot.

He walks, almost casually, a half block to Embarcadero.

He's humming when he jogs down the steps to the BART station, still humming as he catches the train home.

You did it, sailor.

Part One

DO YOU KNOW THIS MAN?

Chapter 3

I WAS OFF DUTY that Saturday morning in early November, called to the scene of a homicide because *my business card* had been found in the victim's pocket.

I stood inside the darkened living room of a two-family house on Seventeenth Street, looking down at a wretched little scuzzball named Jose Alonzo. He was shirtless, paunchy, slumped on a sagging couch of indeterminate color, his wrists cuffed behind him. His head hung to his chest, and tears ran down his chin.

I had no pity for him.

"Was he Mirandized?" I asked Inspector Warren Jacobi, my former partner who now reported to me. Jacobi had just turned fifty-one and had seen more homicide victims in his twenty-five years on the job than any ten cops should see in a lifetime.

"Yeah, I did it, Lieutenant. Before he confessed." Jacobi's fists twitched at his sides. Disgust crossed his timeworn face.

"Do you understand your rights?" I asked Alonzo.

He nodded and began sobbing again. "I shouldn'ta done it, but she made me so *mad*."

A toddler with a dirty white bow in her hair, wet diapers sagging to her dimpled knees, clung to her father's leg. Her wailing just about broke my heart.

"What did Rosa do to make you *mad?*" I asked Alonzo. "I really want to know."

Rosa Alonzo was on the floor, her pretty face turned toward the flaking caramel-colored wall, her head split open by the iron her husband had used to knock her down, then take her life.

The ironing board had collapsed around her like a dead horse, and the smell of burned spray starch was in the air.

The last time I'd seen Rosa, she'd told me how she couldn't leave her husband because he'd said he'd hunt her down and kill her.

I wished with all my heart she'd taken the baby and run.

Inspector Richard Conklin, Jacobi's partner, the newest and youngest member of my squad, walked into the kitchen. Rich poured cat food into a bowl for an old orange tabby cat that was mewing on the red Formica table. *Interesting.*

"He could be alone here for a long time," Conklin said over his shoulder.

"Call animal control."

"Said they were busy, Lieutenant." Conklin turned on the taps, filled a water bowl.

Alonzo spoke up.

"You know what she said, Officer? She said, 'Get a job.' I just *snapped,* you understand?"

I stared at him until he turned away from me, cried out to his dead wife, "I didn't mean to do it, Rosa. *Please. Give me another chance.*"

Jacobi reached for the man's arm, brought him to his feet, saying, "Yeah, she forgives you, pal. Let's take a ride."

The baby launched a new round of howls as Patty Whelk from Child Welfare came through the open door.

"Hey, Lindsay," she said, stepping around the victim, "who's Little Miss Precious?"

I picked up the child, took the dirty ribbon out of her curls, and handed her over to Patty.

"Anita Alonzo," I said sadly, "meet the system."

Patty and I exchanged helpless looks as she jostled the little girl into a comfortable position on her hip.

I left Patty rummaging in the bedroom for a clean diaper. While Conklin stayed behind to wait for the ME, I followed Jacobi and Alonzo out to the street.

I said, "See ya," to Jacobi and climbed into my three-year-old Explorer parked next to six yards of garbage out by the street. I'd just turned the key when my Nextel bleeped on my belt. *It's Saturday. Leave me the hell alone.*

I caught the call on the second ring.

It was my boss, Chief Anthony Tracchio. An unusual tightness strained his voice as he raised it over the keening sound of sirens.

"Boxer," he said, "there's been a shooting on one of the ferries. The *Del Norte*. Three people are dead. A couple more wounded. I need you here. Pronto."

Chapter 4

I HAD A REALLY BAD FEELING, thinking ahead to whatever hell had brought the chief out of his comfy home in Oakland *on a Saturday.* The bad feeling mushroomed when I saw half a dozen black-and-whites parked at the entrance to the pier, and two more patrol cars up on the sidewalk at either end of the Ferry Building.

A patrolman called out, "This way, Lieu," and waved me down the south driveway leading to the dock.

I drove past the police prowlers, ambulances, and fire rigs, and parked outside the terminal. I opened my door and stepped out into the sixty-degree haze. About a twenty-knot breeze had whipped up a stiff chop on the bay, making the *Del Norte* rock at her mooring.

The police activity had excited the crowd, and a thousand people shifted between the Ferry Building and the farmer's market, taking pictures, asking cops what had happened. It was as if they could smell gunpowder and blood in the air.

I ducked under the barrier tape cordoning off the dock, nodded to cops I knew, looked up when I heard Tracchio call my name.

The chief was standing at the mouth of the *Del Norte*.

He was wearing a leather blazer and Dockers, and sporting his signature Vitalis comb-over. He signaled to me to come aboard. *Said the spider to the fly.*

I headed toward him, but before I got five feet up the gangway, I had to back up and let two paramedics pass with a rolling stretcher bouncing between them.

I dropped my eyes to the victim, a large African American woman, her face mostly covered with an oxygen mask, an IV line running into her arm. Blood soaked the sheet tucked tightly over her body.

I felt a pain in my chest, my heart catching on a full second before my brain put it together.

The victim was Claire Washburn!

My best friend had been shot on the ferry!

I grabbed the gurney, stopping its forward motion and causing the brassy blond paramedic bringing up the rear to bark at me, "Lady, out of the way!"

"I'm a *cop*," I said to the paramedic, pulling open my jacket to show her my badge.

"I don't care if you're *God*," said the blonde. "We're getting her to the ER."

My mouth was hanging open and my heart was pounding in my ears.

"Claire," I called out, walking quickly now alongside the stretcher as the gurney rumbled over the gangway and onto the asphalt. "Claire, *it's Lindsay.* Can you hear me?"

No answer.

"What's her condition?" I asked the paramedic.

"Do you understand that we have to get her to the *hospital?*"

"Answer me, goddamn it!"

"I don't freaking know!"

I stood helplessly by as the paramedics opened the ambulance doors.

More than ten minutes had passed since I'd gotten Tracchio's call. Claire had been lying on the deck of the ferry all that time, losing blood, trying to breathe with a bullet hole ripped into her chest.

I gripped her hand, and tears immediately filled my eyes.

My friend turned her face to me, her eyelids fluttering as she forced them open.

"Linds," she mouthed. I moved her mask aside. "Where's Willie?" she asked me.

I remembered then—Claire's youngest son, Willie, was working for the ferry line on the weekends. That's probably why Claire had been on the *Del Norte*.

"We got separated," Claire gasped. "I think he went after the shooter."

Chapter 5

CLAIRE'S EYES ROLLED UP, and she slipped away from me. The knees of the gurney buckled, and the paramedics slid the stretcher out of my grasp and into the ambulance.

The doors slammed. The siren started up its blaring *whoop,* and the ambulance carrying my dearest friend headed into traffic toward San Francisco General.

Time was working against us.

The shooter was gone, and Willie had gone after him.

Tracchio put his hand on my shoulder. "We're getting descriptions of the doer, Boxer —"

"I have to find Claire's son," I said.

I broke away from Tracchio and ran toward the farmer's market, scanning faces as I pushed past the slow-moving crowd. It was like walking through a herd of cattle.

I looked into every fricking produce stall and in between them, raked the aisles with my eyes, searching desperately for Willie — but it was Willie who found *me.*

He shoved his way toward me, calling my name. "Lindsay! Lindsay!"

The front of his T-shirt was soaked with blood. He was panting, and his face was rigid with fear.

I grabbed his shoulders with both hands, tears welling up again.

"*Willie,* where are you hurt?"

He shook his head. "This isn't my blood. My mom's been *shot.*"

I pulled him to me, hugged him to my chest, felt some of my terrible fear leaving me. At least Willie was okay.

"She's on her way to the hospital," I said, wishing I could add, *She'll be fine.* "You saw the shooter? What does he look like?"

"He's a skinny white man," Willie said as we bumped through the mob. "Has a beard, long brown hair. He kept his eyes *down,* Lindsay. *I never saw his eyes.*"

"How old is he?"

"Like, maybe a few years younger than you."

"Early thirties?"

"Yeah. And he's taller than me. Maybe six foot one, wearing cargo pants and a blue Windbreaker. Lindsay, I heard him say to my mom that she was supposed to stop the shooting. That it was her job. What's *that* supposed to mean?"

Claire is chief medical examiner of San Francisco. She's a forensic pathologist, not a cop.

"You think it was personal? That he targeted your mom? Knew her?"

Willie shook his head. "I was helping to tie up the boat when the screaming started," he told me. "He shot some other people first. My mom was the last one. He had a gun right up to her head. I grabbed an iron pipe," he said. "I was going to brain him with it, but he shot at me. Then he jumped overboard. I went after him—but I lost him."

It really hit me then.

What Willie had *done*. My voice was loud, and I grabbed his shoulders.

"What if you'd caught up with him? Willie, did you think about that? That 'skinny white man' was *armed*. He would have *killed* you."

Tears jumped out of Willie's eyes, rolled down his sweet, young face. I relaxed my grip on his shoulders, took him into my arms.

"But you were very brave, Willie," I said. "You were very brave to stand up to a killer to protect your mom.

"I think you saved her life."

Chapter 6

I KISSED WILLIE'S CHEEK through the open patrol-car window. Then Officer Pat Noonan drove Willie to the hospital and I boarded the ferry, joining Tracchio in the open front compartment of the *Del Norte*'s top deck.

It was a scene of unforgettable horror. Bodies lying where they'd fallen on the thirty or forty square yards of bloody fiberglass deck, footprints leaving tracks in all directions. Articles of clothing had been dropped here and there — a red baseball cap was squashed underfoot, mixed with paper cups and hot dog wrappers and newspapers soaked in blood.

I felt a sickening wave of despair. The killer could be anywhere, and evidence that might lead us to him had been lost every time a cop or a passenger or a paramedic walked across the deck.

Plus, I couldn't stop thinking about Claire.

"You okay?" Tracchio asked me.

I nodded, afraid that if I started to cry, I wouldn't be able to stop.

"This is Andrea Canello," Tracchio said, pointing to

the body of a woman in tan pants and a white blouse lying up against the hull. "According to that fellow over there," he said, pointing to a teenager with spiky hair and a sunburned nose, "the doer shot her first. Then he shot her son. A little kid. About nine."

"The boy going to make it?" I asked.

Tracchio shrugged. "He lost a lot of blood." He pointed to another body, a male Caucasian, white haired, looked to be in his fifties, lying halfway under a bench.

"Per Conrad. Engineer. Worked on the ferry. Probably heard the shots and tried to help. And this fellow," he said, indicating an Asian man lying flat on his back in the center of the deck, "is Lester Ng. Insurance salesman. Another guy who could have been a hero. Witnesses say it all went down in two or three minutes."

I started picturing the scene in my head, using what Willie had told me, what Tracchio was telling me now, looking at the evidence, trying to fit the pieces into something that made sense.

I wondered if the shooting spree had been planned or if something had set the shooter off and, if so, what that trigger had been.

"One of the passengers thinks he saw the shooter sitting alone before the incident. Over there," Tracchio told me. "Thinks he was smoking a cigarette. A package of Turkish Specials was found under a table."

I followed Tracchio to the stern, where several horrified passengers sat on an upholstered bench that wrapped around the inner curve of the railing. Some of them were blood spattered. Some held hands. Shock had frozen their faces.

Uniforms were still taking down the witnesses' names

and phone numbers, getting statements. Sergeant Lexi Rose turned toward us, saying, "Chief, Lieutenant. Mr. Jack Rooney here has some good news for us."

An elderly man in a bright-red nylon jacket stepped forward. He wore big-frame eyeglasses and a digital Mini-cam about the size of a bar of soap hanging from a black cord around his neck. He had an expression of grim satisfaction.

"I've got him right here," Rooney said, holding up his camera. "I got that psycho right in the act."

Chapter 7

THE HEAD OF THE Crime Scene Unit, Charlie Clapper, crossed the gangway with his team and came on board moments after the witnesses were released. Charlie stopped in front of us, greeted the chief, said, "Hey, Lindsay," and took a look around.

Then he dug into the pockets of his herringbone tweed jacket, pulled out latex gloves, and snapped them on.

"This is a fine kettle of fish," he said.

"Let's try to stay positive," I said, unable to conceal the edge in my voice.

"Cockeyed optimist," he said. "That's me."

I stood with Tracchio as the CSU team fanned out, putting out markers, photographing the bodies and the blood that was spattered everywhere.

They dug out a projectile from the hull, and they bagged an item that might lead us to a killer: the half-empty packet of Turkish cigarettes that had been found under a table in the stern.

"I'm going to take off now, Lieutenant," Tracchio told

me, looking down at his Rolex. "I have a meeting with the mayor."

"I want to work this case—personally," I said.

He gave me a hard, unblinking stare. I'd just pushed a hot button on his console, but it couldn't be helped.

Tracchio was a decent guy, and mostly I liked him. But the chief had come up through the ranks by way of administration. He'd never worked a case in his life, and that made him see things one way.

He wanted me to do my job from my desk.

And I did my best work on the street.

The last time I'd told Tracchio that I wanted to work cases "hands-on," he'd told me that I was ungrateful; that I had a lot to learn about leading a command, that I should do my goddamned job and feel lucky about my promotion to lieutenant.

He reminded me now, sharply, that one of my partners had been killed on the street and that only months ago, Jacobi and I had both been shot in a desolate alley in the Tenderloin. It was true. We'd both nearly died.

Today, I knew he couldn't turn me down. My best friend had a slug through her chest, and the shooter was free.

"I'll work with Jacobi and Conklin. A three-man team. I'll have McNeil and Chi back us up. Pull in the rest of the squad as needed."

Tracchio nodded reluctantly, but it was a green light. I thanked him and called Jacobi on my cell. Then I phoned the hospital, got a kindhearted nurse on the line who told me that Claire was still in surgery.

I left the scene with Jack Rooney's camera in hand, planning to look at the video back at the Hall, see the shooting for myself.

I walked down the gangway and muttered, "Nuts," before I reached the pavement. Reporters from three local TV stations and the *Chronicle* were waiting for me. I knew them all.

Cameras clicked and zoomed. Microphones were pushed up to my face.

"Was this a terrorist attack, Lieutenant?"

"Who did the shooting?"

"How many people were killed?"

"Give me a break, guys. The crime just happened this morning," I said, wishing these reporters had grabbed Tracchio or any one of the other four dozen cops milling around the perimeter who'd love to see themselves on the six o'clock news.

"We'll release the names of the victims after we've contacted their families.

"And we *will* find whoever did this terrible thing," I said with both hope and conviction. "He *will not* get away."

Chapter 8

IT WAS TWO O'CLOCK in the afternoon when I introduced myself to Claire's doctor, Al Sassoon, who was standing with Claire's chart in hand at the hub of the ICU.

Sassoon was in his midforties, dark haired, with laugh lines fanning out from the corners of his mouth. He looked credible and confident, and I trusted him immediately.

"Are you investigating the shooting?" he asked me.

I nodded. "Yes, and also, Claire's my friend."

"She's a friend of mine, too." He smiled, said, "So here's what I can tell you. The bullet broke a rib and collapsed her left lung, but it missed her heart and major arteries.

"She's going to have some pain from the rib and she's going to have a chest tube inside her until that lung fully expands. But she's healthy and she's lucky. And she's got good people here watching out for her."

The tears that had been dammed up all day threatened to overflow. I lowered my eyes and croaked, "I'd like to talk to her. Claire's assailant killed three people."

"She'll wake up soon," Sassoon told me. He patted my shoulder and held open the door to Claire's room, and I walked inside.

The back of Claire's bed was raised to make it easier for her to breathe. There was a cannula in her nose and an IV bag hanging from a pole, dripping saline into a vein. Under her thin hospital gown, her chest was swaddled in bandages, and her eyes were puffy and closed. In all the years I've known Claire, I've never seen her sick. I've never seen her *down*.

Claire's husband, Edmund, had been sitting in the armchair beside the bed, but he jumped to his feet the moment I walked in the door.

He looked awful, his features twisted with fear and disbelief.

I set down my shopping bag and went to him for a long hug, Edmund saying into my hair, "Oh, God, Lindsay, this is too much."

I murmured all the things you say when words are just plain inadequate. "She'll be on her feet soon, Eddie. You know I'm right."

"I wonder," Edmund said when we finally stepped apart. "Even saying she heals up okay. Have *you* gotten over being shot?"

I couldn't answer. The truth was, I still woke up some nights sweating, knowing I'd been dreaming again about that bad night on Larkin Street. I could still feel the impact of those slugs in my mind, remembering the helplessness and the knowledge that I might die.

"And what about Willie?" Edmund was saying. "His whole world turned inside out this morning. Here, let me help you with that."

Edmund held the sides of the shopping bag apart so that I could extract from it a big silver get-well balloon. I tied the balloon to the frame of Claire's bed, then reached over and touched her hand. "Has she said anything?" I asked.

"She opened her eyes for a couple of seconds. Said, 'Where's Willie?' I told her, 'He's home. Safe.' She said, 'I gotta get back to work,' then she conked out. That was a half hour ago."

I searched my mind for the last time I'd seen Claire before the shooting. Yesterday. We'd waved good-bye in the parking lot across from the Hall as we'd left work for the day. Just a casual flap of our hands.

"See ya, girlfriend."

"Have a good one, Butterfly."

It had been such an ordinary exchange. Taking life for granted. *What if Claire had died today? What if she had died on us?*

Chapter 9

I WAS GRIPPING CLAIRE'S HAND as Edmund returned to the armchair, switched on the overhead TV with the remote. Keeping the sound on low, he asked, "You've seen this, Lindsay?"

I looked up, saw the disclaimer—"What you're about to see is very graphic. Parental discretion is advised."

"I saw it right after the shooting," I told Edmund, "but I want to see it again."

Edmund nodded, said, "Me, too."

And then Jack Rooney's amateur film of the ferry shooting came on the screen.

Together, we watched again what Claire had lived through only hours before. Rooney's film was grainy and jumpy, first focusing on three tourists smiling and waving at the camera, a sailboat behind them, and then a beauty shot of the Golden Gate Bridge.

The camera panned across the ferry's open top deck, past a gaggle of kids feeding hot dog buns to the seagulls. A little boy wearing a backward red baseball cap was drawing on a table with a Sharpie. That was Tony Canello.

A lanky bearded man sitting near the railing plucked at his own arm distractedly.

The shot froze, and a spotlight encircled the bearded man.

"That's *him*," Edmund said. "Is he crazy, Lindsay? Or is he a premeditated killer, biding his time?"

"Maybe he's both," I said, my eyes pinned to the screen as a second clip followed the first. An ebullient crowd clung to the railing as the ferry pulled into dock. Suddenly the camera swung to the left, focusing on a woman, her face screwed up in horror as she grabbed at her chest and then collapsed.

The little boy, Tony Canello, turned toward the camera. His face had been digitally pixilated by the news producers so that his features were a blur.

I winced as he jerked and spun away from the gunman.

The camera's eye jumped around crazily after that. It looked as though Rooney had been bumped, and then the picture stabilized.

I covered my mouth and Edmund gripped the arms of the chair as we watched Claire stretch out her hand toward the shooter. Even though we couldn't hear her over the screams of the crowd, it was clear that she was asking for the gun.

"What bravery," I said. "My God."

"Too damned brave," Edmund muttered, running his hand over the top of his silvering head. "Claire and Willie, *both* of them, too damned brave."

The shooter's back was to the camera as he pulled the trigger. I saw the gun buck in his hand. Claire grabbed at her chest and went down.

Again, the point of view shifted to horrified faces in a roiling crowd. Then the gunman was on the screen in a crouch, his face turned away from the camera. He stepped on Claire's wrist, shouting into her face.

Edmund cried out, *"You sick son of a bitch!"*

Behind me, Claire moaned in her bed.

I turned to look at her, but she was still asleep. My eyes flashed back to the television as the shooter turned and his face came into view.

His eyes were down, his beard swallowing the lower half of his face. He was coming toward the cameraman, who finally lost his nerve and stopped filming.

"He shot at Willie after that," Edmund said.

And then, there I was on the TV screen, my hair tangled from my race through the farmer's market, Claire's blood transferred from Willie's T-shirt to my jacket, a wide-eyed look of shocked intensity on my face.

My voice was saying, "Please call us with any information that could lead to this man."

My face was replaced with a freeze-frame shot of the killer. The SFPD phone number and Web address crawled under a title in big letters at the bottom of the screen.

DO YOU KNOW THIS MAN?

Edmund turned to me, his face stricken. "Have you got anything yet, Lindsay?"

"We have Jack Rooney's video," I said, stabbing my finger at the TV. "We have nonstop media coverage and about two hundred eyewitnesses. We'll find him, Eddie. I swear we will."

I didn't say what I was thinking: *If this guy gets away, I shouldn't be a cop.*

I stood, gathered up my shopping bag.

Eddie said, "Can't you wait a few minutes? Claire will want to see you."

"I'll be back later," I told him. "There's someone I have to see right now."

Chapter 10

I LEFT CLAIRE'S ROOM on the fifth floor and took the stairs to the Pediatric ICU on two. I was bracing myself for what was sure to be an awful, heart-wrenching interview.

I thought about young Tony Canello, watching his mother taking a bullet an instant before being shot himself. I had to ask this child if he'd ever seen the shooter before, if the man had said anything before or after firing the gun, if he could think of any reason why he and his mom had been targeted.

I shifted my shopping bag from my right hand to my left as I took the last flight of stairs, knowing that how I handled this interview was going to stay with this little boy forever.

The police department keeps a stash of teddy bears to give to children who've been traumatized, but those small toys seemed too cheap to give to a kid who'd just seen his mother violently killed. I'd stopped off at the Build-A-Bear Workshop before coming to the hospital and had a bear custom-made for Tony. Before it was dressed in a soccer outfit, a fabric heart had been stitched inside the bear's chest, along with my wish that Tony would get well soon.

I opened the door to the second floor and stepped into the pastel-painted corridor of the Pediatric Unit. Cheery murals of rainbows and picnics lined the walls.

I found my way to the Pediatric ICU and flashed my badge for the nurse at the desk, a woman in her forties with graying hair and large brown eyes. I told her that I had to talk to my witness and that I wouldn't take more than a couple of minutes.

"You're talking about Tony Canello? The little boy who was shot on the ferry?"

I said, "I have about three questions. I'll make it as easy on him as possible."

"Ah, I'm sorry, Lieutenant," the nurse said, holding my eyes with hers. "His surgery was touch and go. The gunshot wound involved several major organs. I'm sorry to tell you we lost him about twenty minutes ago."

I sagged against the nurses' station.

The nurse was speaking to me, asking if she could get me anything or anyone. I handed her the shopping bag with the Build-A-Bear inside and asked her to give it to the next kid who came into the ICU.

Somehow, I found my car in the lot and headed back to the Hall of Justice.

Chapter 11

THE HALL IS A GRAY granite cube of a building that takes up a full block on Bryant Street. Its grungy and dismal ten floors house the superior court, the DA's offices, the southern division of the SFPD, and a jail taking up the top floor.

The medical examiner's office is in an adjacent building, but you can get there by way of a back door in the Hall's ground floor. I pushed open the steel-and-glass doors at the rear of the lobby, exited out the back of the building, and headed down the breezeway that led to the morgue.

I opened the door to the autopsy suite and was immediately enveloped by frosty air. I walked through the place as if I owned it, a habit encouraged by my best friend, Claire, the chief medical examiner.

But of course Claire wasn't on the ladder taking overhead shots of the deceased woman on the table. The deputy chief, a fortysomething white man, five eight or so with salt-and-pepper hair and black horn-rimmed glasses, had taken her place.

"Dr. G.," I said, barreling into the autopsy room.

"Watch where you're stepping, Lieutenant."

Dr. Humphrey Germaniuk had been in charge of the ME's office for about six hours, and already stacks of his papers lined the walls in neat rows. I used the toe of my shoe to straighten the pile that I'd accidentally dislodged, lined it up just right.

I knew Germaniuk to be a perfectionist, fast with a joke, and great on the witness stand. In fact, he was as qualified to be CME as Claire was, and some said that if Claire ever stepped down, Dr. G. would be a shoo-in for her job.

"How's it going with Andrea Canello?" I asked, nearing the body on the autopsy table. Dr. G.'s "patient" was nude, lying faceup, the gunshot wound centered between her breasts.

I leaned in for a closer look, and Dr. Germaniuk stepped between me and the dead woman's body.

"No trespassing, Lieutenant. This is a cop-free zone," he cracked—but I could see he wasn't kidding. "I've already had a suspected child abuse, a traffic fatality, and a woman whose head was opened up with a steam iron.

"The ferry victims are going to be an all-day sucker, and I'm just getting started. If you have any questions, ask me now. Otherwise, just leave your cell number on my desk. I'll call you when I'm done."

Then he turned his back on me and began to measure Andrea Canello's gunshot wound.

I stepped away, my head throbbing from the angry outburst I was keeping in check. I couldn't afford to alienate Dr. G., besides which, he was within his rights. Without Claire, the already understaffed ME's office was in a state of emergency. Germaniuk barely knew me, and he had to protect his department, his job, the rights of his patients, and the overall integrity of the investigation.

And he had to autopsy every one of the ferry victims himself.

If a second pathologist got in on this multiple homicide, a good defense attorney would pit the two pathologists against each other, look for inconsistencies that would undermine their testimonies.

Assuming we would find the psycho who killed these people.

And also assuming we would bring him to trial.

It was almost four in the afternoon. If Andrea Canello was Germaniuk's first ferry victim, his all-day sucker was going to be an all-night sucker, too.

Still, I had my own problems. Four people were dead.

The more time that passed, the more likely the ferry shooter would get away.

"Dr. G."

He turned from his diagram and scowled.

"Sorry if I came on too strong, but the shooter killed four people, and we don't know who he is or where to find him."

"Don't you mean three?" Germaniuk said. "I have only three victims."

"This woman's little boy, Tony Canello, died a half hour ago at San Francisco General," I told him. "He was nine. That's four dead, and Claire Washburn is sucking air through a chest tube."

A wave of sympathy swept the indignation from Dr. Germaniuk's face. The edge was gone from his voice when he said, "Tell me how I can help you."

Chapter 12

DR. GERMANIUK USED A SOFT PROBE to gently explore the wound that had torn through Andrea Canello's chest. "It looks like a K-5 right through the heart. I wouldn't swear to it until the firearms examiner says so, but it looks to me like she was shot with a .38."

It's what I'd thought from the video, but I wanted to be certain. Jack Rooney's camera lens had swung away from Andrea Canello as soon as she was shot. If she'd lived for a moment, if she knew her killer, she might have called out his name.

"Could she have lived after she was shot?"

"Not a chance," Germaniuk told me. "Slug to the heart like that, she was dead before she hit the deck."

"That's some shooting," I said. "Six slugs, five direct hits. With a *revolver*."

"Crowded ferry boat, lots of people. Bound to hit some of them," said Dr. G. matter-of-factly.

We both looked up when the stainless steel doors to the rear of the autopsy suite banged open and a tech wheeled a gurney inside, calling out, "Dr. G., where do you want this?"

The body on the stretcher was sheeted, about fifty inches long. *"This"* was a child.

"Leave him," Germaniuk said to the tech. "We'll take it from here."

The doctor and I stepped over to the gurney. He pulled the sheet down.

Just looking at the dead child was enough to tear out my heart. Tony's skin was a mottled blue color, and he had a freshly stitched twelve-inch incision across his skinny little chest. I fought an impulse to put my hand on his face, touch his hair, do something to comfort a child who'd had the bad luck to be standing in a madman's line of fire.

"I'm so sorry, Tony."

"Here's my card," Germaniuk said, digging it out of his lab coat pocket, putting it in my hand. "Call my cell phone if you need me. And when you see Claire...tell her I'll come to the hospital when I can. Tell her we're all pulling for her—and that we're not going to let her down."

Chapter 13

MY SQUAD HAD MOVED their chairs and herded up around me. They were throwing out questions and trying out theories about the *Del Norte* shooter when my cell phone rang. I recognized the number as Edmund's and took the call.

Edmund's voice was hoarse and breaking when he said, "Claire just came out of X-ray. She's got internal bleeding."

"Eddie, I don't get it. What happened?"

"The bullet bruised her liver.... They have to operate on her—again."

I'd been lulled by Dr. Sassoon's smile when he'd said that Claire was as good as home free. Now I felt nauseated with fear.

When I arrived at the ICU waiting room, it was half full of Claire's family and friends, plus Edmund and Willie and Reggie Washburn, Claire and Edmund's twenty-one-year-old who'd just flown in from the University of Miami.

I hugged everyone, sat down beside Cindy Thomas and Yuki Castellano, Claire's best girlfriends and mine, the four of us making up the entire membership of what we half jokingly call the "Women's Murder Club." We huddled together, waiting for news in that cheerless room.

Throughout the long, tense hours, we camouflaged our fear by topping one another's kick-butt Claire stories. We downed bad coffee and Snickers bars from the vending machines, and during the early morning hours, Edmund asked us to pray.

We all joined hands as Eddie asked God to please spare Claire. I knew we were all hoping that if we stayed close to her and had enough faith, she wouldn't die.

During those grueling hours, I flashed back to the time I'd been shot—how Claire and Cindy had been there for me.

And I remembered other times when I'd waited in rooms much like this one. When my mom had cancer. When a man I'd loved had been shot in the line of duty. When Yuki's mom had been felled by a stroke.

All of them had died.

Cindy said, "Where is that son-of-a-bitch shooter right now? Is he having a smoke after his dinner? Sleeping in a nice soft bed, planning another shooting spree?"

"He's not sleeping in a bed," Yuki said. "Ten bucks says that dude is sleeping in a Maytag box."

At around five in the morning, a weary Dr. Sassoon came out to give us the news.

"Claire's doing fine," he said. "We've repaired the damage to her liver, and her blood pressure is picking up. Her vital signs are good."

A cheer went up, and spontaneously we all started to clap. Edmund hugged his sons, tears in all their eyes.

The doctor smiled, and I had to admit—he was a warrior.

I made a quick trip home to take a sunrise run around Potrero Hill with Martha, my border collie.

Then I called Jacobi as the sun rose over the roof of my car. I met him and Conklin at the elevator bank inside the Hall at eight.

It was Sunday.

They'd brought coffee and donuts.

I loved these guys.

"Let's get to work," I said.

Chapter 14

CONKLIN, JACOBI, AND I had just settled into my glass-cubicle office in the corner of the squad room when Inspectors Paul Chi and Cappy McNeil entered the dingy twenty-by-thirty-foot workspace that's home base to the twelve members of the homicide crew.

Cappy easily weighs two hundred fifty pounds, and the side chair creaked when he sat in it. Chi is lithe. He parked his small butt on my credenza next to Jacobi, who was having one of his not-infrequent bouts of coughing.

With all the seats taken, Conklin chose to stand behind me, his back against the window and its view of the on-ramp to the freeway, one foot casually crossing the ankle of the other.

My office felt overcrowded, like a shot glass stuffed with a fistful of crayons.

I could feel heat coming off Conklin's body, making me too aware of his six-foot-one, perfectly proportioned frame, his light-brown hair falling over his brown eyes, his twenty-nine-year-old looks reminding me of a Kennedy cousin crossed with maybe a U.S. Marine.

Chi had brought the Sunday *Chronicle* and placed it on the desk in front of me.

The shooter's photo, a fuzzy still shot taken from Jack Rooney's low-resolution movie footage, was on the front page, and under it was the caption DO YOU KNOW THIS MAN?

We all leaned in to study that furred face again.

The shooter's dark hair hung around to his jaw, and his beard hid everything from his top lip down to his Adam's apple.

"Jesus Christ," said Cappy. We all looked at him.

"What? I'm saying he *looks* like Jesus Christ."

I said, "We won't be getting anything back from the lab on a Sunday morning, but we have this."

I took the photocopy of the brown-wrapped package of Turkish Specials out of my in-box.

"And we have all this."

I put my hand on the two-inch pile of witness statements, phone messages, and e-mail printouts that our PA, Brenda, had taken off the SFPD Web site yesterday.

"We can divvy it up," said Jacobi.

Loud discussion followed, until Chi said emphatically, "*Hey.* Cigarettes are big business. Any place that's going to sell a brand like Turkish Specials is going to be one of your mom-and-pop stores. And one of those moms or pops might remember this shooter."

I said, "Okay. You guys run with it."

Jacobi and Conklin took two-thirds of the witness statements out to their desks in the squad room and got on the phones while Chi and McNeil made a few calls before hitting the streets.

Alone in my office, I looked over what Brenda had gathered on the victims—all solid citizens, every one.

Was there a connection between the killer and any of the people he'd shot?

I started dialing the numbers on the witness statements, but nothing in the first few calls lifted me out of my seat. Then I reached a fireman who'd been standing only ten feet from Andrea Canello when the shooter opened fire.

"She was yelling at her kid when the shooter popped her," the witness said. "I was about to tell her to take it easy. The next minute, uh, she was dead."

"What was she saying? Do you remember?"

" 'You're driving me crazy, buddy.' Something like that. Terrible to think ... Did the boy make it?"

"I'm sorry to say, no, he didn't."

I made more notes, trying to fit fragments together into pieces, pieces into a whole. I slugged down the last of my coffee and dialed the next person on my list.

His name was Ike Quintana, and he had called late yesterday afternoon, saying maybe he'd been friends with the shooter some fifteen years before.

Now Quintana said to me, "It looks like the same guy for sure. If that's him, we were both at Napa State Hospital in the late '80s."

I gripped the phone, pressing my ear hard against the receiver. Didn't want to miss a syllable.

"You know what I mean?" Quintana asked me. "We were both locked up in the cuckoo's nest."

Chapter 15

I SCRIBBLED A STAR next to Ike Quintana's phone number.

"What's your friend's name?" I asked him, pressing the receiver against my ear. But suddenly Quintana was evasive.

"I don't want to say, in case it turns out *not* to be him," he said. "I have a picture. You can come over and look, if you come now. Otherwise, I have a lot of things to do today."

"Don't you dare leave home! We're on our way!"

I went out to the squad room, said, "We've got a lead. I have an address on San Carlos Street."

Conklin said, "I want to keep working the phones. New videos of the shooting have been e-mailed to our Web site."

Jacobi stood, put on his jacket, said, "I'm driving, Boxer."

I've known Jacobi for ten years, worked as his partner for three before I was promoted to lieutenant. During the time Jacobi and I were a team, we'd developed a deep friendship and an almost telepathic connection. But I don't think either of us acknowledged how close we were until the night we were shot down by coked-up teenagers. Being near death had bonded us.

Now he drove us to a crappy block on the fringes of the Tenderloin.

We looked up the address Ike Quintana had given me, a two-story building with a storefront church on the ground floor and a couple of apartments on top.

I rang the doorbell, and a buzzer sounded. I pulled at the dull metal door handle, and Jacobi and I entered a dark foyer. We climbed creaking stairs into a carpeted hallway smelling of mildew.

There was a single door on each side of the hallway.

I rapped on the one marked 2R, and a long half minute later, it squeaked open.

Ike Quintana was a white male, midthirties. He had black hair sticking up at angles and he was oddly dressed in layers. An undershirt showed in the V of his flannel shirt, a knitted vest was buttoned over that, and an open, rust-colored cardigan hung down to his hips.

He wore blue-striped pajama bottoms and brown felt slippers, and he had a kind of sweet, gappy smile. He stuck out his hand, shook each of ours, and asked us to come in.

Jacobi stepped forward, and I followed both men into a teetering tunnel of newspapers and clear plastic garbage bags filled with soda bottles that lined the hallway from floor to ceiling. In the parlor, cardboard boxes spilled over with coins and empty detergent boxes and ballpoint pens.

"I guess you're prepared for anything," Jacobi muttered.

"That's the idea," said Quintana.

When we reached the kitchen, I saw pots and pans on

every surface, and the table was a layered archive of newspaper clippings covered by a tablecloth, then more newspaper layers and a tablecloth over that, again and again making an archeological mound a foot high.

"I've been following the Giants for most of my life," Quintana said shyly. He offered us coffee, which Jacobi and I declined.

Still, Quintana lit a flame on the gas stove and put a pot of water on to boil.

"You have a picture to show us?" I asked.

Quintana lifted an old wooden soapbox from the floor and put it on the pillowy table. He pawed through piles of photographs and menus and assorted memorabilia that I couldn't make out, his hands flying over the papers.

"Here," he said, lifting out a faded five-by-seven photo. "I think this was taken around '88."

Five teenagers—two girls and three boys—were watching television in an institutional-looking common room.

"That's me," said Quintana, pointing to a younger version of himself slouched in an orange armchair. Even then, he had layered his clothing.

"And see this guy sitting on the window seat?"

I peered at the picture. The boy was thin, had long hair and an attempt at a beard. His face was in profile. It could be the shooter. It could be anyone.

"See how he's pulling at the hairs on his arm?" Quintana said.

I nodded.

"That's why I think it could be him. He used to do that for hours. I loved that guy. Called him *Fred-a-lito-lindo*. After a song he used to sing."

"What's his real name?" I asked.

"He was very depressed," Quintana said. "That's why he checked into Napa. Committed, you know. There was an accident. His little sister died. Something with a sailboat, I think."

Quintana turned off the stove, walked away. I had a fleeting thought: *What miracle has prevented this building from burning to the ground?*

"Mr. Quintana, don't make us ask you again, okay?" Jacobi growled. "What's the man's name?"

Quintana returned to the table with his chipped coffee cup in hand, wearing his hoarder's garb and the confidence of a rich man to the manor born.

"His name is Fred. Alfred Brinkley. But I really don't see how he could have killed those people," Quintana said. "Fred is the sweetest guy in the world."

Chapter 16

I CALLED RICH CONKLIN from the car, gave him Brinkley's name to run through NCIC as Jacobi drove back to Bryant Street.

Chi and McNeil were waiting for us inside MacBain's Beers O' the World Pub, a dark saloon sandwiched between two bail-bond shacks across from the Hall.

Jacobi and I joined them and ordered Foster's on tap, and I asked Chi and McNeil for an update.

"We interviewed a guy at the Smoke Shop on Polk at Vallejo," said Chi, getting right into it. "Old geezer who owns the place says, 'Yeah, I sell Turkish Specials. About two packs a month to a regular customer.' He takes the carton off the shelf to show us — it's down two packs."

Conklin came in, took a seat, and ordered a Dos Equis and an Angus burger, rare.

Looked like he had something on his mind.

"My partner gets excited," said Cappy, "by a carton of cigarettes."

"So who's the fool?" Chi asked McNeil.

"Get to it, okay?" Jacobi grumbled.

The beer came, and Jacobi, Conklin, and I lifted our glasses to Don MacBain, the bar's owner, a maverick former SFPD captain whose portrait hung in a frame over the bar.

Chi continued, "So the geezer says this customer is a Greek guy, about eighty years old—but 'hold on a minute,' he says. 'Let me see that picture again.'"

Cappy picked up where Chi left off. "So I push the photo of the shooter up to his snoot, and he says, '*This* guy? I used to see this guy every morning when he bought his paper. *He's* the guy who did the shootings?'"

Jacobi called the waitress over again, said, "Syd, I'll have a burger, too, medium rare with fries."

Chi talked over him.

"So the Smoke Shop geezer says he doesn't know our suspect's name but thinks he used to live across the street, 1513 Vallejo."

"So we go over there—" Cappy said.

"Please put me out of my misery," Jacobi said. His elbows were on the table, and he was pressing his palms into his eye sockets, waiting for this story to pay out or be over.

"And we got a name," Cappy finished. "The apartment manager at 1513 Vallejo positively IDed the photo. Told us that the suspect was evicted about two months ago, right after he lost his job."

"Drumroll please," said Chi. "The shooter's name is Alfred Brinkley."

It was sad to see the disappointment on the faces of McNeil and Chi, but I had to break it to them.

"Thanks, Paul. We know his name. Did you find out where he used to work?"

"Right, Lieu. That bookstore, uh, Sam's Book Emporium on Mason Street."

I turned to Conklin. "Richie, you look like the Cheshire cat. Whatcha got?"

Conklin had been leaning back in his chair, balancing it on its rear legs, clearly enjoying the banter. Now the front legs of his chair came down, and he leaned over the table. "Brinkley doesn't have a sheet. But...he served at the Presidio for two years. Medical discharge in '94."

"He got into the army after being in a nuthouse?" Jacobi asked.

"He was a kid when he was at Napa State," said Conklin. "His medical records are sealed. Anyway, the army recruiters wouldn't have been too picky."

The fuzzy image of the shooter was starting to come clear. Scary as it was, I knew the answer to what had been messing with my mind since the shooting.

Brinkley was a sure-shot marksman because he'd been trained by the army.

Chapter 17

AT NINE THE NEXT MORNING, Jacobi, Conklin, and I parked our unmarked cars on Mason near North Point. We were two blocks from Fisherman's Wharf, a tourist area crammed with huge hotels, restaurants, bike rentals, and souvenir shops, where sidewalk vendors were setting up their curbside tag sales.

I was feeling keyed up when we entered the cool expanse of the huge bookstore. Jacobi badged the closest desk clerk, asking if she knew Alfred Brinkley.

The clerk paged the floor manager, who walked us to the elevator and down to the basement, where he introduced us to the stockroom manager, a dark-skinned man in his thirties, name of Edison Jones, wearing a threadbare Duran Duran T-shirt and a nose stud.

We arrayed ourselves around the stockroom — concrete walls lined with adjustable shelves, corrugated metal doors opening to the loading dock, guys rolling carts of books all around us.

"Fred and I were buddies," Jones said. "Not like we hung out after work or anything, but he was a bright bulb and I liked him. Then he started getting weird." Jones dialed down the volume on a TV resting atop a metal table crowded with invoices and office supplies.

" 'Weird' like how?" Conklin asked.

"He'd say to me sometimes, 'Did you hear what Wolf Blitzer just said to me?' Like the TV was talking to him, y'know? And he was getting twitchy-like, humming and singing to himself. Made management uneasy," Jones said, lightly running a hand across his T-shirt. "When he started missing work, it gave them a reason to ax him.

"I saved his books," Jones told us. He reached up to a shelf, pulled down a box, set it on the table.

I opened the flaps, saw heavy stuff in there by Jung, Nietzsche, and Wilhelm Reich. And there was a dog-eared paperback of *The Origin of Consciousness in the Breakdown of the Bicameral Mind* by Julian Jaynes.

I picked the paperback out of the box.

"That was his pet book," said Edison. "Surprised he didn't come back for it."

"What's it about?"

"According to Fred, Jaynes had a theory that, until about three thousand years ago, the hemispheres of the human brain weren't connected," Jones said, "so the two halves of the brain didn't communicate directly."

"And the point is?" Jacobi asked.

"Jaynes says that back then, humans believed that their own thoughts came from outside themselves, that their thoughts were actually commands from the gods."

"So Brinkley was... what?" Jacobi asked. "Hearing voices from the television gods?"

"I think he was hearing voices *all* the time. And they were telling him what to do."

Jones's words sent chills out to my fingertips. More than forty-eight hours had passed since the ferry shooting. While dead ends piled up, Brinkley was still out there somewhere. Taking orders from voices. Carrying a gun.

"You have any idea where Brinkley is now?" I asked.

"I saw him hanging out in front of a bar about a month ago," Jones said. "He was looking pretty ragged. Beard all grown out. I made a joke that he was returning to the wild, and he got a wacky expression on his face. Wouldn't look me in the eye."

"Where was this?"

"Outside the Double Shot Bar on Geary. Fred doesn't drink, so maybe he was living in the hotel over the bar."

I knew the place. The Hotel Barbary was one of the several dozen "tourist hotels" in the Tenderloin, rent-by-the-hour rooms used by prostitutes, junkies, and the nearly destitute. It was one step above the gutter, and not much of a step.

If Fred Brinkley had been living at the Hotel Barbary a month ago, he might still be there now.

Chapter 18

THE WEATHERMAN SAID it would rain, but the sun was high and milky overhead. When Fred Brinkley held out his hand, *he could see right through it.*

He headed for the dark of the underground, jogging down the steps into the Civic Center BART, where he used to go when he still had his job.

Brinkley lowered his eyes, marking off his paces on the familiar white marble-tiled floor with black granite borders, walking steadily across the mezzanine, not looking up at the corporate slaves buying their tickets and flowers and bottled water for their commute. He didn't want to pick up any thoughts from their hamster-wheel brains, didn't want to see the prying looks coming from their hooded eyes.

He took the escalator down to the tunnels, but instead of feeling calmer, he realized that the deeper he went, the more agitated, angry, he became.

The voices were on him again, calling him names.

Ducking his head, Brinkley kept his eyes on the floor, and he sang inside his mind, *Ay, ay, ay, ay, BART-*

a-lito-lindo, trying to quash the voices, trying to shut them down.

As soon as he got off the escalator on the third level down, he realized his mistake. The platform was packed with deadheads going home from work.

They were like thunderclouds, with their dark coats, their eyes boring into him, closing in and trapping him where he stood.

Pictures he'd seen on the wall of TVs in the electronics-shop window streamed into Fred's mind: *the images of himself, shooting the people on the ferry.*

He did that!

Brinkley sidled through the crowd, mumbling and singing under his breath until he stood at the edge of the platform, standing on one square only, his toes curled over the void.

Still, he felt the hate and condemnation all around him, and his own fury rose. The white tile walls seemed to pulse and billow. Fred could see, out of the corners of his eyes, people turning toward him, reading his mind.

He wanted to yell, *I had to do it! Watch out. You could be next.*

He stared down onto the rails, not moving or looking at anyone, keeping his hands in his pockets, the right one curled around Bucky.

They know, the voices roared in unison. *They see right through you, Fred.*

A sharp voice called out from behind him, *"Hey!"* Brinkley turned to see a woman with a sharp jaw and tiny black eyes shaking a finger at him.

"He's the *one*. He was on the ferry. *He was there.* That's the ferry shooter. Someone call the police."

Things were breaking up now. Everyone knew the bad thing he'd done.

Dog shit. Loser.

Ay, ay, ay, ayyyyyyy.

Fred pulled Bucky out of his pocket, waved it above the crowd. People all around him screamed and shrank away.

The tunnel roared.

Silver-and-blue bullet cars streaked into the station, the noise obliterating all other sound and thought.

The train stopped, and clots of people boiled out of the cars like rats, others washing back in, buffeting Fred like a tide, slamming him into a pylon.

Knocking the breath right out of him.

Freeing himself, wading against the throng, Fred made his way to the escalator. In long, bounding strides, he bolted up past the rodent people on the moving stairway, finding his way up to the air on the street.

The voice inside his head yelled, *Go! Get your ass out of here!*

Chapter 19

THE DIGITAL CLOCK on the microwave read 7:08. I was physically wrung out and mentally fried after combing the Tenderloin all day, coming up with nothing more than a list of all the places where Alfred Brinkley *didn't* live.

I wasn't just frustrated, either. I felt dread. Fred Brinkley was still out there.

I put a Healthy Choice macaroni and cheese into the microwave, pressed the minute button five times.

As my dinner revolved, I ran the day through my mind again, searching for anything we might have overlooked in our tour of six dozen sleazy hotels, the interviews with useless desk clerks and scores of low-rent tenants.

Martha brushed up against me, and I stroked her ears, poured dog chow into a bowl. She lowered her head, wagged her plumey tail.

"You're a good girl," I said. "Light of my life."

I had just cracked open a beer when my doorbell rang. *What now?*

I limped to the window to see who had the audacity to

ring my bell—but I didn't know the man staring up at me from the sidewalk.

He was clean shaven, half in shadow—holding up an envelope.

"What do you want?"

"I have something for you, Lieutenant. It's urgent. I have to deliver this to you personally."

What was he? A process server? A tipster? Behind me, the microwave beeped, alerting me that dinner was ready.

"Leave it in the mailbox!" I shouted down.

"I could do that," said my visitor. "But you said on TV, 'Do you know this man?' Remember?"

"Do you know him?" I called.

"I *am* him. I'm the one who did it."

Chapter 20

I HAD AN INSTANT of stunned confusion.

The ferry shooter was at my door?

Then I snapped to.

"I'll be right there!" I shouted down.

I grabbed my gun and holster from the back of a chair, clipped my cuffs to my belt. As I rounded the second-floor landing, I called Jacobi on my cell phone, knowing full well that I couldn't wait for him to arrive.

I could be walking into a shooting gallery, but if the man downstairs was Alfred Brinkley, I couldn't chance letting him get away.

My Glock was in my hand as I cracked the front door a couple of inches, using it as a blind.

"Keep your hands where I can see them," I called out.

The man looked volatile. He seemed to hesitate, move back into the street, then forward toward my doorway. His eyes darted everywhere, and I could make out that he was singing under his breath.

God, he was crazy—and he was dangerous. Where was his gun?

"Hands up. Stay where you are!" I yelled again.

The man stopped walking around. He raised his hands, flapping his envelope side to side like a white flag.

I scanned his face, trying to match what I saw against my mental picture of the shooter. This guy had shaved, and he'd done a poor job of it. Wisps of beard showed dark against his pale skin.

In every other way, I saw a match. He was tall, skinny, wearing clothes similar or identical to those worn by the shooter about sixty hours ago.

Was this Alfred Brinkley? Had a violent killer simply rung my doorbell to turn himself in? Or was this a different kind of lunatic, looking for a spotlight?

I stepped out onto the moon-shadowed sidewalk, gripping my Glock in both hands, pointing at the man's chest. The unwashed smell of him wafted toward me.

"It's *me*," he said, staring down at his shoes. "You said you're looking for me. I saw you on TV. In the video store."

"Get on the ground," I barked at him. "Facedown, with your fingers entwined on top of your head where I can see them."

He swayed on his feet. I shouted, *"Get down—do it now!"* and he dropped to the sidewalk and placed his hands on his head.

With my gun pressed to the back of his skull, I ran my hands over the suspect's body, checking for weapons, images from Rooney's video flickering through my mind the whole time.

I pulled a gun from his jacket pocket, stuck it into the back of my waistband, and searched for more weapons. There were none.

I holstered my Glock and yanked the cuffs from my belt.

"What's your name?" I asked, dragging back each stick-thin arm until the cuffs snapped around his wrists. Then I picked the envelope up from the sidewalk and stuffed it into my front pocket.

"Fred Brinkley," he said, his voice filling with agitation. "You know me. You said to come in, remember? 'We *will* find whoever did this terrible thing.' I wrote it all down."

The pictures from the Rooney video looped in my head. I saw this man shoot five people. *I saw him shoot Claire.*

I took his wallet from his hip pocket with a shaking hand, flipped it open, saw his driver's license by the dim light of the streetlamp across the road.

It *was* Alfred Brinkley.

I had him.

I read Brinkley his rights and he waived them, saying again, "I did it. I'm the ferry shooter."

"How did you find me?" I asked.

"Your address is on the Internet. At the library," Brinkley told me. "Lock me up, okay? I think I could do it again."

Jacobi's car pulled up just then, brakes squealing. He bolted out of the driver's seat with his gun in hand.

"You couldn't wait for me, Boxer?"

"Mr. Brinkley is cooperating, Jacobi. Everything is under control."

But seeing Jacobi, knowing that the danger was over, sent waves of relief through me, making me want to laugh and cry and shout *woo-hoooo* all at the same time.

"Nice work," I heard Jacobi say. I felt his hand on my shoulder. I gulped air, trying to calm myself as Jacobi and I got Brinkley to his feet.

As we folded him into the backseat of Jacobi's car, Brinkley turned toward me.

"Thank you, Lieutenant," he said, his crazy eyes still darting, his face crumpling as he broke into tears. "I knew you would help me."

Chapter 21

JACOBI FOLLOWED ME into my office, our nerves strung so tight we could have played them like guitars. As we waited for Brinkley to be processed, we hunched over my desk, drinking coffee, talking over what we needed to do next.

Brinkley had confessed to being the ferry shooter, and he'd refused counsel. But the written statement he'd given me was a rambling screed of nonsense about white light, and rat people, and a gun named "Bucky."

We had to get Brinkley's confession on the record, show that while Alfred Brinkley might be mentally disturbed, he was rational *now*.

After I called Tracchio, I phoned Cindy, who was not only my good friend but top dog on the *Chronicle*'s crime desk, to give her a heads-up on Brinkley's capture. Then I paced around the squad room, watching the hands of the clock crawl around the dial as we waited for Tracchio to arrive.

By 9:15 Alfred Brinkley had been printed and photographed, his clothes swapped out for a prison jumpsuit so that his garments could be tested for blood spatter and gunshot residue.

I asked Brinkley to let a medical tech take his blood, and I told him why: "I want to make sure you're not under the influence of alcohol or drugs when we take your confession."

"I'm clean," Brinkley told me, rolling up his sleeve.

Now Brinkley waited for us in Interview Room Number Two, the box with the overhead video camera that worked most of the time.

Jacobi and I joined Brinkley in the gray-tiled room, pulling out the chairs around the scratched metal table, taking our seats across from the killer.

My skin still crawled when I looked at his pale and scruffy face.

Remembered what he'd said.

"I'm the one who did it."

Chapter 22

BRINKLEY WAS JUMPY. His knees were thumping the underside of the table, and he had crossed his cuffed wrists so that he could pluck at the hairs on his forearm.

"Mr. Brinkley, you understand that you have the right to remain silent?" I asked him. He nodded as I took him through Miranda once more. And he said 'yes' when I asked, "Do you understand your rights?"

I put a waiver in front of him, and he signed it. I heard a chair scraping in the observation room behind the glass, and the faint whir of the camera overhead. This interview was on.

"Do you know what day of the week this is?"

"It's Monday," he told me.

"Where do you live?"

"BART stations. Computer stores. The library sometimes."

"You know where you are right now?"

"The Hall of Justice, 850 Bryant Street."

"Very good, Mr. Brinkley. Now, can you tell me this:

did you travel on the *Del Norte* ferry on Saturday, the day before yesterday?"

"Yep, I did. It was a really nice day. I found the ticket when I was at the farmer's market," he said. "I don't think it was a crime to use that ticket, was it?" he asked.

"Did you take it from someone?"

"No, I found it on the ground."

"We'll just let it slide, then," Jacobi told Brinkley.

Brinkley looked calmer now and much younger than his years. It was starting to irk me that he seemed childish, even harmless. Like some kind of victim himself.

I had a thought about how he would come across to a jury. *Would they find him sympathetic?*

"Not guilty" by reason of the likability factor as well as being freaking insane?

"On the return trip, Mr. Brinkley—" I said.

"You can call me Fred."

"Okay, Fred. As the *Del Norte* was docking in San Francisco, did you pull a gun and fire on some of the passengers?"

"I had to do it," he said, his voice breaking, suddenly strained. "The mother was... listen, *I did a bad thing.* I know that, and I want to be punished."

"Did you shoot those people?" I insisted.

"Yes, I did it! I shot that mother and her son. And those two men. And that other woman who was looking at me like she knew everything inside my head. I'm really sorry. I was having a very nice time until it all went wrong."

"But you planned this shooting, didn't you?" I asked, keeping my voice level, even giving Brinkley an encouraging smile. "Isn't it true that you were carrying a loaded gun?"

"I always carry Bucky," Brinkley said. "But I didn't want to hurt those people. I didn't *know* them. I didn't even think they were *real* until I saw the video on TV."

"Is that right? So why'd you shoot them?" Jacobi asked.

Brinkley stared over my head into the glass of the two-way mirror. "The voices told me to do it."

Was that the truth? Or was Brinkley staging his insanity defense right now?

Jacobi asked him what kind of voices he was talking about, but Brinkley had stopped answering. He dropped his chin toward his chest, mumbling, "I want you to lock me up. Will you do that? I really need some sleep."

"I'm pretty sure we can find you an empty cell on the tenth floor," I said.

I knocked on the door, and Sergeant Steve Hall came into the interrogation room. He stood behind the prisoner.

"Mr. Brinkley," I said as we all came to our feet, "you've been charged with the murders of four people, attempted murder of another, and about fourteen lesser crimes. Make sure you get a good lawyer."

"Thank you," Brinkley said, looking me in the eyes for the first time. "You're an honorable person. I really appreciate all you've done."

Chapter 23

THE NEWSPAPER WAS WAITING outside my front door the next morning, the headline huge over Cindy's by-line: FERRY SHOOTER IN DRY DOCK.

When I arrived at the Hall of Justice, a knot of reporters was waiting for me.

"How do you feel, Lieutenant?"

"Fantastic," I said, grinning. "Doesn't get any better than this."

I answered questions, praised my team, and smiled for a few pictures before going into the building, taking the elevator to the third floor.

When I walked through the gate to the squad room, Brenda struck a little gong she kept at her station and then stood up and hugged me. I could see the flowers on my desk from across the room.

I gathered everyone together and thanked them for all they'd done, and when Inspector Lemke asked if I could give lessons in how to conjure up murderers, we all cracked up.

"I've got the nose-twitching part down pat," he said, "but nothing happens."

"You gotta twitch your nose, cross your arms, and blink at the same *time!*" Rodriguez shouted.

I was pouring coffee for myself in the lunchroom before diving into the thick pile of paperwork taking up half my desktop when Brenda peeked around the doorway, saying, "The chief is on line one."

I went to my office, moved a huge basket of flowers from my desk. Glanced at the small card sticking up between the roses. There were a whole lot of X's and O's on the note from Joe, my wonderful guy.

I was still smiling when I pressed the blinking button on my phone, the chief's voice all mellow, asking me to come upstairs to his office.

"Let me get the team," I said, but he told me, "No, just come by yourself."

I let Brenda know I'd be back in a few minutes and took the stairs to Tracchio's walnut-paneled office on the fifth floor.

The chief stood up when I entered, reached his meaty hand across his desk, grasping mine, saying, "Boxer, bringing down that wackjob makes this a good day for the SFPD. I want to thank you again for your excellent work."

I said, "Thanks, Chief. And thanks for backing me up." I was readying to leave—but an embarrassed look came over the chief's face, a look I hadn't seen him wear before.

He gestured for me to sit down and he did the same, rolling his chair back and forth on the acrylic rug-protector a couple of times before locking his hands across his midsection.

"Lindsay, I've come to a conclusion that I've been fighting tooth and nail."

He was going to give me more manpower?

A bigger overtime budget?

"I've watched firsthand how you worked this case, and I'm impressed at how much tenacity and determination you showed in the investigation."

"Thanks—"

"And so I have to admit that you were right and I was wrong."

Right about what?

My mind raced ahead of his words, trying to gain a half second on him—and failing.

"As you've told me," Tracchio continued, "you belong on the street, not chained to a desk. And I get it now. I finally understand. Simply put, administrative work is a waste of your talent."

I stared at the chief as he put a badge down on the desktop in front of me.

"Congratulations, Boxer, on your well-earned *demotion* to sergeant."

Chapter 24

SUDDENLY I WAS DIZZY with disbelief.

I heard Tracchio speaking, but it was as if his desk had shot back through the wall and he was talking to me from somewhere over the freeway.

"You'll have a dotted-line reporting relationship to me. Keep your current pay grade, of course..."

Inside my head, I was screaming, *Demotion? You're demoting me? Today?*

I made a grab for the edge of his desk, needing to hold on. I saw Tracchio fall back into his chair, the expression on his face telling me that he was as stunned by my reaction as I was by his announcement.

"What is it, Boxer? Isn't this what you wanted? You've been nagging me for months—"

"No, I mean, *yes*. I *have*. But I wasn't expecting—"

"Come on, Boxer. What are you telling me? I spent all night clearing this up and down the line because you *said* it's what you wanted."

I opened my mouth, closed it again. "Give me some time to get my head around this, okay, Tony?" I sputtered.

"I give up," Tracchio said, picking up his stapler and banging it down on his desk. "I don't understand you. I never will. I give up, Boxer!"

I don't remember leaving the chief's office, but I do remember a long walk to the stairway, a strained smile on my face as people called out their congratulations when I passed their desks.

My mind was cycling on a short loop.

What the hell had I been thinking?

And what did I want?

I found the stairwell and was leaning heavily on the banister, making my way down to the squad room, when I saw Jacobi coming up the other way.

"*Warren,* you're not going to *believe* this."

"Let's get out of here," he said.

We took the stairs to the ground floor and out onto Bryant, heading toward the Flower Mart.

"Tracchio called me last night," Jacobi said as we walked. I looked up at him. Jacobi and I have never had any secrets from each other, but I read pain on his face, and that jolted me.

"He offered me the job, Lindsay. Your job. But I told him I wouldn't take it unless it was okay with you."

The rumble under my feet was surely the Caltrain coming into the station, but it felt like an earthquake.

I knew what I was supposed to say: *Congratulations. Brilliant choice. You'll be great, Jacobi.*

But I couldn't get out the words.

"I need some time to think, Jacobi. I'm taking the day off," I sputtered.

"Sure, Lindsay. Nobody's going to do anything unless—"

"Maybe *two* days."

"Lindsay, stop! Talk to me."

But I was gone.

I jaywalked across the street. Got my car out of the lot and drove down Bryant to Sixth, and from there got onto 280 South, heading toward Potrero Hill.

I jerked my phone off my belt and autodialed Joe's cell phone as I drove, listened to the ring tone as I floored my Explorer and took it into the fast lane.

It was one p.m. in Washington.

Pick up, Joe!

The ring went into his voice mail, so I left a message: *"Call me. Please."*

Then I phoned San Francisco General.

I asked the operator to put me through to Claire.

Chapter 25

I WAS HOPING TO HEAR Claire's voice, but Edmund answered the phone. He sounded as if he'd spent another night sleeping in a chair.

"How is she?" I asked through the crimp in my throat.

"Having another MRI," he said.

"Tell Claire we got the shooter," I said. "He confessed, and we've got him locked up."

I told Edmund that I'd check in with Claire later, then I dialed Joe again. This time I got the voice mail at his office, so I tried him at home.

Got his voice mail there, too.

I braked at the light on Eighteenth Street, tapped my fingers impatiently against the steering wheel, stepped on the gas as the light turned green.

An old memory came into my mind—the day I'd been promoted to lieutenant on the heels of bringing down the "bride and groom killer," a psycho who'd surely earned a top-ten ranking in the Most-Depraved-Criminal Hall of Fame. At the time, I viewed my promotion as pretty much a political appointment. No woman had held the job before.

I'd stepped up, let them pin a gold shield on me, without ever knowing if the power and responsibility of the job were what I wanted.

I guess I still didn't know.

I *had* asked to be put back on the line, so of course Tracchio didn't understand my reaction. *Shit.* I didn't understand it myself.

But sometimes you couldn't know a thing until you were there.

A dotted-line reporting to Tracchio was bullshit.

I'd be going backward in rank.

Could I handle taking orders from Jacobi?

"I told him I wouldn't take it unless it was okay with you," he'd said.

I needed to talk to Joe.

I pulled the phone back from the passenger seat and hit redial, the sound of Joe's voice on his outgoing message calling up so many memories: the storybook trips we'd taken together, our lovemaking, little things about Joe that I adored—every moment savored because I didn't know when I'd see him again.

What I wouldn't give to be in his arms tonight, to have him wrap me up in his love, and to feel his ability to see the real me. His touch could make the bad feelings go away....

I clicked off my phone without leaving a message, called Joe's other two numbers—same thing.

I pulled my car into a parking spot, set the hand brake, and sat there stupidly, looking at nothing, wishing that I could see Joe.

And then a bright idea broke through.

Hey, I can.

Chapter 26

I DIDN'T LOOK LIKE ANYONE ELSE in the flight lounge, all men in gray suits and red or blue ties—and me. I'd dressed in a new butter-colored cashmere V-neck, tight jeans, and a waist-skimming tweed jacket. My hair gleamed like a halo. Men stole glances, gave my ego a boost.

As I waited for the plane to board, I checked things off in my mind: That Martha's dog sitter was on duty. That I'd locked up my gun and badge in my dresser drawer. That I'd left my cell phone in my car. Actually, leaving my cell phone was an oversight, but I didn't need a shrink to tell me that by shedding my hardware, I was telling the Job to go straight to hell.

I was traveling light, but I *had* brought the essential stuff: lipstick and my round trip business-class ticket to Reagan National that Joe had given me with his keys and a note saying, *"This is your 'come-to-Joe' pass and it's good anytime. XOXO, Joe."*

I felt a little reckless as I boarded the plane. Not only

was I leaving town with a major conflict unresolved but something else was giving me the jitters.

Joe had made surprise visits to me, but I'd never dropped in unannounced on *him.*

The glass of preflight champagne helped settle me down, and as soon as the plane lifted off, I lowered my seat into the reclining position and slept, waking up only when the pilot's voice announced our imminent descent into DC.

Once on the ground, I gave a cab driver Joe's address in northwest DC.

A half hour later, the cab swooped around the plantings and fountains in front of the deluxe, L-shaped Kennedy-Warren Apartment Complex. And only minutes after that, I stood in the densely carpeted top-floor hallway of the historic wing, ringing Joe's doorbell.

Well, I'm here.

When he didn't answer, I rang the bell again. Then I slipped the first key into the lower lock, used the second key on the dead bolt, and opened the door.

I called out, "Joe?" as I stepped into his unlit foyer. I called again as I approached the kitchen.

Now I was asking myself, *Where* was *Joe?*

Why hadn't he answered any of his phones?

The kitchen opened into a large, attractive area that was both a dining and a living room. Hardwood floors glowed under the stream of light pouring through the windows at the far end, and I saw a terrace beyond.

I noted that the richly upholstered and dark-wood furnishings were in neat, apple-pie order.

My second look made my heart slam to a stop.

A woman was curled up on a sofa, turned toward the

windows, reading a magazine, the white cords of an iPod dangling from her ears.

I was too shocked to move.

Or speak a word.

Chapter 27

MY HEART RATE ZOOMED as my focus narrowed to the woman on the couch, a sandwich and cup of tea beside her on the coffee table.

I took in her black tank top and workout pants, the thick, blond-streaked hair knotted behind her head, her bare feet.

My body felt bloodless except for the tingling in my fingertips. *Had Joe been leading a double life while I was in San Francisco, waiting for his calls and visits?*

My face flushed with anger but also shame. I didn't know whether to shout or run.

How could Joe have been cheating on me?

The woman must have caught my reflection in the glass. She dropped her magazine, put her hands to her face, and screamed.

I screamed, too. *"Who the hell are you?"*

"Who are *you!*" she shouted back, her hair tumbling out of its knot as she ripped the iPod out of her ears.

"I'm Joe's girlfriend," I said. I felt naked and raw, wishing I had a badge to flash at her. Any badge.

Oh, Joe, what have you done?

"I'm Milda," she said, jumping up from the couch, leading me into the kitchen. "I work here. I clean house for Mr. Molinari."

I laughed, not out of humor but out of shock.

She yanked a check out of her pants pocket and stuck it out for me to see.

But I was barely focusing on her. Images from the last few days were flying around inside my head.

And now this young woman's presence was undoing whatever hold I had over my emotions.

"I finished early and I just thought I'd sit for a few minutes," she said as she washed the dishes she'd used. "Please don't tell him, okay?"

I nodded numbly. "No. Of course not."

"I'm leaving now," she said, turning off the taps. "I don't want to be late to pick up my son, so I'm going now, okay?"

I nodded.

I went down a hall, pushed open the door to the bathroom. I opened the medicine chest and scanned the boxes and bottles, looking for nail polish, tampons, makeup.

Coming up empty, I went to the bedroom, a large carpeted space with a view of the courtyard. I threw open Joe's closet door, checked the floor for women's shoes, ran my hands through the rack. No skirts, no blouses. *What was I doing?*

I knew Joe, didn't I?

I turned back to the bed and was about to undo the bedding and inspect the linens when I saw a photo on the night table. It was of me and Joe six months ago in Sausalito, his arm around me as the breeze whipped my hair across my face. We both looked in love.

I pressed my hands to my eyes.

I was so ashamed. The sobs simply poured out of me. I just stood there in Joe's bedroom and cried.

And then I left and went back to California.

Part Two

BROWN-EYED GIRL

Chapter 28

MADISON TYLER HOPSCOTCHED over the lines in the sidewalk, then raced back to her nanny's side, grabbing her hand as they walked toward Alta Plaza Park, Madison saying, "Were you *listening,* Paola?"

Paola Ricci squeezed Madison's small hand.

Sometimes the little girl's enchanting five-year-old precocity was almost more than Paola could understand.

"Of course I was listening, darling."

"As I was saying," the girl said in the funny grown-up way she had, "when I play Beethoven's *Bagatelle,* the first notes are an ascending scale, and they look like a blue ladder—"

She trilled the notes.

"Then, the next part, when I play C-D-C, the notes are pink-green-pink!" she exclaimed.

"So you *imagine* that those notes have colors?"

"No, Paola," the little girl said comically, patiently. "The notes *are* those colors. Don't you see colors when you sing?"

"Nope. I guess I'm a ninny," Paola said. "A ninny-nanny."

"I don't know what a ninny-nanny *is*," Madison said, her dazzling smile setting off sparks in her big brown eyes. "But it sounds very funny."

The two laughed hard, Madison grabbing Paola around the waist, burying her face in the young woman's coat as they passed the exclusive Waldorf School, only a block and a half from where Madison lived with her parents.

"It's Saturday," Madison whispered to Paola. "I don't have to even *look* at school on Saturday."

Now the park was only a block away, and seeing the stone walls surrounding it, Madison got more excited and changed subjects.

"Mommy says I can have a red Lakeland terrier when I get a little older," Madison confided as they crossed Divisadero. "I'm going to name him 'Wolfgang.'"

"What a serious name for a little dog," Paola said, intent on crossing the street safely. She barely glanced at the black minivan idling outside the park's fence. Expensive black minivans were as common as crows in Pacific Heights.

Paola swung Madison's arm, and the child jumped up onto the curb, then stopped suddenly as someone got out of the vehicle and came quickly toward them.

Madison said to her nanny, "Paola, who is that?"

"What's wrong?" Paola called to the man stepping out of the van.

"Trouble at home. You've both got to come with us right now. Madison, your mom took a fall down the stairs."

Madison stepped out from behind her nanny's back, shouting, "My daddy told me never to ride with strangers! And believe me, you're *strange*."

The man picked up the child like a bag of birdseed, and as she shouted, *"Help! Put me down,"* he tossed her into the backseat of the van.

"Get in," the man said to Paola. He was pointing a handgun at her chest.

"Either get in or kiss this kid good-bye."

Chapter 29

RICH CONKLIN AND I had just returned to the squad room after a grim morning of investigating a brutal drive-by shooting when Jacobi waved us into his office.

We crossed the gray linoleum floor to the glass box and took our seats, Conklin perched on the edge of the credenza where Jacobi used to sit, me in the side chair next to Jacobi's desk, watching him get comfortable in the chair that was once mine.

I was still trying to get used to this turn of events. I looked around at the mess Jacobi had made of the place in just under two weeks: newspapers piled on the floor and windowsill, food odors coming out of the trash can.

"You're a pig, Jacobi," I said. "And I mean that in the barnyard sense."

Jacobi laughed, a thing he'd done more in the last few days than he'd done in the last two years, and despite the chop to my ego, I was glad that he wasn't huffing up hills anymore. He was a great cop, good at managing the unmanageable, and I was working myself around to loving him again.

Jacobi coughed a few times, said, "We've got a kidnapping."

"And *we're* catching it?" Conklin asked.

"Major Crimes has been on it for a few hours, but a witness came forward and now it looks like there could be a murder," said Jacobi. "We'll be coordinating with Lieutenant Macklin."

A humming sound came from the computer as Jacobi booted up, a thing he'd never done before getting his new badge. He pulled a CD off the pile of crap on his desk and clumsily slid it into the CD/DVD tray of his computer.

He said, "Little girl, age five, was going to the park with her nanny at nine this morning when they were snatched. The nanny is Paola Ricci, here on a work visa from Cremona, Italy. The child is Madison Tyler."

"Of the *Chronicle* Tylers?" I asked.

"Yep. Henry Tyler is the little girl's father."

"Did you say there's a witness to the kidnapping?"

"That's right, Boxer. A woman walking her schnauzer before going to work saw a figure in a gray coat exit a black minivan outside Alta Plaza Park on Scott Street."

"What do you mean, 'figure'?" Conklin asked.

"All she could say was a person in a gray coat, didn't know if it was a man or a woman because said person was turned away from her and she only looked up for a second. Likewise, she couldn't identify the make of the vehicle. Said it happened too fast."

"And what makes this a possible homicide?" I asked.

"The witness said that as soon as the car rounded Divisadero, she heard a pop. Then she saw blood explode against the back window of the van."

Chapter 30

JACOBI CLICKED HIS MOUSE a few times, then swung the laptop around so Conklin and I could see the video that was playing on the screen.

"This is Madison Tyler," he said.

The camera was focused on a small blond-haired child who came out from behind curtains onto a stage. She was wearing a simple navy-blue velvet dress with a lace collar, socks, and shiny red Mary Janes.

She was absolutely the prettiest little girl I'd ever seen, with a look of intelligence in her eyes that canceled any notion that she was a baby pageant queen.

Applause filled Jacobi's office as the little girl climbed onto a piano seat in front of a Steinway grand.

The clapping died away, and she began to play a piece of classical music I didn't recognize, but it was complicated and the child didn't seem to make any mistakes.

She finished the piece with a flourish, stretching her arms as far as they could go down the keyboard, releasing the last notes to loud bravos and rousing applause.

Madison turned and said to the audience, "I'll be able to do much better when my arms grow."

Fond laughter bubbled over the speakers, and a boy of about nine came out from the wings and gave her a bouquet.

"Have the parents gotten a call?" I asked, tearing my eyes from the video of Madison Tyler.

"It's still early, but no, they haven't heard anything from anyone," said Jacobi. "Not a single word. Nothing about a ransom so far."

Chapter 31

CINDY THOMAS WAS WORKING from the home office she'd set up in the small second bedroom of her new apartment. CNN was providing ambient sound as she typed, immersed in the story she was writing about Alfred Brinkley's upcoming trial. She thought of not answering the phone when it rang next to her elbow.

Then she glanced at the caller ID — and grabbed the phone off the hook.

"Mr. Tyler?" she said.

Henry Tyler's voice was eerily hollow, nearly unrecognizable. She almost thought he was playing a joke, but that wasn't his style.

Listening hard, gasping and saying, *"No...oh, no,"* she tried hard to understand the man who was crying, losing his thoughts, and having to ask Cindy what he'd been saying.

"She was wearing a blue coat," Cindy prompted.

"That's right. A dark-blue coat, red sweater, blue pants, red shoes."

"You'll have copy in an hour," Cindy said, "and by then

you'll have heard from those bastards saying how much you have to pay to get Maddy back. You *will* get her back."

Cindy said good-bye to the *Chronicle*'s associate publisher, put down the receiver, and sat still for a moment, gripping the armrests, reeling from a sickening feeling of fear. She'd covered enough kidnappings to know that if the child wasn't found today, the chances of finding her alive dropped by about half. It would drop by half again if she wasn't found tomorrow.

She thought back to the last time she'd seen Madison, at the beginning of the summer when the little girl had come to the office with her father.

For about twenty minutes Madison had twirled around in the chair across from Cindy's desk, scribbling on a steno pad, pretending that she was a reporter who was interviewing Cindy about her job.

"Why is it called a '*dead*line'? Do you ever get afraid when you're writing about bad guys? What's the dumbest story you ever wrote?"

Maddy was a delightful kid, funny and unspoiled, and Cindy had felt aggrieved when Tyler's secretary had returned, saying, "Come on, Madison. Miss Thomas has work to do."

Cindy had impetuously kissed the child on the cheek, saying, "You're as cute as *ten* buttons, you know that?"

And Madison had flung her arms around her neck and returned the kiss.

"See you in the funny papers," Cindy had called after her, and Madison Tyler had spun around, grinning. "That's where I'll be!"

Now Cindy turned her eyes to her blank computer

screen, paralyzed with thoughts of Madison being held captive by people who didn't love her, wondering if the girl was tied up inside a car trunk, if she'd been sexually molested, if she was already dead.

Cindy opened a new file on her computer and, after a few false starts, felt the story unspool under her fingers. *"The five-year-old daughter of* Chronicle *associate publisher Henry Tyler was abducted this morning only blocks from her house...."*

She heard Henry Tyler in her head, his voice choked with misery: "Write the story, Cindy. And pray to God we'll have Madison back before we run it."

Chapter 32

YUKI CASTELLANO SAT three rows back in the gallery of Superior Court 22, waiting for the clerk to call the case number.

She'd been with the DA's office only about a month, and although she'd worked as a defense attorney in a top law firm for several years, switching to the prosecution side was turning out to be dirtier, more urgent, and more real than defending white-collar clients in civil lawsuits.

It was exactly what she wanted.

Her former colleagues would never believe how much she was enjoying her new life "on the dark side."

The purpose of today's hearing was to set a trial date for Alfred Brinkley. There was an ADA in the office whose job it was to attend no-brainer proceedings like this one and keep the master calendar.

But Yuki didn't want to delegate a moment of this case.

She'd been picked by senior ADA Leonard Parisi to be his second chair in a trial that mattered very much to Yuki. Alfred Brinkley had murdered four people. It was sheer luck that he hadn't also killed Claire Washburn, one of her dearest friends.

She glanced down the row of seats, past the junkies and child abusers, their mothers and girlfriends, the public defenders in ad hoc conferences with their clients.

Finally she homed in on Public Defender Barbara Blanco, who was whispering to the ferry shooter. Blanco was a smart woman who, like herself, had drawn a hell of a card in Alfred Brinkley.

Blanco had pleaded Brinkley "not guilty" at his arraignment and was certainly going to try to get his confession tossed out before the trial. She would contend that Brinkley was bug-nuts during the crime and had been medicated ever since. And she'd work to get him kicked out of the penal system and into the mental-health system.

Let her try.

The clerk called the case number, and Yuki's pulse quickened as she closed her laptop and walked to the bench.

Alfred Brinkley followed meekly behind his attorney, looking clean-cut and less agitated than he had at his arraignment—which was all to the good.

Yuki opened the wooden gate between the gallery and the court proper, and stood at the bench with Blanco and Brinkley, looking up into the slate-blue eyes of Judge Norman Moore.

Moore looked back at them fleetingly, then dropped his eyes to the docket.

"All right. What do you say we set this matter soon, say Monday, November seventeenth?"

Yuki said, "That's good for the People, Your Honor."

But Blanco had a different idea. "Your Honor, Mr. Brinkley has a long history of mental illness. He should be evaluated pursuant to 1368 to determine his competence to stand trial."

Moore dropped his hands to his desktop, sighed, and said, "Okay, Ms. Blanco. Dr. Charlene Everedt is back from vacation. She told me this morning that she's got some free time. She'll do the psych on Mr. Brinkley."

His eyes went to Yuki. "Ms. Castellano, is it?"

"Yes, Your Honor. This is a delaying tactic," she said, her words coming out clipped and fast, her usual rat-a-tat style. "Defense counsel wants to get her client out of the public eye so that the media flap will die down. Ms. Blanco knows perfectly well that Mr. Brinkley is quite competent to stand trial. He shot and killed four people. He turned himself in. He confessed of his own volition.

"The People want and deserve a speedy trial —"

"I understand what the People want, Ms. Castellano," said the judge, countering her verbal machine gun with a patient drawl. "But we'll get a quick turnaround from Dr. Everedt. Shouldn't take more than a few days. I think the People can wait that long, don't you?"

Yuki said, "Yes, sir," and as the judge said, "Next case," to his clerk, Yuki left the courtroom through the vestibule and out the double courtroom doors.

She turned right, down the dingy marble hall toward her office, hoping that the court-appointed shrink would see what she and Lindsay knew to be true.

Alfred Brinkley might be crazy, but he wasn't legally insane.

He was a premeditated killer four times over. Soon enough, if all went well, the prosecution would get their chance to prove it.

Chapter 33

I TOSSED THE KEYS TO CONKLIN and got into the passenger-side door of the squad car.

Conklin whistled nervously through his teeth as we pulled onto Bryant, headed north on Sixth Street for a few blocks, then went across Market Street and north toward Pacific Heights.

"If there was ever a thing that would make you not want to have kids, this is it," he said.

"Otherwise?"

"I'd want a whole tribe."

We theorized about the kidnapping — whether or not there really had been a murder and if the nanny could have played a part in the abduction.

"She was inside," I said. "She would've known everything that went on in the household. How much money they had, their patterns and movements. If Madison trusted her, the abduction would have been a piece of cake."

"So why pop the nanny?" said Conklin.

"Well, maybe she outlived her usefulness."

"One less person to cut in on the ransom. Still, to shoot her in front of the little girl."

"Was it the nanny?" I asked. "Or did they shoot the child?"

We lapsed into silence as we turned onto Washington, one of the prettiest streets in Pacific Heights.

The Tyler house stood in the middle of the tree-lined block, a stately Victorian, pale yellow with gingerbread under the eaves and plants cascading over the sides of the flower boxes. It was a dream house, the kind of place you never imagined being visited by terror.

Conklin parked at the curb, and we took the Napa stone path six steps up to the front-door landing.

I lifted the brass knocker and let it fall against the striker plate on the old oak door, knowing that inside this beautiful house were two people absolutely steeped in fear and grief.

Chapter 34

HENRY TYLER OPENED THE FRONT DOOR, paling as he seemed to recognize my face. I held up my badge.

"I'm Sergeant Boxer and this is Inspector Conklin—"

"I know who you are," he said to me. "You're Cindy Thomas's friend. From *homicide*."

"That's right, Mr. Tyler, but please . . . we don't have any news about your daughter."

"Some other inspectors were here earlier," he said, showing us down a carpeted hallway to a sumptuous living room furnished authentically in 1800s style—antiques and Persian rugs and paintings of people and their dogs from an earlier time. A piano was angled toward the windows and a zillion-dollar panoramic view of the bay.

Tyler invited us to sit, taking a seat across from us on a velvet camelback sofa.

"We're here because a witness to the kidnapping heard a gunshot," I said.

"A gunshot?"

"We have no reason to think Madison has been harmed, Mr. Tyler, but we need to know more about your daughter and Paola Ricci."

Elizabeth Tyler entered the room, dressed in beige silk and fine wool, her eyes puffy and red from crying. She sat down beside her husband and clasped his hand.

"The sergeant just told me that the woman who saw Madison kidnapped heard a *gunshot!*"

"Oh, my *God*," said Elizabeth Tyler, collapsing against her husband.

I explained the situation again, doing my best to calm Madison's parents, saying we knew only that a gun had been fired. I left out any mention of blood against glass.

After Mrs. Tyler had composed herself, Conklin asked if they'd noticed anyone who seemed out of place hanging around the neighborhood.

"I never saw a thing out of the ordinary," Tyler said.

"We watch out for one another in this neighborhood," said Elizabeth. "We're unabashed snoops. If any of us had seen anything suspicious, we would have called the police."

We asked the Tylers about their movements over the past days and about their habits—when they left the house, when they went to bed at night.

"Tell me about your daughter," I said. "Don't leave anything out."

Mrs. Tyler brightened for a moment. "She's a very happy little girl. Loves dogs. And she's a musical genius, you know."

"I saw a video. She was playing the piano," I said.

"Do you know she has synesthesia?" Elizabeth Tyler asked me.

I shook my head. "What is synesthesia?"

"When she hears or plays music, the notes appear to her in color. It's a fantastic gift—"

"It's a neurological condition," Henry Tyler said impatiently. "It has nothing to do with her abduction. This has got to be about money. What else could it be?"

"What can you tell us about Paola?" I asked.

"She spoke excellent English," Tyler said. "She's been with us only a couple of months. When was it, sweetie?"

"September. Right after Mala went home to Sri Lanka. Paola was highly recommended," Mrs. Tyler said. "And Maddy took to her instantly."

"Do you know any of Paola's friends?"

"No," Mrs. Tyler told us. "She wasn't allowed to bring anyone to the house. She had Thursdays and Sunday afternoons off, and what she did on those days, I'm sorry, we really don't know."

"She was always on her cell phone," Tyler said. "Madison told me that. So she had to have friends. What are you suggesting, Inspector? You think she was behind this?"

"Does that seem possible to you?"

"Sure," said Tyler. "She saw how we live. Maybe she wanted some of this for herself. Or maybe some guy she was seeing put her up to it."

"Right now, we can't rule anything out," I said.

"Whatever it takes, whoever did it," Henry Tyler said, his wife starting to break down beside him, "just please find our little girl."

Chapter 35

PAOLA RICCI'S ROOM in the Tylers' house was compact and feminine. A poster of an Italian soccer team was on the wall opposite her bed, and over the headboard was a hand-carved crucifix.

There were three main doors in the small room, one leading out to the hallway, one opening into a bathroom, and another that connected to Madison's room.

Paola's bed was made up with a blue chenille spread, and her clothes hung neatly in her closet — tasteful jumpers and plain skirts and blouses and a shelf of sweaters in neutral colors. A few pairs of flat-soled shoes were lined up on the floor, and a black leather bag hung from the knob of the closet door.

I opened Paola's handbag, went through her wallet.

According to her driver's license, Paola was nineteen years old.

"She's five nine, brown haired, blue eyed — and she likes her weed."

I waggled the baggie with three joints I'd found in a

zipper pocket. "But there's no cell phone here, Richie. She must've taken it with her."

I opened one of the drawers in Paola's dresser while Conklin tossed the vanity.

Paola had white cotton workaday underwear, and she also had her days-off satin lingerie in tropical colors.

"A little bit naughty," I said, "a little bit nice."

I went into the bathroom, opened the medicine cabinet. Saw her various lotions and potions for clear skin and split ends, and an opened box of Ortho Evra, the patch for birth control.

Who was she sleeping with?

A boyfriend? Henry Tyler?

It wouldn't be the first time a nanny had gotten involved with the man of the house. *Was something twisted going on? An affair gone wrong?*

"Here's something, Lieu," Conklin called out. "I mean, Sarge." I stepped back into the bedroom.

"If you can't call me Boxer," I said, "try Lindsay."

"Okay," he said, his handsome face lighting up with a grin. "Lindsay. Paola keeps a diary."

Chapter 36

AS CONKLIN WENT TO SEARCH Madison's room, I skimmed the nanny's diary.

Paola wrote in beautiful script, using symbols and emoticons to punctuate her exclamatory writing style.

Even a cursory look through the pages told me that Paola Ricci loved America.

She raved about the cafés and shops on Fillmore Street, saying she couldn't wait for nicer weather so that she and her friends could sit outside like she did at home.

She went on for pages about outfits she'd seen in shop windows, and she quoted her San Francisco friends on men, clothes, and media stars.

When mentioning her friends, Paola used only their initials, leading me to guess that she was smoking pot with ME and LK on her nanny's nights out.

I looked for references to Henry Tyler, and Paola referred to him infrequently, but when she did, she called him "Mr. B."

However, she embellished the initial of someone she called "G."

Paola reported charged looks and sightings of "G," but I got the clear impression that whoever he was, she was more anticipating having sex with "G" than actually having it.

The person mentioned most often in Paola's diary was Maddy. That's where I really saw Paola's love for the child. She'd even pasted some of Madison's drawings and poems onto the pages.

I read nothing about plans, assignations, or vengeance.

I closed Paola's little red book, thinking it was the journal of an innocent abroad.

Or maybe she'd planted this diary to make us think so.

Henry Tyler followed Conklin and me out to the front step. He grabbed my arm.

"I appreciate your downplaying this for my wife, but I understand why you're here. Something may have already happened to my daughter. Please, keep me up to date on everything. And I insist that you tell me the truth."

I gave the distraught Henry Tyler my cell phone number and promised to check in often during the day. Techs were wiring up the Tylers' phone lines, and inspectors from the Major Crimes Squad were canvassing the houses on Washington Street when Conklin and I left.

We drove to Alta Plaza Park, a historic, terraced gem of a place with breathtaking views.

Along with the nannies and toddlers and dog owners recreating within the park's tranquil greens were cops doing interviews.

Conklin and I joined the canvass, and between us all, we talked to every nanny and child who knew Madison, including one nanny with the initials ME, the friend Paola had mentioned in her diary.

Madeline Ellis broke into tears, telling us about her fear for Paola and Maddy.

"It's like everything I know has been turned upside down," she said. "This place is supposed to be safe!"

Madeline rocked the carriage with a baby inside, her voice choking as she said, "She's a nice girl. And she's very young for her age."

She told us that the "G" in Paola's diary was George, last name unknown, a waiter at the Rhapsody Café. He had flirted with Paola, and she with him — but Madeline was positive that Paola and George had never had a date.

We found George Henley working the tables outside the Rhapsody Café on Fillmore, and we questioned him. We drilled him, tried to scare him, but my instincts told me he wasn't involved in a kidnapping or a murder.

He was a kid, just a regular kid, working his way through night school, trying to get his degree in fine arts.

George wiped his hands on his apron, took Paola's driver's license from my hand, looked at her picture.

"Oh, sure. I've seen her around here with her girl-friends," he said. "But until this minute, I never knew her name."

Chapter 37

THE SUN WAS GOING DOWN on Pacific Heights as we left the apartment of a handyman named Willy Evans who lived over the garage of one of the Tylers' neighbors. Evans was a creep with unbelievably dirty fingernails and two dozen terrariums inhabited by snakes and lizards. But as slithery as Willy Evans was, he had a solid alibi for the time Madison and Paola were abducted.

Conklin and I buttoned our coats and joined the canvass of the neighborhood, showing pictures of Paola and Madison to homeowners just returning from work.

We scared the hell out of a lot of innocent people and didn't get a single lead in return.

Back at the Hall, we converted our notes and thoughts into a report, noting the interviews we'd done and that the Devines, a family living next door to the Tylers, were on vacation before, during, and after the abduction and weren't interviewed, and that Paola Ricci's friends thought she was a saint.

A deep sadness was weighing on me.

The only witness to the abduction had told Jacobi that

she'd heard a pop and saw blood explode on the inside of the rear window of the van at nine this morning.

Did the blood belong to Paola?

Or had the child put up a struggle and gotten a bullet to shut her up?

I said good night to Conklin and drove to the hospital.

Claire was sleeping when I came into her room.

She opened her eyes, said, "Hi, sugar," and fell back asleep. I sat with her for a while, leaned back in the leatherette armchair and even dozed fitfully for a moment or two before kissing my friend's cheek and telling her good-bye.

I parked my Explorer on the uphill slope a few doors from my apartment and got out my keys, thoughts of Madison Tyler still cycling through my mind as I walked up the hill.

I had to blink a couple of times to make sure I wasn't hallucinating.

Joe was waiting outside my apartment, sitting on the steps, a leash looped around his wrist, an arm around Martha.

He stood and I walked into his big hug, swayed with him in the moon shadows.

It felt so good to be in his arms.

Chapter 38

AS FAR AS I KNEW, Joe had never found out about my misadventure in Washington, and now didn't seem like the time to tell him.

"You've fed Martha?" I asked, hugging him closer, reaching my arms up around his neck for his kiss.

"Walked her, too," he murmured. "And I bought a roasted chicken and some vegetables for the human folk. Wine's in the fridge."

"Someday, I'm going to walk into my apartment and shoot you by accident."

"You wouldn't do that, would you, Blondie?"

I pulled back, smiled up at his face, saying, "No, I wouldn't do it, Joe."

"You're my girl."

Then he kissed me again, a true toe curler, and my body melted against his. We walked up the stairs to my apartment, Martha barking and herding us together, making us laugh so hard we were weak by the time we got to the top floor.

As was our habit...the food had to wait.

Joe took off my clothes and his, turned on the shower until the temperature was just right, and once we were both inside the stall, put my hands on the wall and washed me gently and slowly, working me up until I wanted to scream. He wrapped me in a bath sheet and walked me to my bed, lowered me down, turned on the small lamp by the night table, the one with the soft pink light. He unwrapped me as if this were our first time together, as if he were just now discovering my body.

And that gave me the time to admire his broad chest, the way the pattern curls led my eyes downward—and when I reached out to touch him, he was ready.

"Just lie back," he said into my ear.

The brilliant thing about going so long without Joe was that when I was with him, there was the element of "the unknown" along with the safety of familiarity.

I lay back on the pillows, my palms turned up, and Joe drove me crazy as he kissed me everywhere, ran teasing fingers over hot spots and pressed his hard body against mine.

I was dissolving in the heat, but as much as I was dying for him, something else was going on in my head. I was fighting my feelings for Joe, and I didn't know why.

Then the answer came: *I don't want to do this.*

Chapter 39

I FELT *CRAZY,* wanting Joe and not wanting him at the same time.

I rationalized at first that I was still swimming in worry for Madison and Paola, but what came to mind was my shame at showing up at Joe's place nearly two weeks ago, needing him so much, feeling as though I'd gone where I didn't belong.

He was lying beside me now, his hand on the plane of my belly.

"What is it, Lindsay?"

I shook my head—*No, nothing's wrong*—but Joe turned me toward him, made me look into his deep blue eyes.

"I had a horrible day," I told him.

"Sure," he said, "that's not new. But your mood is."

I felt tears spring from my eyes, and that embarrassed me. I didn't want to be vulnerable with Joe. Not now anyway.

"Start talking, Blondie," he said.

I rolled toward him and put my arm over his chest, tucked my head under his jaw. "I can't take this, Joe."

"I know, I know how you feel. I want to move here, but it's not the right time."

My breathing slowed as he talked about the current state of the war, next year's elections, the bombings in major cities, and the focus on Homeland Security.

At some point, I stopped listening. I got out of bed and put on a robe.

"Are you coming back?" Joe asked.

"There it is," I said. "I'm *always* asking myself that question about you."

Joe started to protest, but I said, "Let me talk."

I sat on the edge of the bed, said, "As good as this can be, that's how *bad* it is because I can't count on you, Joe. I'm too old for jack-in-the-box love."

"Linds—"

"You know I'm right. I don't know when I'll be seeing you, if I'll reach you when I call. Then you're here, and then you're gone, and I'm left behind, missing you.

"We have no time to relax together, be normal, have a life. We've talked and talked about your moving here, but we both know it's impossible."

"Lindsay, I swear—"

"I can't wait for the next administration or the war to be over. Do you understand?"

He was sitting up now, legs over the side of the bed, so much love in his face I had to turn away.

"I love you, Lindsay. Please, let's not fight. I have to leave in the morning."

"You have to leave *now,* Joe," I heard myself say. "It kills me to say this, but I don't want any more well-intentioned promises," I said. "Let's end this, okay? We had a great time. Please? If you love me, let me go."

After Joe kissed me good-bye, I lay on my bed, staring at the ceiling for a long time, tears soaking my pillow. I wondered what the hell I had done.

Chapter 40

IT WAS SATURDAY NIGHT, almost midnight. Cindy was sleeping in the bedroom of her new apartment at the Blakely Arms—alone—when she was awoken by a woman shouting her lungs out in Spanish on a floor somewhere over her head.

A door slammed, there were running footsteps, then a hinge creaked and another door slammed, this one closer to Cindy's apartment.

Maybe it was the door to the stairwell?

She heard more shouting, this time down on the street. Men's voices rose up to her third-floor windows, then there was the sound of scuffling.

Cindy was having thoughts she'd never had in her old apartment building.

Was she safe here?

Was the great buy she got on this place a poor bargain after all?

She threw back the covers, left her bedroom, and went out to her new airy living room and foyer. She peeked through the peephole—saw no one. She twisted the knob of the dead bolt, left-right-left-right, before going to her desk.

She ran her hands through her hair, pulled it up into a band. *Jeez. Her hands were shaking.*

Maybe it wasn't just the nightlife in the building. Maybe she was giving herself the creeps because of the story she was writing about child abduction. Since Henry Tyler's phone call, she'd been surfing the Web, reading more than she'd ever known about the thousands of children who were abducted in the United States every year.

Most of those kids were taken by family members, found, and returned. But a few hundred children every year were strangled, stabbed, or buried alive by their abductors.

And the majority of those kids were murdered within the first hours of their abduction.

Statistically it was far more likely that Madison had been grabbed by an extortionist than a child-molesting, murdering freak. The only problem with that scenario was that it left a huge, chilling question in her mind.

Why hadn't the Tylers been contacted about paying a ransom?

Cindy was halfway back to her bedroom when the doorbell rang. She froze, heart jumping inside her chest. *She didn't know a soul in this building.*

So who could be ringing her doorbell?

The bell rung again, insistently.

Clutching her robe, Cindy went to the door and peered through the peephole. She couldn't believe who was peering back.

It was Lindsay.

And she looked like hell.

Chapter 41

I WAS ABOUT TO TURN AND GO when Cindy opened the door in her pink PJs, her curls rubber banded into a pom-pom on the top of her head. She was looking at me as if she'd just seen the dead.

"You okay?" I asked.

"*Me?* I'm fine, Lindsay. I live here, remember? What's wrong with *you?*"

"I would've called," I said, hugging my friend, using the moment to try to get a grip on myself. But clearly Cindy had scanned and memorized the shock on my face. And frankly she didn't look so good herself. "But I didn't know I was coming until I was here."

"Come in, and for God's sake, sit down," she said, staring at me anxiously as I made for the couch.

Cardboard cartons were stacked against the walls, and layers of Bubble Wrap wafted around my feet.

"What's happened, Lindsay? As Yuki would say, 'You look like you've been dragged through a duck's ass.'"

I managed a weak laugh. "That's about how I feel."

"What can I get you? Tea? Maybe something stronger."

"Tea would be great."

I fell back onto the sofa cushions, and a few minutes later, Cindy returned from the kitchen, pulled up a footstool to sit on, and handed me a mug. "Talk to me," she said.

No joke, Cindy was a perfect paradox: all pink ruffles and curls on the outside, never leaving home without lipstick and the perfect shoes, but inside that girlie-girl was a bulldog who would get a grip on your leg and hang on until you had no choice but to tell her what she wanted to know.

I suddenly felt idiotic. Just seeing Cindy changed my mood for the better, and I no longer wanted to open myself up and talk about Joe.

"I wanted to see your apartment."

"Give. Me. A. Break."

"You're relentless—"

"Blame it on my choice of career."

"And proud of it."

"Ab-solutely."

"Bitch." I found myself laughing.

"Go ahead. Get it off your chest," she said. "Give me your best shot."

"Calling you a bitch *was* my best shot."

"Okay, then. What gives, Linds?"

I covered my face with a throw pillow, shutting out the light, feeling myself tumbling down. I sighed. "I broke up with Joe."

Cindy grabbed the pillow away from my face.

"You're kidding, right?"

"Be nice, okay, Cindy? Or I'll throw up on your rug."

"Okay, okay, so why did you do *that?* Joe's smart.

He's gorgeous. He loves you. You love him. What's wrong with you?"

I pulled my knees up and hugged them tight with my arms. Cindy sat down next to me on the couch. She put an arm around me.

I felt as if I were holding on to a skinny tree while being lashed by a tidal wave. I'd been crying so much lately. I thought I might be losing my mind.

"Take your time, honey. I'm here. The night is young. Sort of."

So I gave in, blurted out the story about my totally embarrassing trip to DC and how I felt about the whole mood-swinging affair with Joe. "It really, really hurts, Cindy. But I did the right thing."

"It's not just because you got your feelings hurt when he wasn't home and you saw that girl?"

"No. *Hell no.*"

"Oh, God, Linds, I didn't mean to make you cry. Lie down here. Close your eyes."

Cindy pushed me gently onto my side, put a pillow under my head. A moment later, a blanket floated over me. The light went off, and I felt Cindy tuck me in.

"It's not over, Linds. Trust me. It's not over."

"You're wrong once in a while, you know," I muttered.

"Wanna bet?" Cindy kissed my cheek. And then I was swept along by whatever dream featured me in a starring role. I sunk into a deep hole of agonized sleep, waking only as sunlight streamed through Cindy's bare windows.

I forced myself to sit up, swung my legs off the couch, saw the note from Cindy on the coffee table saying she'd gone out for rolls and coffee.

Then the day hit me for real.

Jacobi and Macklin were having a staff meeting this morning at eight. Every cop on the Tyler-Ricci case would be there—*except me.*

I scribbled a note to Cindy, stuck my feet in my shoes, and raced out the door.

Chapter 42

JACOBI ROLLED HIS EYES when I edged past him, slipped into a seat in the back of the squad room. Lieutenant Macklin gave me a short, glancing stare as he summarized the meeting so far. In the absence of any information regarding the whereabouts of Madison Tyler and Paola Ricci, we were assigned to interview registered sex offenders.

"Patrick Calvin," I read from our list as Conklin and I got into the squad car. "Convicted sex offender, recently released on probation after serving time for the sexual abuse of his own daughter. She was six when it happened."

Conklin started the car. "There's no understanding that kind of garbage. You know what? I don't *want* to understand it."

Calvin lived in a twenty-unit, U-shaped stucco apartment building at Palm and Euclid on the fringe of Jordan Park, about a mile and a half from where Madison Tyler lived and played. A blue Toyota Corolla registered to Calvin was parked on the street.

I smelled bacon cooking as we crossed the open patio area at the front entrance, climbed the outside stairs, knocked on Calvin's aggressively red-painted door.

The door opened, and a tousle-haired white male no more than five foot three stood in the doorway, wearing plaid pajamas and white socks.

He looked about fifteen years old, making me want to ask, "Is your father home?" But the faint gray shadow on his jowls and the prison tats on his knuckles gave Pat Calvin away as a former inmate of our prison system.

"Patrick Calvin?" I said, showing him my badge.

"What do you want?"

"I'm Sergeant Boxer. This is Inspector Conklin," I said. "We have a few questions. Mind if we come in?"

"Yes, I mind. What do you *want?*"

Conklin has an easy way about him, a trait I frankly envy. I'd seen him interrogate murdering psychos with a kind of sweetness, good cop to the max. He'd also taken care of that poor cat at the Alonzo murder scene.

"Sorry, Mr. Calvin," Conklin said now. "I know it's early on a Sunday morning, but a child is missing and we don't have a lot of time."

"What's that got to do with me?"

"Get used to this, Mr. Calvin," I said. "You're on parole—"

"You want to search my house, is that it?" Calvin shouted. "This is a goddamned free country, isn't it? You don't have a warrant," Calvin spat. "You have *shit.*"

"You're getting awful steamed up for an innocent man," Conklin said. "Makes me wonder, you know?"

I stood by as Conklin explained that we could call Calvin's parole officer, who would have no problem letting us in. "Or we could get a warrant," Conklin said. "Have a couple of cruisers come screaming up to the curb, show your neighbors what kind of guy you are."

"So . . . mind if we come in?" I asked.

Calvin countered my scowl with a dark look of his own. "I've got nothing to hide," he said.

And he stepped aside.

Chapter 43

CALVIN'S PLACE WAS SPARSELY DECORATED in early Ikea: lightweight blond wood. There was a shelf of dolls over the TV—big ones, little ones, baby dolls, and dolls in fancy dresses.

"I bought them for my daughter," Calvin snarled, dropping into a chair. "In case she can ever visit me."

"What is she now? Sixteen?" Conklin asked.

"Shut up," Calvin said. "Okay? Just shut up."

"Watch your mouth," Conklin said before he disappeared into Calvin's bedroom. I took a seat on the sofa and whipped out my notebook.

I shook off the image of a young girl, now a teen, who'd had the terrible misfortune to have this shit as a father, and asked Calvin if he'd ever seen Madison Tyler.

"I saw her on the news last night. She's very cute. You could even say *edible*. But I don't know her."

"Okay, then," I said, gritting my teeth, feeling a sharp pang of fear for Madison. "Where were you yesterday morning at nine a.m.?"

"I was watching TV. I like to stay on top of the current

cartoon shows so I can talk to little girls on their level, you know what I mean?"

At five ten, I'm a head taller than Calvin and in better shape, too. Violent fantasies were roiling in my mind, just as they had when I'd arrested Alfred Brinkley. I was stressing too much, too much...

"Can anyone vouch for your whereabouts?"

"Sure. Ask Mr. Happy," Pat Calvin said, patting the fly of his pajama bottoms, grabbing himself there. "He'll tell you anything you want to know."

I snapped. I grabbed Calvin's collar, bunching up the flannel tight around his neck. His hands flew out as I lifted him off his chair, thumped him against the wall.

Dolls scattered.

Conklin came out of the bedroom as I was about to thump Calvin again. My partner pretended that he didn't see anything crazy in my face and leaned casually against the door frame.

I was alarmed at how close I was to the edge. What I didn't need now was a complaint for police brutality. I released Calvin's pajamas.

"Nice photo collection you have, Mr. Calvin," Conklin said conversationally. "Pictures of little kids playing in Alta Plaza Park."

I shot a look at Conklin. Madison and Paola were snatched from the street just outside that park.

"Did you see my camera?" Calvin said defiantly. "Seven million megapixels and a 12x zoom. I shot those pictures from a block away. I know the *rules*. And I didn't break *any* of them."

"Sergeant," Conklin said to me, "there's a little girl in one of those pictures, could be Madison Tyler."

I got Jacobi on the phone, told him that Patrick Calvin had photos we should look at more closely.

"We need two patrolmen to sit on Calvin while Conklin and I come in to write up a warrant," I said.

"No problem, Boxer. I'll send a car. But I'll have Chi take care of the warrant and bring Calvin in."

"We can handle it, Jacobi," I said.

"You *could*," Jacobi said, "but a child matching Madison Tyler's description was just called in from Transbay security."

"She's been seen?"

"She's there right now."

Chapter 44

THE TRANSBAY TERMINAL on First and Mission is an open-air, rusty-roofed, concrete-block shed. Inside the cinder-block shell, half-dead fluorescent lights sputter overhead, throwing faint shadows on the homeless souls who camp out in this oppressive place so that they can use the scant facilities.

Even in daytime this terminal is creepy. I felt an urgent need to find Madison Tyler and get her the hell out of here.

Conklin and I jogged down the stairs to the terminal's lower level, a dark, dingy space dominated by a short wall of ticket booths and a security area.

Two black women wearing navy-blue pants and shirts with PRIVATE SECURITY SERVICES patches sewn to their pockets sat behind the desk.

We flashed our badges and were buzzed in.

The security office was glassed in on two sides, painted grimy beige on the other two, and furnished with two desks, unmatched file cabinets, three exit doors with keypad access, and two vending machines.

And there, sitting beside the stationmaster's desk, was a little girl with silky yellow hair falling over her collar.

Her blue coat was unbuttoned. She had on a red sweater over blue pants. And *she wore shiny red shoes.*

My heart did a little dance. We'd found her.

Oh, my God, Madison was safe!

The stationmaster, a big man, fortysomething with gray hair and matching mustache, stood up to introduce himself.

"I'm Fred Zimmer," he said, shaking our hands. "And we found this little lady wandering all by herself about fifteen minutes ago, weren't you, honey? I couldn't get her to talk to me."

I put my hands on my knees and looked into the little girl's face. She'd been crying, and I couldn't get her to look me in the eyes.

Her cheeks were dirt streaked and her nose was running. Her lower lip was swollen and she had a scrape along the side of her left cheek. I threw Richie a look. My relief at seeing Madison alive was swamped by a new concern for what had been done to her.

She looked so *traumatized* that I was having a hard time matching up her face to the image of the little dazzler I'd seen playing the piano on videotape.

Conklin stooped to the little girl's level.

"My name is Richie." He smiled. "Is your name Maddy?"

The child looked at Conklin, opened her mouth, and said, "Mahhh-dy."

I thought, *This little girl has been scared to death.*

I took her small hands in mine. They were cold to the touch, and she stared right through me.

"Call EMS," I said softly, trying not to frighten her further. "Something's wrong with this child."

Chapter 45

CONKLIN AND I WERE PACING RESTLESSLY outside the hospital's emergency room when the Tylers rushed in and embraced us like family.

I was feeling high. One part of this frightening, godawful story was over. And I was hoping that right after she saw her parents, Madison would come back to herself. Because I had some questions for her—starting with, "Did you get a good look at the guys who kidnapped you?"

"She was sleeping when we last looked in on her," I told the Tylers. "Dr. Collins just stopped by and said he'll be back in...let's see...about ten minutes."

"I have to ask," Elizabeth Tyler said softly, "was Maddy harmed in any way?"

"She looks like she's been through an ordeal," I said to Madison's mom. "She wasn't given any kind of invasive exam because the doctors were waiting for your consent."

Elizabeth Tyler covered her mouth with both hands, stifled her tears.

"You should know she's barely said anything to anyone."

"That's not like Maddy."

"Maybe she was warned not to talk or she would be hurt—"

"Oh, *God.* Those animals!"

"Why would they kidnap Maddy, then abandon her without trying to get a ransom?" Tyler was asking as we entered the ER.

I let the question hang, because I didn't want to say what I was thinking: *Pedophiles don't ask for ransom.* I stood aside so that the Tylers could enter Maddy's curtained stall in the ER ahead of me, thinking how overjoyed Madison would be when she saw her parents again.

Henry Tyler squeezed my arm and whispered, "Thank you," as he went through the curtains. I heard Elizabeth Tyler calling her daughter's name—then cry out with an agonized moan.

I jumped aside as she ran past me. Henry Tyler emerged next and put his face right up to mine.

"Do you know what you've done?" he said, his face scarlet with rage. "That girl isn't Madison. Do you understand? That's not Madison. *That's not our baby!*"

Chapter 46

I APOLOGIZED TO THE TYLERS sincerely and profusely as they exploded all over me in the hospital parking lot, then stood flat-footed as their car tore past me, leaving rubber on the asphalt. My cell phone rang on my hip, and eventually I answered it.

It was Jacobi. "A woman just called saying her daughter is missing. The child is five. Has long blond hair."

The caller's name was Sylvia Brodsky, and she was hysterical. She'd lost track of her daughter, Alicia, while shopping for groceries. Alicia must have wandered away, Mrs. Brodsky told the 911 operator, adding that her daughter was autistic.

Alicia Brodsky could barely speak a word.

Not long after Jacobi's call, Sylvia Brodsky came to the hospital and claimed her daughter, but Conklin and I weren't there to see it.

We were back in our Crown Vic, talking it over, me taking responsibility for jumping the gun, saying, "I should have been more forceful when I told the Tylers that *maybe* we'd found their daughter, but we couldn't be *sure*.

But I did say that we needed them to make a positive ID, didn't I, Rich? You heard me."

"They stopped listening after you said, 'We may have found your daughter.' Hey, it all clicked, Lindsay. She said her name was Maddy."

"Well. Something like that."

"The red shoes," he insisted. "How many five-year-old blond-haired kids have blue coats and red patent leather shoes?"

"Two, anyway." I sighed.

Back at the Hall, we interrogated Calvin for two hours, squeezed him until he wasn't smirking anymore. We looked at the digital photos still inside his camera, and we examined the photos Conklin had found in his bedroom.

There were no pictures of Madison Tyler, but we kept our hopes up until the last frame that Calvin might have accidentally photographed the kidnapping in progress.

That maybe he'd caught the black van in his lens.

But the Memory Stick in his camera showed that he hadn't been taking pictures at Alta Plaza Park yesterday.

Patrick Calvin made me sick, but the law doesn't recognize causing revulsion as a criminal offense.

So we kicked him. Turned him loose.

Conklin and I interviewed three more registered sex offenders that day, three average-looking white males you'd never pick out of a crowd as sexual predators.

Three men whose alibis checked out.

I finally called it quits at around seven p.m. Emotionally speaking, my tank was dry.

I entered my apartment, threw my arms around Martha, and promised her a run after my shower to rinse the skeezy images out of my brain.

There was a note from Martha's sitter on the kitchen counter. I went to the fridge, cracked open a Corona, and took a long pull from the bottle before reading it.

Lindsay, hi, when I didn't see your car, I took Martha for a walk! ☹ Remember I told you my parents are letting me have the house in Hermosa Beach through Christmas? I should take Martha with me. It would be good for her, Lindsay!!!
Let me know. K.

I felt sick knowing that I'd abandoned my dog without calling her sitter. And I knew Karen was right. I wasn't doing Martha any good right now. My new hours included double shifts and all-work weekends. I hadn't taken a real break since the ferry shooting.

I stooped down for a kiss, lifted Martha's silky ears, looked into her big brown eyes.

"You want to run on the beach, Boo?"

I picked up the phone and dialed Karen's number.

"Excellent," she said. "I'll pick her up in the morning."

Chapter 47

IT WAS MONDAY MORNING, half past dawn.

Conklin and I were at the construction site below Fort Point, the huge brick fort that had been built on the edge of the San Francisco peninsula during the Civil War and now stood in the shadow of the Golden Gate Bridge.

A damp breeze kicked up whitecaps on the bay, making the fifty-degree temperature feel more like thirty-five.

I was shaking, either because of the windchill factor or from my sickening sense of what we were about to find.

I zipped up my fleece-lined jacket, put my hands inside my pockets as the whipping wind brought moisture to my eyes.

A welder who was working on the bridge retrofit came toward us with containers of coffee from the "garbage truck," a food wagon outside the chain-link fence that separated the construction site from the public area.

The welder's name was Wayne Murray, and he told me and Conklin how when he'd come to work that morning, he'd seen something weird hung up on the rocks below the fort.

"I thought at first it was a seal," he said mournfully.

"When I got closer, I saw an arm in the water. I never saw a dead body before."

Car doors slammed, men coming through the chain-link gate, talking and laughing—construction workers, EMS, and a couple of Park Service cops.

I asked them to rope off the area.

I turned my eyes back to the dark lump down on the rocks below the seawall, a white hand and foot trailing in the foam-flecked water that streamed toward the ocean.

"She wasn't dumped here," Conklin said. "Too much chance of being seen."

I squinted up at the silhouette of the bridge security officer patrolling the structure with his AR-15 semiautomatic rifle.

"Yeah. Depending on the time and the tides, she could have been dropped off one of the piers. The perps must've thought she'd float out to sea."

"Here comes Dr. G.," Conklin said.

The ME was chipper this morning, his damp white hair still showing comb marks, his waders pulled up to midchest, his nose pink under the bridge of his glasses.

He and one of his assistants took the lead, and we joined them, walking awkwardly across the jagged rocks that sloped at a forty-five-degree angle, fifteen feet down to the lip of the bay.

"Hang on, there. Be careful," Dr. Germaniuk said as we approached the body. "Don't want anyone to fall and touch something."

We stood our ground as Dr. G. scrambled down the boulders, approached the body, put his scene kit down. Using his flashlight, he began his preliminary in situ assessment.

I could see the body pretty well in his beam. The victim's face was darkened and swollen.

"Got some skin slippage here," Dr. G. called up to me. "She's been in the water a couple of days. Long enough to have become a floater."

"Does she have a gunshot wound to the head?"

"Can't tell. Looks like she's been banged up on the rocks. I'll give her a head-to-toe X-ray when we get her back to home base."

Dr. G. photographed the body twice from each angle, his flash popping every second or two.

I took note of the girl's clothing—the dark coat, the turtleneck sweater, her short hair, similar to the distinctive bowl cut I'd seen in her driver's license picture when I'd gone through her wallet two days before.

"We both know that's Paola Ricci," Conklin said, staring down at the body.

I nodded. Except that yesterday we'd blown it, broken the Tylers' hearts by jumping to conclusions.

"Right," I said. "But I'll believe it when we get a positive ID."

Chapter 48

CLAIRE WAS SITTING UP IN BED when I walked through the door of her hospital room. She stretched out her arms, and I hugged her until she said, "Take it easy, sugar. I've got a hole in my chest, remember?"

I pulled back, kissed her on both cheeks, and sat down beside her.

"What's the latest from your doctor?"

"He said I'm a big, strong girl…" And then Claire started coughing. She held up the hand that wasn't covering her mouth, managing to finally say, "It hurts only when I cough."

"You're a big, strong girl and … what?" I pressed her.

"And I'm going to be fine. Getting out of this joint Wednesday. Then some time at home in bed. After that I should be good to go."

"Thank God."

"I've been thanking God since that asshole shot me, whenever that was. You lose track of time when you don't have an office job."

"It happened two weeks ago, Butterfly. Two weeks and two days."

Claire pushed a box of chocolates toward me, and I took the first one my hand fell on.

"You been sleeping in the trunk of your car?" she asked me. "Or did you trade Joe in for an eighteen-year-old boyfriend?"

I poured water for both of us, put a straw in Claire's glass, handed it to her, said, "I didn't trade him in. I just kinda let him go."

Claire's eyebrows shot up. "No, you didn't."

I explained what happened, aching as I talked. Claire watched me warily but kindly. She asked a few questions but mostly let me spill.

I sipped some water. Then I cleared my throat and told Claire about my new rank with the SFPD.

Shock registered in her eyes. Again. "You got yourself bumped down to the street *and* you told Joe to hit the bricks— at the same time? I'm worried about you, Lindsay. Are you sleeping? Taking vitamins? Eating right?"

No. No. No.

I threw myself back into the armchair as a nurse came in, bearing a tray with Claire's medication and dinner.

"Here you go, Dr. Washburn. Down the hatch."

Claire slugged down the pills, pushed her tray away once the nurse had gone. "Slop du jour," she said.

Had I eaten today? I didn't think so. I appropriated Claire's meal, mashing the overcooked peas and meatloaf together on the fork, getting to the ice-cream course before telling her that we had identified Paola Ricci's body.

"The kidnappers shot the nanny within a minute of taking her and the child. Couldn't get rid of her fast enough. But that's all I've got, Butterfly. We don't know who did it, why, or where they've taken Madison."

"Why haven't those shits called the parents?"

"That's the million-dollar question. Way too long without a ransom request. I don't think they want the Tylers' money."

"Damn."

"Yeah." I dropped the plastic spoon onto the tray and leaned back in the chair again, staring out at nothing.

"Lindsay?"

"I've been thinking that they'd shot Paola because she'd witnessed Madison's kidnapping."

"Makes sense."

"But if Madison witnessed Paola's murder... they're not going to let the child live after that."

Part Three

THE ACCOUNTING

Chapter 49

CINDY THOMAS LEFT her Blakely Arms apartment, crossed the street at the corner, and began her five-block walk to her office at the *Chronicle*.

Two floors above Cindy's apartment, facing the back of the building, a man named Garry Tenning was having a bad morning. Tenning gripped the edges of the desk in his workroom and tried to stifle his anger. Down in the courtyard, five floors below, a dog was barking incessantly, each shrill note stabbing Tenning's eardrums like a skewer.

He knew the dog.

It was Barnaby, a rat terrier who belonged to Margery Glynn, a lumpen, dishwater-blond single mother of god-awful Baby Oliver, all of them living on the ground floor, usurping the back courtyard as if it were *theirs*.

Again, Tenning pressed on his special Mack's ear-plugs, soft wax that conformed exactly to the shape of his ear holes. And still he could hear Barnaby *yappa-yappa-yipping* through his Mack's.

Tenning rubbed the flat of his hand across the front of

his T-shirt as the dog's brainless yapping ripped the fabric of his repose. The tingling was starting now in his lips and fingers, and his heart was palpitating.

God*damn* it.

Was a little quiet too much to ask?

On the computer screen in front of him, neat rows of type marched down the screen — chapter six of his book, *The Accounting: A Statistical Compendium of the Twentieth Century.*

The book was more than a conceit or a pet project. *The Accounting* was his raison d'être and his legacy. He even cherished the rejection letters from publishers turning down his book proposal. He lovingly logged these rejections into a ledger, filing the originals in a folder inside his lockbox.

He'd get his laugh when *The Accounting* was published, when it became a critical reference work for scholars all over the world — and for generations to come.

Nobody would be able to take that away from him.

As Tenning *willed* Barnaby to shut the hell up, he ran his eyes down the line of numbers — the fatal lightning strikes since 1900, the inches of snowfall in Vermont, the verified sightings of cows sucked into the air by tornadoes — when a garbage truck began its halting clamor up the block.

He thought his fricking skull would crack open.

He wasn't crazy, either.

He was having a perfectly reasoned response to a horrific assault on the senses. He clapped his hands over his ears, but the squeals, screeches, galvanized shimmies, came through — *and they set off Oliver!*

The goddamned baby.

How many times had he been interrupted by that baby?

How many times had his thoughts been derailed by that shitty-ass rat dog?

The pressure in Tenning's chest and head was building. If he didn't *do* something, he would explode.

Garry Tenning had had it.

Chapter 50

EVEN WITH QUIVERING FINGERS, Tenning quickly tied the laces of his bald-treaded Adidas, stepped out into the hallway, and locked the apartment door behind him, pocketing his big bunch of keys.

He used the fire stairs to get down to the basement level — he never took the elevator.

He passed the laundry room and entered the boiler room, where the senior furnace mumbled in its pipes and the hateful new furnace roared with freshly minted enthusiasm.

An eighteen-inch length of pipe with a rusted ball joint affixed to one end leaned against the concrete-block wall. Tenning hefted it, socked the ball joint into the cupped palm of his hand.

He turned right, walking down the incline toward the blinking light of the EXIT sign, murderous ideas igniting in his mind like a chain of firecrackers.

The lock bar on the exit door opened against his forearm. He stood for a minute in the sunshine, getting his bearings. Then he turned the brick corner of the building, heading toward the patio of keystones and the planters that were added since the building's conversion.

Seeing Tenning coming toward him, Barnaby started yapping. He lunged at the leash connecting his collar to the chain-link fence.

Beside him was the baby carriage, where Oliver Glynn fretted in the dappled shade. He was howling, too.

Tenning felt a flame of hope rush through him.

Two birds with one stone.

Clutching the valve-capped pipe, he edged along the side of the building toward the shrieks and howls of the Nasty Little Animals.

Just then, Margery Glynn, her bland blond hair knotted up and stabbed into place with a pencil, stepped out of her apartment. She bent low, displaying several square feet of milky-white thigh, and lifted Oliver out of his carriage.

Tenning watched, unseen.

The baby quieted instantly, but Barnaby only changed his tune, his excited yips *stabbing, stabbing, stabbing*.

Mistress Margery shushed him, put one hand under the baby's ass, and pressing his wet face to her deflated bosom, carried him inside her apartment.

Tenning advanced on Barnaby, who paused midyowl and licked his chops, hoping for a pat perhaps or a run in the park. Then he sent up his yapping alarm—again.

Tenning lifted his club and swung it down hard. Barnaby squealed, made a feeble grab for Tenning's arm as the club rose high against the cloudless sky and then slammed down a second time.

The rat dog was completely still.

As Tenning stuffed its body into a garbage bag, he thought, *RIBP*.

Rest in bloody peace.

Chapter 51

THREE DAYS HAD PASSED since Madison Tyler had been taken from Scott Street and her nanny murdered only a few yards from Alta Plaza Park.

We were all in the squad room that morning: Conklin, four homicide inspectors from the night tour doing overtime, Macklin, a half-dozen cops from Major Crimes, and me.

Macklin looked around the small room and said, "I'll make this quick so we can get to work. We've got nothing. Nothing but the talent in this room. So let's keep doing what we're doing, good solid police work. And for those of you who pray—put in a word for a miracle."

He handed out assignments, asked for questions—got none. Chairs scraped as everyone scrambled. I looked over the new list of pervs Conklin and I were assigned to interview.

I got up from my desk and crossed the scuffed linoleum floor to Jacobi's office door.

"Come in, Boxer."

"Jacobi, there were two people involved in the abduction. There was the guy who did the coercing and then there was a driver. Pretty odd, don't you think, for a pedophile to partner up?"

"Got any other ideas, Boxer? I'm wide open."

"I want to go back to square one. The witness. I want to talk to her."

"After all these years, I can't believe you want to double check an interview of mine," Jacobi groused. "Hang on. I have her statement right here."

I sighed as Jacobi moved his coffee, his Egg McMuffin, his newspaper, lifted a pile of manila folders. He sorted through those, found the one he was looking for, flapped it open.

"Gilda Gray. Here's her number."

"Thanks, Lieu," I said, reaching for the folder. I felt a pang, as if I'd made a slip of the tongue. I'd never called Jacobi "Lieu" before. I hoped he'd missed it, but no. Jacobi beamed at me.

I smiled at him over my shoulder, walked back to the face-to-face desk arrangement I have with Conklin. Dialed Gilda Gray's number and got her on the phone.

"I can't come in now. I've got a presentation with a client at nine thirty," she protested.

"A child is *missing,* Ms. Gray."

"Look, I can tell you everything in about ten seconds over the phone. I was walking our dog on Divisadero. I was following her, getting the newspaper into position, when the little girl and her nanny crossed the street."

"Then what happened?"

"My attention was on Schotzie. I was looking *down,* lining up that newspaper, you know? I thought I heard a child call out—but when I looked up, all I saw was someone in a gray coat sliding open a door to a black minivan. And I saw the back of the nanny's coat as she got inside."

"Someone in a gray coat. Gotcha. Did you see the person at the wheel?"

"Nope. I put the newspaper in the trash, and I heard the van turn the corner. Then, like I've *said,* I heard a loud pop and saw what looked like blood splattering against the back window. It was horrible..."

"Anything you can tell me about the man in the gray coat?"

"I'm pretty sure he was white."

"Tall, short, distinguishing features?"

"I didn't pay any attention. I'm sorry."

I asked Ms. Gray when she could come in and look at mug shots, and she said, "You've got mug shots of the backs of people's heads?"

I said, "Thanks anyway," and hung up.

I looked into Conklin's light-brown eyes. Got lost there for half a second.

"So we're still on perv patrol?" he asked.

"Yeah, we are, Rich. Bring your coffee."

Chapter 52

KENNETH KLASSEN WAS WASHING his silver Jaguar when we parked on the uphill slope outside his home on Vallejo.

He was a white male, forty-eight, five ten, your average-to-good-looking porno auteur with artificially enhanced features: good hair weave, quality nose job, aquamarine contact lenses, dental veneers—the works.

According to his sheet, Klassen had been caught in an online chat-room sting setting up a date with someone he thought was a twelve-year-old girl—turned out to be a forty-year-old cop.

Klassen had cut a deal with the DA. In exchange for ratting out a child pornographer, he got a lengthy probation and a hefty fine. He was *still* making adult porn, which was completely legal, even in the upscale neighborhood of Pacific Heights.

A look of delight brightened Klassen's face as Conklin and I left our Crown Vic on the curb and came toward him.

"Well, well, well," he said, shutting off the hose, looking from me to Conklin and back to me. Sizing us up.

Then his smile hardened as he made us as cops.

"Kenneth Klassen," I said, flashing my badge, "I'm Sergeant Boxer. And this is Inspector Conklin. We have some questions for you. Mind if we come inside?"

"Come wherever you like, Sergeant." Klassen smirked, holding the hose gun in front of himself as if it were cocked and ready to go.

"Shut up, asshole," Conklin said mildly.

"Joke, Officer," Klassen said, grinning. "I was just kidding around. Come on in."

We followed Klassen up the front steps; through an oaken door, a spiffy foyer, and a contemporary parlor; and out to a glass conservatory extending off the kitchen. Ferns, gardenias, and large pots of cacti abounded.

Klassen offered us wicker-basket chairs suspended by chains from overhead beams, and a Chinese man of indeterminate age appeared at the edge of the room, crossed his left hand over his right wrist, and waited.

"Can Mr. Wu get you anything, Officers?" he asked.

"No, thanks," I said.

"So what brings you into my life on this otherwise magnificent morning?"

I balanced uncomfortably on the edge of the basket chair and got my notebook out as Conklin walked around the conservatory, picking up the odd piece of erotic statuary, moving potted plants a couple of inches here and there.

"Make yourself at home," Klassen called out to Conklin.

"Where were you on Saturday morning?" I asked.

"Saturday," he said, leaning back, patting his hair, a look coming over his face as though he were remembering a particularly sweet dream.

"I was making *Moonlight Mambo*," he said. "Shot it

right here. I'm directing a series of twenty-minute films. What I call 'bedroom shorts.'" He grinned.

"That's just great. I'd like the names and phone numbers of everyone who can vouch for your whereabouts."

"Am I suspected of something, Sergeant?"

"Let's just say we think of you as a 'person of interest.'"

Klassen leered at me as though I'd paid him a compliment. "You have lovely skin. You don't spend a penny on makeup, do you?"

"Mr. Klassen, don't screw around with me. Names and phone numbers, please."

"No problem. I'll print out a list."

"Good. Have you seen this child?" I asked, showing him the class photo of Madison Tyler that I'd kept in my jacket pocket for the last three days.

I hated to let Klassen pass his slimeball eyes over Madison's lovely face.

"That's the newspaper guy's kid, right? I've seen her on the news. Look," Klassen said, smiling, nearly blinding me with his sparkling choppers, "I can make this very easy for all of us, all right? Come with me."

Chapter 53

THE ELEVATOR IN KLASSEN'S PANTRY was a knotty-pine box about the size of a double-wide coffin. Conklin, Klassen, and I stepped inside, and I lifted my eyes to where the number board should have been, seeing only the numbers "one" and "four"—no stops in between.

The car opened on the top floor, a bright forty-by-fifty-foot space with furniture, lights, rolled-up carpets, and backdrops stacked against the walls. A high-tech computer station took up a back corner.

It was a wide-open space, but I scanned it anyway for signs of a child.

"It's all done digitally these days," Klassen was saying. He straddled a stool in front of a flat-screen monitor. "You shoot it, download it, and edit it all in one room."

He threw a switch, rolled his mouse, and clicked an icon labeled *Moonlight Mambo*.

"This is the rough cut I shot on Saturday," Klassen told us. "It's my time-dated alibi—not that I need one. I started shooting at seven, and we worked the whole day."

Latin music came through the computer's speakers,

then images jumped onto the screen. A young dark-haired woman wearing something black and scanty lit candles in one of the now-disassembled bedroom sets.

The camera panned the room, stopping at the bed—where Klassen fondled himself and uttered cornball come-ons as the woman did a seductive striptease.

"Ah, jeez," I muttered.

Conklin stepped between me and the computer monitor.

"I'll take a copy of that," he said.

"My pleasure." Klassen slipped a CD out of the drawer, put it in a red plastic case, and handed it to Conklin.

"You have any pictures or films of children on this computer?"

"Hell, no. I'm not into kiddie porn," Klassen huffed. "Besides being in violation of my deal, it's not my thing."

"Yeah, that's terrific," Conklin said smoothly. "So now I'd like to take a quick search through your computer files while the sergeant walks through your house."

"Looks like a neat place, Mr. Klassen," I said. "I love what you've done with it."

"What if I say it's not okay?"

"We'll take you in for questioning while we get a warrant," Conklin told him. "Then we'll impound your computer and search your house with dogs."

"The stairs are that way."

I left Conklin and Klassen at the computer console and strolled downstairs, poking my head into every room, opening doors, checking closets, looking and listening, hoping with all my heart to find a little girl.

Mr. Wu was changing the sheets in a second-floor bedroom when I showed him my badge and the picture of Madison Tyler.

"Have you seen this little girl?" I asked him.

He shook his head vigorously — no. "No children here. Mr. Klassen not like children. No children here!"

Ten minutes later, I was taking deep breaths of cold, clean air on the front steps when Conklin joined me, closing the heavy oaken door behind him.

"Well, that was fun," I said.

"His alibi is going to check out," said Conklin, folding a list of names and numbers into his notebook.

"Yeah, I know it will. Rich, you think that guy is straight?"

"I think he'll twitch for anything that moves."

Klassen was in his driveway when Conklin and I got into our squad car. He lifted a hand, gave us another cheese-eating smile, said, "Buh-bye."

He was whistling to himself, buffing the silver haunch of his Jaguar, when our humble Ford shot away from the curb.

Chapter 54

CONKLIN AND I SAT ACROSS from each other in the squad room. Beside my phone was a pile of unreturned messages from various tipsters who'd reported seeing Madison Tyler everywhere—from Ghirardelli Square to Osaka, Japan.

Dr. Germaniuk's autopsy report of Paola Ricci was open in front of me. Bottom line—cause of death: gunshot to the head. Manner of death: homicide.

Dr. G. had stuck a Post-it note to his report. I read it out loud to my partner.

Sergeant Boxer,

   Clothing went to crime lab. I did a sexual-assault kit, just to say I've been there, but don't count on it coming back with anything positive due to total submersion, etc. Bullet was through and through. No projectile recovered.

Regards, H. G.

"Dead girl. Dead end," Conklin said, running his hands through his hair. "The kidnappers have no problem with murder. And that's all we know."

"So what are we missing? We have a half-baked sighting from a witness who gave us nondescriptions of the perps and the car. We have no plate number, no physical evidence from the scene—no cigarette butts, no chewing gum, no shell casings, no tread marks. *And no freaking ransom note*."

Conklin leaned back in his chair, said to the ceiling, "The perps acted like muscle, not like sexual predators. Shooting Paola within a minute of capturing her? What's that?"

"It's like the shooter was itchy. High on crack. Like the job was subbed out to gangbangers. Or Paola was excess baggage, so they offed her. Or she put up a fight and someone panicked," I said. "But you know, Richie, you're right. Totally right."

His chair creaked as he returned it to an upright position.

"We have to turn this investigation on its head. Work on solving Paola Ricci," I said, planting my hand palm down on the autopsy report. "Even dead, she could lead us to Madison."

Conklin was putting in a call to the Italian Consulate when Brenda swiveled her chair toward me. She covered the mouthpiece of her phone with her hand.

"Lindsay, you've got a caller on line four, won't identify himself. Sounds . . . scary. I asked for a trace."

I nodded, my heartbeat ticking up a notch. I stabbed the button on the phone console.

"This is Sergeant Boxer."

"I'm only going to say this once," said the digitally altered voice that sounded like a frog talking through Bubble Wrap. I signaled to Conklin to pick up on my line.

"Who is this?" I asked.

"Never mind," said the voice. "Madison Tyler is fine."

"How do you know?"

"Say something, Maddy."

Another voice came over the line, breathy, young, broken. "Mommy? Mommy?"

"Madison?" I said into the phone.

The frog voice was back.

"Tell her parents they made a big mistake calling the police. Call off the dogs," said the caller, "or we'll hurt Madison. Permanently. If you back off, she'll stay alive and well, but either way, the Tylers will never see their daughter again."

And then the phone went dead.

"Hello? *Hello?*"

I jiggled the hook until I got a dial tone, then I slammed the phone down.

"Brenda, get the Call Center."

"What was *that? 'They made a big mistake calling the police?'*" Conklin shouted. "Lindsay, did that little girl sound like Madison?"

"Jesus Christ, I couldn't tell. *I don't know.*"

"What the *hell?*" Conklin said, hurling a phone book against the wall.

I felt dizzy, physically sick.

Was Madison really fine?

What did it mean that her parents shouldn't have called the police? Had there been a ransom demand or a phone call that we didn't know about?

Everyone in the squad room was looking at me, and Jacobi was standing behind me, literally breathing down my neck, when the radio room called back with the result of the phone trace.

The caller had used a no-name cell phone, and the location couldn't be traced.

"The voice was altered," I told Jacobi. "I'll send the tape to the lab."

"Before you do that, get the parents to listen to it. Maybe we can get a positive ID on the child's voice."

"Could still be a sicko getting his rocks off," Conklin said as Jacobi walked away.

"I hope that's what it is. Because we're not 'calling off the dogs.' Not even close."

I couldn't say what I was thinking.

That we'd just heard Madison Tyler's last words.

Chapter 55

BRENDA FREGOSI HAD BEEN the homicide squad
assistant for some years and, at only twenty-five years old,
was a natural mother hen.

She was clucking sympathetically as I spoke to Henry
Tyler on the phone, and when I hung up, she handed me a
message slip.

I read her spiky handwriting: *"Claire wants you to
come to the hospital at six this evening."*

It was almost six now.

"How did she sound?" I asked.

"Fine, I think."

"Is this all she said?"

"This is what she said exactly: 'Brenda, please tell
Lindsay to come to the hospital at six. Thanks a lot.'"

I'd just seen Claire *yesterday. What was wrong?*

I drove toward San Francisco General, my mind
swirling with terrible, sinking thoughts. Claire once
told me this thing about brain chemistry, the nub of it
being that when you're feeling good, you can't ever
imagine feeling bad again. And when you're feeling

bad, it's impossible to imagine a time when you won't be circling the drain.

As I sucked on an Altoids, a little girl's voice was crying, "Mommy," in my head, and it was mixed up with the bad knee-jerk reaction I had to hospitals ever since my mother died in one almost fifteen years ago.

I parked in the hospital lot, thinking about how good it had been having Joe to talk to when I felt this low, frustrated from three days of staggering blindly into dead ends.

My thoughts turned back to Claire as I stepped into the hospital elevator. I stared at my fried reflection in the stainless steel doors. I fluffed my bangs uselessly as the car climbed upward, then when the doors slid open, I stepped out into the antiseptic stink and cold white light of the post-op unit.

I wasn't the first to arrive at Claire's room. Yuki and Cindy had already moved chairs up to her bed, and Claire was sitting up, wearing a flowered nightgown and a *Mona Lisa* smile on her face.

The Women's Murder Club was assembled — but why?

"Hey, everyone," I said, walking around the bed, kissing cheeks. "You look gorgeous," I said to Claire, my relief that this wasn't a life-support emergency bringing me almost to the point of giddiness. "What's the occasion?"

"She wouldn't tell until you got here," Yuki said.

"Okay, okay!" Claire said. "I do have an announcement to make."

"You're *pregnant*," said Cindy.

Claire burst out laughing, and we all looked at Cindy.

"You're crazy, girl reporter," I said. A baby was the last

thing Claire needed at age forty-three, with two near-grown-up sons.

"Give us a clue," Yuki blurted out. "Give us a category."

"You guys! Stomping on my surprise with your cleats on," said Claire, still laughing.

Cindy, Yuki, and I swiveled our heads toward her.

"I had some blood work done," said Claire. "And Miss Cindy, as usual, is *right*."

"Ha!" Cindy cried out.

Claire said, "If I hadn't been in this hospital, I probably wouldn't have even *known* I was pregnant until I started having contractions."

We were all yelling now. "What did you say?" "You're not putting us on?" "How far along are you?"

"The sonogram shows that my little one is fine," said Claire, serene as a Buddha. *"My wonder child!"*

Chapter 56

I HAD TO PULL MYSELF AWAY from the celebration, overdue as I was for Tracchio's meeting back at the Hall. As I entered his office, the chief was offering leather-upholstered armchairs to the Tylers, while Jacobi, Conklin, and Macklin dragged up side chairs, circling the wagons around the chief's large desk.

The Tylers looked as if they'd been sleeping standing up for the last eighty-four hours. Their faces were gray, their shoulders slumped. I knew they were painfully suspended between hope and despair as they waited to hear the audiotape.

A tape recorder was set up on Tracchio's desk. I leaned over and pressed the play button, and a terrifying, evil voice alternating with mine filled the room.

A little girl's voice cried out, *"Mommy? Mommy?"*

I pressed the recorder's stop key. Elizabeth Tyler reached out toward the tape recorder, then turned, grabbed her husband's arm, buried her face into his coat, and sobbed.

"Is that Madison's voice?" Tracchio asked.

Both parents nodded—yes.

Jacobi said, "The rest of this tape is going to be even more difficult for you to hear. But we're feeling optimistic. When this call came in, your daughter was alive."

I pressed the play button again, watched the Tylers' faces as they heard the kidnapper say that Madison was fine but that she would never be seen again.

"Mr. and Mrs. Tyler, do you have any idea why the kidnapper said you 'made a big mistake calling the police'?" I asked.

"No idea at all," Henry Tyler snapped. "Why would they feel threatened? You've turned up *nothing*. You don't even have a *suspect*. Where is the FBI? Why aren't they trying to find Madison?"

Macklin said, "We *are* working with the FBI. We're using their sources and their databases, but the FBI won't actively work this case unless we have some reason to believe that Madison was taken out of state."

"So tell them that she was!"

Jacobi said, "Mr. Tyler, what we're asking is, did you receive a communication from the kidnapper telling you not to call the police? Anything like that happen?"

"Nothing," said Elizabeth Tyler. "Henry? Did you hear from them at the office?"

"Not a word. I swear."

I was thinking about Paola Ricci as I looked at the Tylers. I said, "You told us that Paola Ricci was highly recommended. Who recommended her?"

Elizabeth Tyler leaned forward. "Paola came to us directly through her service."

"What kind of service is that?" Macklin asked, stress showing in the grinding of his jaw.

"It's an employment agency," said Elizabeth Tyler. "They screen, sponsor, and train well-bred girls from overseas. They get their work papers and find them jobs. Paola had tremendous references from the agency and from back home in Italy. She was a very proper young woman. We loved her."

"The service gets their fees from the employers?" Jacobi asked.

"Yes. I think we paid them eighteen thousand dollars."

The mentioning of money sent a prickling sensation along the tops of my arms and a swooping feeling in my stomach.

"What's the name of this service?" I said.

"Westbury. No, the Westwood Registry," said Henry Tyler. "You'll speak to them?"

"Yes, and please don't say anything about this call to anyone," Jacobi cautioned the Tylers. "Just go home. Stay near your phone. And leave the Westwood Registry to us."

"You'll be in touch with them?" asked Henry Tyler again.

"We'll be all over them."

Chapter 57

CINDY WAS ON THE PHONE with Yuki, loading the dishwasher as she talked.

"He's just too funny," Cindy said about Whit Ewing, the good-looking reporter from the *Chicago Tribune* she'd met about a month ago at the Municipal Hospital trial.

"The guy with the glasses, right? The one who tore out of the courtroom by way of the emergency exit? Set off the alarm?" Yuki chuckled, remembering.

"Yeah. See... and he can goof on himself. Whit says he's Clark Kent's nerdy younger brother." Cindy laughed. "He's been threatening to fly into town and take me out to dinner. He's even angling to be assigned to the Brinkley trial."

"Oh, so wait a minute," Yuki said. "You're *not* thinking of doing what Lindsay did. I mean, Whit lives in Chicago. Why start up an LDR when they're so freaking doomed?"

"I'm thinking... it's been a while since I've had any, uh, fun."

"Been a while for me, too." Yuki sighed. "I not only don't remember *when,* I don't remember with *whom!*"

Cindy cackled, then Yuki put her on hold so she could take an incoming call. When Yuki came back on the line, she said, "Hey, girl reporter, Red Dog wants me. Gotta scoot."

"Go, go," Cindy said. "See you in court."

Cindy hung up and turned on the dishwasher, then emptied the trash can. She tied a knot in the bag, went out into the hallway, and hit the elevator call button, and when the car clanked to a stop, she checked to make sure it was empty before she got in.

She thought again about Whit Ewing, and about Lindsay and Joe, and about how long-distance relationships were, by definition, roller-coaster rides.

Fun for a while, until they made you sick.

And now here was another reason to have a boyfriend who stayed in town—the sheer creepiness of living in this building alone. She hit B for "basement," and the newly paneled old elevator rocked as it descended. A minute later, Cindy stepped out into the dank bowels of the building.

As she walked toward the trash area, she heard the sound of a woman crying, a sobbing that echoed and was joined by the screaming of a baby!

What now?

Cindy rounded a bend in the underground vault of the building and saw a blond-haired woman about her own age holding a baby over her shoulder.

There was a black trash bag lying open at the woman's feet.

"What's wrong?" Cindy asked.

"My *dog*," the stricken woman cried. "Look!"

She bent, spread open the mouth of the trash bag so

that Cindy could see the small black-and-white dog that was covered with blood.

"I left him outside for only a few minutes," she said, "just to take the baby into my apartment. *Oh, my God.* I called the police to report that someone had stolen him, but *look*. Someone who lives here did this. *Someone who lives here beat Barnaby to death!*"

Chapter 58

IT WAS WEDNESDAY MORNING, 8:30 a.m., four days after Madison Tyler's abduction. Conklin and I were parked in a construction zone near the corner of Waverly and Clay, steam from our coffee condensing on the car windows as we watched the traffic weave around double-parked delivery vans, pedestrians spilling into the narrow, gloomy streets of Chinatown.

I was eyeballing one building in particular, a three-story redbrick house halfway down Waverly. Wong's Chinese Apothecary was on the ground floor. The top two floors were leased to the Westwood Registry.

My gut was telling me that we'd find at least partial answers in that house — a link between Paola Ricci and the abduction... *something.*

At 8:35 the front door to the brick house opened and a woman stepped out, took the trash down to the curb.

"Time to rock and roll," said Conklin.

We crossed the street and intercepted the woman before she disappeared back inside. We flashed our badges.

She was white, thin, midthirties, dark hair falling

straight to her shoulders, her prettiness marred by the worry lining her brow.

"I've been wondering when we'd hear from the police," she said, one hand on the doorknob. "The owners are out of town. Can you come back on Friday?"

"Sure," Conklin said, "but we have a couple of questions for you *now,* if you don't mind."

Brenda, our squad assistant, swoons over Conklin, says he's a "girl magnet," and it's true. He doesn't work it. He's just got this natural, hunky appeal.

I watched as the dark-haired woman hesitated, looked at Conklin, then opened the door wide.

"I'm Mary Jordan," she said. "Office manager, bookkeeper, den mother, and everything else you can think of. Come on in..."

I shot a grin at Conklin as we followed Ms. Jordan across the threshold and down a hallway to her office. It was a small room, her desk at an angle facing the door. Two ladder-back chairs faced the desk, and a framed picture of Jordan surrounded by a dozen young women, presumably nannies, hung on the wall behind her.

I found Jordan's apparent anxiety noteworthy. She chewed on her lower lip, stood up, moved a stack of three-ring binders to the top of a file cabinet, sat down, picked at her watch strap, twiddled a pencil. I was getting seasick just watching her.

"What are your thoughts on the abduction of Paola and Madison Tyler?" I asked.

"I'm at a complete loss," Jordan said, shaking her head, and then she continued, barely pausing to take a breath.

Jordan said that she was the registry's only full-time employee. There were two tutors, both women, who worked when needed. Apart from the co-owner, a fifty-year-old white man, there were no men associated with the registry and no minivans, black or otherwise.

The owners of the Westwood Registry were Paul and Laura Renfrew, husband and wife, Ms. Jordan told us. At the moment, Paul was calling on potential clients north of San Francisco and Laura was off recruiting in Europe. They'd left town before the kidnappings.

"The Renfrews are nice people," Jordan assured us.

"And how long have you known them?"

"I started working for the Renfrews just before they relocated from Boston, about eight months ago. The business isn't breaking even yet," Jordan went on. "Now, with Paola dead and Madison Tyler...gone...that's not very good publicity, is it?"

Tears filled Mary Jordan's eyes. She pulled a pink tissue from a box on her desk, blotted her face.

"Ms. Jordan," I said, leaning across her desk, "something's eating at you. What is it?"

"No, really, I'm fine."

"The hell you are."

"It's just that I *loved* Paola. And I'm the one who matched her up with the Tylers. It was *me*. If I hadn't done that, Paola would still be alive!"

Chapter 59

"THE RENFREWS HAVE AN APARTMENT down here," Ms. Jordan said as she walked us around the administrative floor. She pointed to the green-painted, padlocked door at the end of a hallway.

"Why the padlock?" I asked.

"They lock up only when they're both away," Jordan said. "It's a good thing. This way I don't have to worry about the girls poking around where they don't belong."

The bumping sound of footsteps came through the floor above.

"The common room is over there," Jordan said, continuing the tour. "The conference room is on your right, and the dorm is upstairs," she said, looking up at the wooden stairway.

"The girls live at the registry until we place them with families. I live up there, too."

"How many girls are here?" I asked.

"Four. After Laura gets back from her trip, we'll probably bring over four more."

Conklin and I spent the remainder of the morning

interviewing the young women as they came downstairs, one by one, to the conference room. They ranged in age from eighteen to twenty-two, all European, with good-to-excellent English.

None had a clue or a suspicion or a bad thought about the Renfrews or about Paola Ricci.

"When Paola was here, she said her prayers on her knees every night," a girl named Luisa insisted. "She was a virgin!"

Back at Ms. Jordan's desk, the Renfrews' office manager threw up her hands when we asked her if she had any idea who might have kidnapped Paola and Madison. When she answered a ringing phone, Conklin asked me, "Want me to bust that padlock?"

"Want your next career to be with the sanitation department?"

"It could be worth it."

"You're dreaming," I said. "Even if we had probable cause, Madison Tyler isn't in there. The den mother would spill."

We were leaving the house, walking down the front steps, when Mary Jordan called out, caught up with us, clutched Conklin's arm.

"I've been debating with myself. This could be gossip or just plain wrong, and I don't want to make trouble for anyone," she said.

"You can't worry about that, Mary," Conklin said. "Whatever you think you know, you've got to tell us."

"I'd just started with the Renfrews," Jordan said, darting her eyes to the door of the house, then back to Conklin.

"One of the girls told me something and made me

swear not to tell. She said that a graduate of the registry left her employers without notice. I'm not talking about bad manners— the Renfrews had her passport. That girl couldn't get another job without it."

"Was the missing girl reported to the police?"

"I think so. All I know is what I was told. And I was told that Helga Schmidt went missing and was never heard from again."

Chapter 60

THE TENANTS' MEETING HAD HEATED UP to a full boil by the time Cindy got there. A couple hundred people, more or less, were crammed into the lobby. President of the Board Fern Galperin was a small, pretty woman with wire-frame glasses, her head barely visible over the crowd as she tried to quell the clamor.

"One at a time," Ms. Galperin shouted. "Margery? Please go on with what you were saying."

Cindy saw Margery Glynn, the woman she'd met in the garbage room yesterday, sitting on a love seat, jammed between three other people.

Glynn cried out, "The police sent me a *form* to fill out. They're not going to do anything about Barnaby, and Barnaby was family. Now I feel even more at risk because he's gone. Should I get another dog? Or should I get a *gun?*"

"I feel as scared and sick as you do," Galperin said, clutching her own small dog to her bosom. "But you can't be serious about getting a gun! Anyone else?"

Cindy put down her computer bag, whispered to a

striking brunette woman standing next to the refreshment table, "What's going on?"

"You know about Barnaby?"

"Afraid so. I was in the garbage room when Margery found him."

"Nasty, huh? Barnaby was kind of a pest, but for somebody to kill him? It's certifiably crazy. What is this... *New York?*"

"Catch me up, will you? I'm new here."

"Sure, okay. So Barnaby wasn't the first. Mrs. Neely's poodle was found dead in a stairwell, and that poor woman blamed *herself* because she'd forgotten to lock her door."

"I take it someone in the building doesn't care for dogs."

"I mean, yeah," the brunette woman continued. "But there's more. A month ago, Mr. Franks, a real nice guy who lived on the second floor, had a moving van come, like, in the middle of the night. He left Fern a packet of threatening letters that had been slipped under his door over a number of months."

"What kind of threats?"

"*Death threats.* Can you believe it?"

"Why didn't he call the police?"

"I guess he did. But the letters were anonymous. The cops asked a few questions, then let the whole thing drop. Typical crap."

"And I assume Mr. Franks had a dog?"

"No. He had a *stereo.* I'm Debbie Green, by the way." The woman smiled broadly. "2F." She shook Cindy's hand.

"I'm Cindy Thomas. 3B."

"Nice to meet you, Cindy. Welcome to *A Nightmare at the Blakely Arms*."

Cindy smiled uncertainly. "So aren't you scared?"

"Kinda." Debbie sighed. "But my apartment is fantastic.... I'm dating someone now. I think I've talked him into moving in."

"Lucky you." Cindy turned her attention back to the meeting as a stooped elderly gentleman was recognized by the board president.

"Mr. Horn."

"Thank you. What bothers me the most is the stealth," he said. "The notes under the doors. The murdered pets. I think Margery is on to something. If the police can't help us, we must form a tenants' patrol—"

Voices erupted, and Ms. Galperin cried out, "People, raise your hands, please! Tom, you have something to say?"

A man in his thirties stood up. He was slight and balding, standing far across the room from Cindy.

"A tenants' patrol scares the hell out of me," he said. "Whoever is terrorizing the Blakely Arms could sign up to be on a patrol—and then he wouldn't have to sneak around. He could walk the halls with impunity. How scary would that be?

"About three hundred eighty-five people live in this building, and more than half of us are here tonight. The odds are nearly fifty-fifty that our own private terrorist is in this room. *Right now.*"

Chapter 61

YUKI HAD NEVER SEEN Leonard Parisi *mad* before. "Red Dog," as he was called, was red haired, tall, more than two hundred pounds, usually affable and avuncular—but right now his dark eyes were pumping bullets as he pounded the conference table with his fist.

Platters of leftover Chinese food jumped.

The five new ADAs around the table looked shocked, with the exception of David Hale, who'd had the bad judgment to remark that the Brinkley case was a "slam dunk."

"There's no such thing as a slam dunk," Parisi roared. *"O. J. was a slam dunk."*

"Robert Durst," said Yuki.

"Bingo," Parisi said, staring around at all of them. "Durst *admitted* that he killed his neighbor, chopped him into a dozen parts, and dumped him into the ocean—and a jury of his peers found him *'not guilty.'*

"And that's our challenge with Brinkley, David. We have a taped confession and more witnesses than we can count. The *crime* was caught on tape. And still, it's not a slam dunk."

"But, Leonard," Hale said, "that tape of the crime makes the killer in the *act*. It's admissible and indisputable."

Parisi grinned. "You're quite the bulldog, David. Good for you. You all know about Rodney King?" Parisi asked, loosening his tie.

"Rodney King, a black parolee, refused to exit his car after he was stopped for speeding. He was pulled out of his vehicle and struck fifty-six times by four white cops—a massive, bloody beating, all caught on video-tape. The case went to trial. The cops were *acquitted,* and so began the race riots in LA.

"So the tape didn't make the case a slam dunk. And maybe this is why: First time you see the Rodney King tape, you're horrified. Second time, you're outraged. But once you see it for the *twentieth time,* your brain has been around every corner of that scene, and you remember it, sure, but the shock power's gone.

"Everyone in this country with a television set has seen Jack Rooney's tape of Alfred Brinkley shooting those people over and over and over again. By now it's lost its shock power. Understand?

"That said, the tape *is* in. We *should* win this case. And we're going to do everything we can to put Brinkley on death row.

"But we're going against a smart and tenacious attorney in Barbara Blanco," Parisi said, leaning back in his chair. "And she isn't working this crap public-defender job for the money. She believes in her client, and the jury is going to feel that.

"We've got to be prepared for anything. And that's the end of today's lecture."

A respectful silence fell over the conference room. Len Parisi was definitely "da man" around here.

"Yuki, anything we forgot to go over?"

"I think we're covered."

"Feeling good?"

"Feeling great, Len. I'm ready to go. Can't wait."

"Sure. You're twenty-eight. But I need my beauty sleep. I'll see you here at seven thirty a.m. Everyone else, stay tuned. We'll have a postmortem at close of day tomorrow."

Yuki said good night to her colleagues and left the room, feeling charged up and lucky that tomorrow morning, she'd be Leonard Parisi's second chair.

And despite Parisi's cautionary rant, Yuki did feel confident. Brinkley wasn't O. J. or even Robert Durst. He had no star wattage, no media appeal. Only weeks ago he was sleeping on the street with a loaded gun in his pocket. *He'd killed four total strangers.*

No way a jury would chance letting that maniac back on the streets of San Francisco again. *Would they?*

Part Four

THE PEOPLE VS. ALFRED BRINKLEY

Chapter 62

YUKI PUT HER BRIEFCASE next to Leonard's on the table outside Department 21. They passed through the metal detectors, walked through the first set of double doors into the small anteroom, then through the second set of doors and directly into the courtroom.

There was a definite buzz from the gallery as Red Dog, at six two in navy-blue pinstripes, walked next to Yuki, at five three in heels, a hundred pounds in her pearl-gray suit, down the center aisle of the courtroom. Leonard yanked open the gate that separated the gallery from the bar, let her go ahead of him. Then he followed and immediately began setting up at the prosecution table.

Yuki's thrill of anticipation was cut sharply with first-day jitters. There was nothing more she could do to prepare, and she couldn't bear to wait. She straightened her lapels and her stack of papers, glanced at her watch. Court was due to begin in five minutes sharp, and the defense table was *empty*.

The room stirred again, and what she saw almost stopped her heart. She nudged Leonard, and he turned.

Alfred Brinkley was coming up the aisle. His beard had been shaved, his long hair had been buzzed short, and he was wearing a blue polyester suit and tie, looking about as dangerous as rice pudding.

But it wasn't Brinkley who'd made her stomach clench and her mouth drop open.

Barbara Blanco wasn't at Brinkley's side. Instead, there was a man in his early forties, prematurely gray, dressed in a charcoal-gray Brioni suit and yellow-print Armani tie. She knew Brinkley's new attorney.

Everyone did.

"Aw, fuck," Parisi said, smiling stiffly. "Mickey Sherman. You know him, don't you, Yuki?"

"Sure do. We were cocounsel when we defended a friend of mine only months ago."

"Yeah, I remember. Homicide lieutenant charged with wrongful death." Parisi took off his glasses, polished them with his handkerchief, said to Yuki, "What'd I say last night?"

" 'Be prepared for anything.' "

"Sometimes I hate it when I'm right. What can you tell me, apart from the fact that Sherman's never seen a camera he doesn't like?"

"He's a big-picture guy," Yuki said. "Leaves the details to others. Stuff might fall through the cracks."

Yuki was thinking how she'd read that Mickey Sherman had resigned his job as deputy corporation counsel for the City of San Francisco and opened a small private practice. He'd do the Brinkley case pro bono, but the media attention would be a hell of a launching pad for Sherman and Associates—*if he won.*

"Well, he hasn't got a big staff anymore," Parisi said.

"We'll just have to find those cracks and pry them open with a crowbar. Meanwhile, I already see his first big problem."

"Yeah." Yuki nodded. "Alfred Brinkley doesn't look insane. But Len, Mickey Sherman knows that, too."

Chapter 63

YUKI STOOD AT ATTENTION as Judge Norman Moore took the bench, Old Glory on one side, flag of the State of California on the other, thermos of coffee and a laptop in front of him.

The two hundred people in the courtroom sat down as court was called into session.

Judge Moore was known to be fair, with a tendency to let lawyers run out ahead a jot too far before bringing down his gavel.

Now Moore spent a good fifteen minutes instructing the jury before turning his bespectacled blue eyes on Leonard Parisi. "Are the People ready to begin?"

"We are, Your Honor."

Leonard Parisi stood, fastened the middle button of his suit jacket, walked toward the jury box, and greeted the jurors. Red Dog was truly large, his hips broad and his shoulders sloping and wide. His red hair was fuzzy, and his skin was pocked and rough.

Leonard Parisi was no heartthrob, but when he spoke,

he had the stage presence of a character actor, one of the greats like Rod Steiger or Gene Hackman.

You just couldn't keep your eyes off him.

"Ladies and Gentlemen, when you were selected for this jury, you all said that you'd seen the 'Rooney tape' of the *Del Norte* ferry tragedy. You said that you could keep an open mind about the defendant's guilt or innocence. And you promised that you'd judge Mr. Brinkley by what's proven to you *in this courtroom.*

"That's why I want to tell you what it was like November first on the *Del Norte,* so that you will see it fresh in your mind's eye.

"It was a real nice day for a ferry ride," Parisi began. "About sixty degrees, with intermittent sun. A lot of the tourists were wearing shorts because, hey, San Francisco is in California, right?"

Laughter rippled across the courtroom as Parisi warmed to his opening statement.

"It was a beautiful day that turned into a day in *hell* because the defendant, Alfred Brinkley, was on that ferry.

"Mr. Brinkley was penniless, but he'd found a round-trip ticket at the farmer's market and decided to take a ride. He had a loaded gun in his pocket, a revolver that held six rounds.

"On this particular day, Mr. Brinkley rode the ferry to Larkspur without incident, but on the return trip, as the boat was docking in San Francisco, the defendant saw Andrea Canello having a discussion with her little boy, a cute nine-year-old lad by the name of Tony.

"For a reason known only to Mr. Brinkley, he pulled out his gun and shot that thirty-year-old mother in her chest.

"She died almost instantly, right in front of her small

son," Parisi said. "Then Mrs. Canello's boy turned his huge, terrified eyes to face the man who had just shot his mother—and what did Alfred Brinkley do?

"He shot Tony Canello, a little boy who was armed with a *strawberry ice-cream cone*. Tony was in the fourth grade, looking forward to Thanksgiving and to getting a mountain bike for Christmas and to growing up to become a man.

"Mr. Brinkley took all that away from Tony Canello. He died in the hospital later that day."

The pained faces of the jury showed that Parisi had already moved them. One of the jurors, a young woman with shocking magenta hair, bit her lips as tears coursed down her cheeks.

Leonard paused in his speech respectfully and let the juror cry.

Chapter 64

AT THIS POINT, Judge Moore spoke to the six men and six women of the jury. "Do you need to take a break? Okay then, please continue, Mr. Parisi."

"Thank you, Your Honor," Parisi said. He flicked his eyes over to the defense table, saw that Mickey Sherman was whispering to his client, his back turned away from the proceedings, a dismissive gesture meant to show that Parisi's opening hadn't disturbed the defense in the least.

Smart move. Parisi knew he would've done the same thing.

"I've told you that the *Del Norte* was coming into dock when Mr. Brinkley shot Andrea and Tony Canello. The docking operation was noisy, much louder than two shots from a gun.

"But a couple of people understood what had happened.

"Mr. Per Conrad was working on the *Del Norte* as an engineer that day. He was a family man, with a wife and four beautiful kids, and he was about two years away from retirement. He saw Alfred Brinkley with his gun in hand

and he saw the fallen bodies of Andrea and Tony Canello bleeding out on the deck.

"Mr. Conrad moved to disarm Mr. Brinkley, who took aim and shot Mr. Conrad between the eyes.

"Mr. Lester Ng was an insurance broker in Larkspur, coming into San Francisco to make a business call. He, too, was a family man, a former U.S. Air Force pilot. And he, too, tried to wrest Mr. Brinkley's gun away from him. He was shot in the head. Mr. Brinkley's gun was the last thing Mr. Ng saw in his life.

"Both men were selfless. They were heroes. And they died because of it.

"And still Mr. Brinkley was not finished."

Parisi walked over to the jury box, put his hands on the rail, looked at each of the jurors as he spoke.

"Mr. Brinkley was standing beside a woman this community holds in high regard, Dr. Claire Washburn, San Francisco's chief medical examiner. Dr. Washburn was terrified, but she had the presence of mind to say to Mr. Brinkley, 'Okay, son... give me the gun.'

"Instead, Mr. Brinkley gave her a *bullet* in the *chest*. And when Dr. Washburn's teenage son, Willie, went to her assistance, Mr. Brinkley shot at him, too.

"Luckily, the boat bumped the pier at that moment, and Mr. Brinkley's sixth and final shot missed its mark. And because that shot went wild, two brave people, Claire and Willie Washburn, survived, and Dr. Washburn will be a witness in this trial."

Parisi paused, letting the horror of the shooting imprint on the jurors' minds before he spoke again.

"There's no question that everything I've told you actually happened.

"There's no question that without regard to sex, age, race, or reason, Alfred Brinkley shot and killed four people he didn't know, and attempted to kill two others.

"Mr. Jack Rooney, who will also be a witness in this trial, videotaped the shootings, which we will show you. And Mr. Brinkley confessed to these brutal killings, and we'll show you his taped confession, too.

"There is no DNA in this case. No blood-spatter evidence and no partial palm prints or any of the kind of forensic evidence that you see every night on TV crime shows. That's because this case is not a 'whodunit.'

"*We know who did it.* He's sitting right there."

Parisi pointed to the man in the blue suit. Brinkley's head had sunk down on his shoulders so that his neck seemed to have retracted. His dulled eyes stared straight ahead. The man looked so medicated, Parisi wondered how much of this Brinkley even heard or understood.

"The defense is going to try to convince you that Mr. Brinkley is psychotic and therefore not responsible for his actions," Parisi said, walking back to the lectern. "Defense medical experts may have the nerve to stand up here and tell you that the defendant needs 'treatment,' not punishment.

"No problem. We have great doctors treating all our death-row inmates.

"Acting insane does not exempt you from the rule of law. And it doesn't mean that you don't understand that killing people is wrong.

"Ladies and Gentlemen, Alfred Brinkley brought a loaded gun onto the ferry. He targeted his victims with intent and deadly aim. He murdered four of them. And then he ran from the scene of his crime.

"Because Alfred Brinkley knew that what he'd done was wrong.

"The People will prove to you that Mr. Brinkley was legally sane when he committed four acts of murder and two acts of attempted murder. And we will ask you to find him *'guilty'* on all counts.

"We thank you for your attention. I'm sorry I made some of you cry, but these murders are a tragedy."

Chapter 65

YUKI WATCHED MICKEY SHERMAN STAND UP from the defense table and confidently cross the courtroom floor to the podium.

Sherman introduced himself to the jury, his hands-in-pockets demeanor and easy charm captivating them with his first sentence.

"Folks, everything the prosecutor told you is *true,*" he began. It was a daring declaration, Yuki thought. In fact, she'd never heard opposition counsel take that position before.

"You all know what happened on the *Del Norte* on November first," Sherman said. "Mr. Brinkley did in fact bring a loaded gun onto the ferry. He shot those people without regard for the consequences to them — or to himself.

"He was surrounded by two hundred fifty people, some of whom witnessed the shooting. Mr. Brinkley didn't throw his gun away after he fled the *Del Norte*. He didn't get rid of the *evidence*.

"This was not what you'd call a perfect crime. Only an insane person would do these acts and behave in this way.

"So *what* happened is no mystery.

"But *why* it happened is what this trial is about.

"Mr. Brinkley did not understand his actions because when he shot those unfortunate people, *he was legally insane.*

"Since the issue of 'legal insanity' will be the basis for your judgment of Mr. Brinkley and his actions, this is a good time to define the term," Sherman said.

"The issue is this: Did Mr. Brinkley understand the wrongfulness of his acts when he committed the crimes? If he didn't understand that those acts were wrong because he suffered from a mental disease or defect at the time the crimes were committed, then he was 'legally insane.' "

Mickey Sherman paused, shuffled his notes on the lectern, and began speaking again in a tone of voice that Yuki admired and feared. It was soft on the ear, personal, as if he trusted that the jurors wouldn't need theatrics, that his reasoning was not only credible but true.

"Mr. Brinkley has been diagnosed with schizoaffective disorder," Sherman told the jury. "He has an illness, like cancer, or diabetes, a disabling disease that came to him genetically and also through childhood trauma.

"He didn't ask for this disease, but he got it.

"It could have happened to you or me or anyone in this room. And what disease could be worse than to have your *own brain* turn against you and cause you to have thoughts and take actions that are completely against your character and nature?

"I want to say right now that our hearts go out to all the victims of this tragedy. If there was some way we could turn back the clock, if Fred Brinkley could take a magic pill or an injection that would heal him on November first and restore those people's lives, he would do it in a second.

"If he had known that he was mentally ill, Mr. Brinkley would have gotten treatment. But he didn't know why he felt the way he did.

"Mr. Brinkley's life brings true meaning to the expression 'living hell.'"

Chapter 66

MICKEY SHERMAN FELT THE NICE, STEADY flow of adrenaline that came from knowing his stuff and from believing in his client. Brinkley, the poor schmuck, was just waking up to the real world after fifteen years of slow decompensation as his illness had progressed.

And what a sorry world it was. Going on trial for his life under a thick blanket of antipsychotic medication.

It was a damned tragedy all the way around.

"Mr. Brinkley heard voices," Mickey Sherman said as he paced in front of the jury box. "I'm not talking about the 'little voice' we all hear in our own heads, the interior monologue that helps us figure out problems or write a speech or find our car keys.

"The voices in Mr. Brinkley's head were directive, intrusive, overwhelming, and *cruel*.

"These voices taunted him unrelentingly, called him derogatory names—and they goaded him to kill. When he watched television, he believed that the characters and the news anchors were talking directly to him, that they were accusing him of crimes, and *also* that they were telling him what to do.

"And after years of fighting these demons, Fred Brinkley finally obeyed the voices.

"Ladies and Gentlemen, at the time of the shooting, Fred Brinkley was not in touch with reality.

"He didn't know that the people he shot on the ferry were made of flesh and blood. To him they were part of the painful hallucinations in his own mind.

"Afterward, Mr. Brinkley saw the TV news report of himself shooting people on the ferry, and because the pictures were on TV, he realized what he had done. He was so overcome with remorse and guilt and self-hatred that he turned himself in to the police of his own volition.

"He waived all his rights and confessed, because in the aftermath of his crimes, the healthy part of his brain allowed him to understand the horror of his actions.

"That should give you a window into this man's character.

"The prosecution would like you to believe that the hardest decision you'll have to make in this trial is picking your foreperson.

"But you haven't heard the full story yet.

"Witnesses who know Mr. Brinkley and psychiatric professionals who have examined him will attest to Mr. Brinkley's character and his past and present state of mind.

"When you've heard our case in its entirety, I am confident that you will find Fred Brinkley 'not guilty' by reason of mental defect or disease.

"Because the truth is, Fred Brinkley is a good man who is afflicted with a terrible mind-altering disease."

Chapter 67

AT 6:30 THAT NIGHT, Yuki and Leonard Parisi were seated in the cavernous sunken dining room at Restaurant LuLu, an old warehouse turned popular eatery not far from the Hall of Justice.

Yuki felt sharp, part of the A-team. The *winning* A-team. She carved into her rotisserie chicken and Len tucked into his spicy prawn pizza, the two of them reviewing the day as they ate, trying on potential roadblocks, planning how to detonate those roadblocks in their next day's presentation of the People's case against Alfred Brinkley.

Leonard refilled their wineglasses with a sixty-dollar merlot, saying, "Grrrrr. Beware of Team Red Dog."

Yuki laughed, sipped, put her papers into a large leather bag as the dinner plates were taken away. Working as a civil litigator had never felt as good as this.

The large brick oven across the room perfumed the air with burning hickory wood, and as the restaurant and bar filled up, conversation and laughter caromed off the walls and high ceilings.

"Coffee?" Len asked Yuki.

"Sure," she said. "And I'm so stoked, I think I'm gonna go for the profiteroles."

"I'll second that," Leonard said, raising his hand to signal their waitress. And then, in midgesture, his face went slack. Len put his hand on his chest and half stood, leaning against the seat back, which caused the chair to topple over, throwing him onto the floor.

Yuki heard a tray fall behind her. Dishes broke, and someone screamed.

She realized that the scream had come from *her.*

She jumped from her seat, crouched beside the big man who was rolling from side to side and moaning.

"Leonard! Len, where does it hurt?"

He mumbled, but she couldn't make out what he was saying over the roar of concern all around them.

"Can you raise your arms, Len?"

"My *chest,*" he groaned. "Call my wife."

"I can drive him to the hospital," a man was saying over Yuki's shoulder. "My car is right out front."

"Thanks, but that'll take too long."

"Look, the hospital is only *ten minutes*—"

"Please. No, thank you. EMS brings the hospital to *him,* okay?"

Yuki pulled her satchel toward her, emptied it onto the floor, and located her cell phone. She blocked out the well-meaning guy behind her, pictured the traffic jam, the three hours' wait outside the emergency room—which is what would happen if anything but an ambulance took Len to the hospital.

That was the mistake they'd made with her dad.

Yuki gripped Len's hand as she listened intently to the

ring tone. She hissed, *"Come on, come on,"* and when the 911 operator answered, she spoke distinctly and urgently.

"This is an emergency. Send an ambulance to Restaurant LuLu at 816 Folsom. My friend is having a heart attack."

Chapter 68

CONKLIN AND I WERE WORKING phone leads on the Ricci/Tyler case when Jacobi popped out to the squad room, said to us, "You two look like you need some air."

Fifteen minutes later, just before seven p.m., we pulled up to an apartment building near Third and Townsend. Three patrol cars, two fire rigs, and the medical examiner's van had gotten there before us.

"This is weird. I know this place," I told Conklin. "My friend Cindy lives here."

I tried to reach Cindy but got a busy signal on her cell. No answer on her home phone, either.

I looked for but didn't see Cindy among the tenants standing in tight knots on the sidewalk, giving their statements to the uniforms walking among them, looking up at the brick face of the Blakely Arms and the pale curtains blowing out of windows on the fifth floor.

Cindy lived on three. My relief was sudden and short-lived. *Someone* had damned well died prematurely in Cindy's building.

The doorman, a middle-aged man with a sloping forehead

and frizzy gray hair springing out from his hatband, paced outside the main door. He had a fading flower-power look, as if he'd been beached by the '60s revolution. He told us that his name was Joseph "Pinky" Boyd and that he'd been working at the Blakely Arms for three years.

"Miss Portia Fox in 5K," he told us. "She's the one who smelled the gas. She called down to the desk a half hour ago. Yeah," he said, looking at his watch.

"And you called the fire department?"

"Right. They were here in about five minutes."

"Where's the complainant? Miss Fox."

"She's probably outside here. We cleared the whole fifth floor. I saw her...Mrs. Wolkowski. Terrible thing to see someone dead in real life, someone you know."

"Can you think of anyone who'd want to hurt Mrs. Wolkowski?" Conklin asked the doorman.

"Nah. She was a bit of a crank. Complained about getting the wrong mail in her box, scuff marks on the tile, stuff like that. But she was a pussycat for an old girl."

"Mr. Boyd, were you here all day?"

"Since eight this morning."

"You have surveillance cameras?" I asked.

"The tenants have a picture phone for when someone buzzes the bell, and that's it."

"What's downstairs?"

"Laundry room, garbage, bathroom, and a door that leads out to the courtyard."

"A locked door?" Conklin asked. "Is it alarmed?"

"Used to be alarmed," Boyd told us. "But when they did the renovation, it was made into a common space, so the tenants got keys."

"Right. So there's no real security from downstairs," I

said. "Did you see anyone or anything suspicious in the building today?"

Boyd's laugh was tinged with hysteria. "Did I see anyone suspicious? In this building? This is the first day in a month that I *didn't*."

Chapter 69

THE UNIFORMED OFFICER standing at the door to apartment 5J was a rookie—Officer Matt Hartnett, tall guy, looked a little like Jimmy Smits. Sweat beaded his upper lip, and his face was pallid under his dark eyes.

"The vic is Mrs. Irene Wolkowski," Hartnett said, handing the log to me. "Last seen alive this morning in the laundry room around eleven. The husband isn't home from work, and we still haven't been able to reach him. My partner and another team are interviewing the tenants on the street."

I nodded, signed my name and Conklin's into the log. We ducked under the tape that was stretched across the doorway, walked into a scene already crawling with the CSU and the current ME, who was snapping pictures of the victim.

The room stunk of gas.

Windows on two sides were wide open to vent the room, making it seem colder inside the apartment than it was on the street.

The deceased was on her back in the middle of the floor, arms and legs akimbo, a pose that made her defenseless against both the original attack and now the poking and prodding of strangers. The woman appeared to be in her early sixties.

There was blood coming from the back of her head. I saw that it had soaked into the pale gray carpet, the stain parting around a leg of the piano.

And the piano was wrecked!

What was left of the keyboard was blood-smeared and smashed. Keys were dislocated and broken, and many were scattered on the floor as though someone had hammered at the keys repeatedly.

Dr. Germaniuk had set up portable lights to illuminate every corner of the room. It was both well-lived-in and recently furnished. I saw a scrap of plastic wrap still clinging to one of the sofa legs.

Dr. G. said hello to me, pushed his glasses up on his nose with the back of his hand, and put his camera away.

"What have we got?" I asked him.

"Very interesting," Germaniuk said. "Except for the piano and every gas jet on the stove being turned on, nothing else looks disturbed."

The crime scene was organized — that is to say, neat — which nearly always meant that the crime was planned and the killer was smart.

"The victim suffered trauma to her head, front and back," said Dr. G. "Looks to me like two different implements were used. The piano was one of them.

"I'll give you more after I get Mrs. Wolkowski on my table, but I'll tell you this much right now: She's got no rigor — she's warm to the touch, and blanching lividity is just starting. This lady's been dead only a couple of hours, probably less. We just missed the killer."

Chapter 70

I HEARD CINDY'S VOICE at the doorway and broke away from the murder scene long enough to throw my arms around her in the hallway.

"I'm okay, I'm okay," she murmured. "I just got your messages."

"Did you know the victim?"

"I don't think so. Not by name anyway. Let me see her."

The crime scene was off-limits and she knew it, but it was a battle I'd fought and lost with Cindy before. She had that look in her eyes now. Stubborn. Intractable. Canny.

"Stand to the side. Don't touch."

"I know. I won't."

"If anyone objects, you have to leave. And I want your word you will not write anything about the cause of death."

"My word," she said, giving me lip.

I pointed to an empty corner of the room, and Cindy went there. She blanched at the sight of the dead woman on the floor, but as one of the swarm of people in 5J, she went unquestioned.

"That's Cindy?" Conklin asked, tipping his chin toward where she stood on the fringes.

"Yeah. She's trustworthy."

"If you say so."

I introduced Rich to Cindy as Irene Wolkowski's body was wrapped in sheets, zipped into a body bag. We talked over our theories of the crime as the cold wind blew through the apartment.

I said to Conklin, "So let's say the killer is someone she knows. Guy who lives in the building. He rings the bell. Says, 'Hi, Irene. Don't let me interrupt you. That sounds really nice.'"

"Okay. Or maybe it was her husband," Conklin said. "Came home early, killed her, and split. Or maybe a friend. Or a romantic interest. Or a stranger."

"A stranger? I don't see that," Cindy said. "I wouldn't let a stranger into my apartment, would you?"

"Okay, I get that," Conklin said. "But anyway, she's sitting at the piano. The music covers the sound of the door opening, and this nice, thick carpet absorbs the sound of footsteps."

"Right," I agreed.

"Is that her handbag?" Cindy asked.

A woman's shiny black purse rested on a slipper chair. I opened it, took out the wallet, showed Conklin the wad of twenties and a full deck of credit cards.

"So there goes the robbery theory," I said.

"I was there when one of those dogs was found," Cindy said, sketching in the story.

Rich shook his head, hair swinging in front of his eyes. "Sign of a potential psycho killer escalating to... *this?* Talk about overkill. So on the one hand we have the beating and the trashing of the piano. But why bother with the gas?"

"He either wanted to make sure she was discovered," I said, "or he wanted to make sure she was dead." I looked at Cindy. "Not one word of this in the *Chronicle*."

Chapter 71

YUKI COULDN'T STOP THINKING about Len's face, twisting with pain as his heart attack tried to kill him. She'd left him in the hospital last night, stabilized but incapacitated, and called David Hale's answering machine at home. "There's been an emergency. Meet me at the office at six a.m. and be ready to go to court."

Now Yuki sat across from David in the grungy, pine-paneled conference room, her notes and instant coffee in front of her, bringing her fellow ADA up to speed.

"Why aren't we getting a continuance?" he asked her. David was presentable today, in a tan herringbone jacket, blue pants, striped tie. Needed a haircut, but that couldn't be helped. Of all the people available to her at short notice, she'd get the best work from Hale.

"Three reasons," Yuki said, tapping the table with a plastic spoon.

"One, Leonard doesn't want to lose Jack Rooney as a witness. Rooney is frail. He was on vacation when the shooting occurred. We might not be able to get him back when we need him, which means his tape might be excluded."

"Okay."

"Two, Len doesn't want to chance losing Judge Moore."

"Yeah, I get that, too."

"Len says he'll be in court in time to do the summation."

"He said that?"

"Yep, when they were prepping him for surgery. He was lucid and adamant."

"What did his doctor say?"

"His doctor said, and I quote, 'There's a reasonable possibility that the damage to Leonard's heart is reversible.' "

"Did they have to crack open his chest?"

"Yes. I checked with Len's wife. He came through the surgery fine."

"And so he'll be doing a summation in a little more than a *week?*"

"Probably not. And he won't be doing the tarantella, either," Yuki said. "So that brings me to number three. Len said that I'm as prepared as he is, that he's confident in us. And we're not to let him down."

David Hale stared at her, openmouthed, before finally saying, "Yuki, I don't have any trial experience."

"I do. Several years."

"Your experience is in civil cases, not criminal."

"Shut *up,* David. I was a litigator. That counts. So we're gonna give Red Dog our best. We're gonna spend the next three hours going over what we both already know.

"We've got credible eyewitnesses, the Rooney tape, and a jury that is going to be rolling its eyes at the insanity defense.

"It's what Len said at the prep meeting: The more random the crime, the less motive for the killings, the more afraid the jury is going to be that Brinkley will get forty-five minutes in a nuthouse and then go free—"

Yuki stopped to take in the grin spreading across David Hale's face.

"What are you thinking, David? No, I take it back. Please don't say it," Yuki said, trying not to laugh.

"Open-and-shut case," said her new teammate. "Slam dunk."

Chapter 72

YUKI STOOD IN THE WELL of the courtroom, feeling as green as if she were trying her first case. She clutched the edges of the lectern, thought how when Len stood behind this thing, it appeared to be the size of a music stand. She was peering over the top of it like a grade-schooler.

The jury looked at her expectantly.

Could she actually convince them that Alfred Brinkley was guilty of capital murder?

Yuki called her first witness, Officer Bobby Cohen, a fifteen-year veteran of the SFPD, his just-the-facts-ma'am demeanor setting a good solid tone for the People's case.

She took him through what he had seen when he arrived at the *Del Norte,* what he had done, and when she finished her direct, Mickey Sherman had only one question for Officer Cohen.

"Did you witness the incident on the ferry?"

"No, I did not."

"Thank you. That's all I have."

Yuki checked off Cohen in her mind, thinking that although Cohen didn't see the shootings, he'd set the stage

for the jurors, putting the picture of human destruction in
their minds—an image she would now build upon.

She called Bernard Stringer, the fireman who'd seen
Brinkley shoot Andrea and Tony Canello. Stringer lum-
bered to the stand and was sworn in before taking his seat.
He was in his late twenties, with the open-faced, all-
American looks of a baseball player.

Yuki said, "Mr. Stringer, what kind of work do you do?"

"I'm a firefighter out of Station 14 at Twenty-sixth and
Geary."

"And why were you on the *Del Norte* on November
first?"

"I'm a weekend dad," he said, smiling. "My kids just
love the ferry."

"And did anything unusual happen on the day in
question?"

"Yes. I saw the shooting on the top deck."

"Is the shooter in court today?" Yuki asked.

"Yes, he is."

"Can you point him out to us?"

"He's sitting right there. The man in the blue suit."

"Will the court reporter please note that Mr. Stringer
indicated the defendant, Alfred Brinkley. Mr. Stringer,
how far were you standing from Andrea Canello and her
son, Anthony, when Mr. Brinkley shot them?"

"About as far as I am from you. Five or six feet."

"Can you tell us what you saw?"

Stringer's face seemed to contract as he sent his mind
back to that horrific and bloody day. "Mrs. Canello was
straightening the kid out, being kind of rough on him, I
thought.

"Don't get me wrong. She wasn't abusive. It was just

that the kid was taking it hard, and I was thinking about butting in. But I never said anything because the defendant shot her. And then he shot the little boy. And then everything on the boat went crazy."

"Did Mr. Brinkley say anything to either of those victims before firing his gun?"

"Nope. He just lined up his shots. *Bang. Bang.* Really cold."

Yuki let Bernard Stringer's words hang for a moment in the courtroom, then said, "To be clear, when you say it was 'really cold,' you're not talking about the temperature?"

"No, it's the way he killed those people. His face was like ice."

"Thank you, Mr. Stringer. Your witness," Yuki said to the defense counsel.

Chapter 73

YUKI WATCHED MICKEY SHERMAN put his hands in his pockets, walk toward the witness in the reflected golden glow of the oak-paneled walls of the courtroom. His smile was real enough, but the amble, the common-man language, the whole low-key act, was also a cunning cover for Mickey's talent for launching surprise attacks.

Yuki had worked with Sherman at close range before, and she'd learned to recognize his "tell." Sherman would touch his right forefinger to the divot in his upper lip just before he sprang for the witness's throat.

"Mr. Stringer, did Mrs. Canello or Anthony Canello do anything to provoke my client?" Sherman asked.

"No. As far as I could see, they were unaware of him."

"And you say my client looked calm when he shot them?"

"He had a wild look about him *generally,* but when he pulled the trigger, his expression was like I said—cold. Blank. And his hand was steady."

"When you look at him today, does Mr. Brinkley look the way he did on the *Del Norte*?"

"Not really."

"In what way does he look different?"

Stringer sighed, gazed down at his hands before answering. "He looked mangy. I mean, his hair was long. He had a messy beard. His clothes were dirty, and he smelled funky."

"So he looked *mangy*. His face was blank, and *he stank to high heaven*. And you saw him shoot two people *who didn't provoke him. They didn't even know he was there*."

"That's right."

Forefinger to the upper lip.

"So what you're saying is, Fred Brinkley looked and acted like a madman."

Yuki shot to her feet. "*Objection, Your Honor*. Leading the witness."

"Sustained."

Sherman's quiet charm returned.

"Mr. Stringer, did Mr. Brinkley look sane to you?"

"No. He looked as crazy as hell."

"Thank you, Mr. Stringer," Sherman said.

Yuki tried to summon up a question for redirect that could cancel out the words "madman" and "crazy," but what came out of her mouth was "The People call Mr. Jack Rooney."

Chapter 74

JACK ROONEY MADE HIS WAY up the aisle, leaning on his three-legged cane, putting his weight on his left leg, then swinging out his right hip, repeating the awkward yet mesmerizing gait all the way to the witness stand.

Rooney accepted assistance from the bailiff, who put a hand under the man's elbow and helped him up into the chair. Yuki thought that this witness was surely Mickey-proof.

Or was he?

"Thanks for coming all this way, Mr. Rooney," Yuki said when the elderly man was finally seated. Rooney was wearing a red cardigan over a white shirt, red bow tie. His glasses were big and square, perched on a knobby nose, white hair parted and slicked down like that of a little boy on the first day of school.

"My pleasure." Rooney beamed.

"Mr. Rooney, were you on the *Del Norte* ferry on November first?"

"Yes, dear. I was with my wife, Betty, and our two friends, Leslie and Joe Waters. We all live near Albany, you know. That was our first trip to San Francisco."

"And did anything unusual happen on that ferry ride?"

"Oh, I'll say. That fellow over there killed a lot of people," he said, pointing to Brinkley. "I was so scared I almost shit myself."

Yuki allowed herself a smile as laughter rippled out over the gallery. She said, "Will the court reporter please note that the witness has identified the defendant, Alfred Brinkley. Mr. Rooney, did you make a video recording of the shooting?"

"Well, it was supposed to be a movie of the ferry ride—the Golden Gate Bridge and Alcatraz and so forth—but it turned out to be a movie of the shooting. Nice little camera my grandson gave me," he said, holding his thumb and forefinger about three inches apart.

"It's only the size of a Snickers bar, but it takes pictures *and* movies. I just take the pictures, and my grandson puts it on the computer for me. Oh, and I sold the movie to a TV station, and that pretty much paid for the whole darned San Francisco trip."

"Your Honor?" Mickey Sherman said wearily from the counsel table.

Judge Moore leaned across the bench and said, "Mr. Rooney, please answer the questions 'yes' or 'no' unless you're asked for a fuller explanation, all right?"

"Certainly, Your Honor. I'm sorry. I've never done this before."

"That's okay."

Yuki interlaced her fingers in front of her, asked, "You gave me a copy of the video, didn't you, sir?"

"Yep, I did."

"Judge, permission to show a copy of this video and enter it into evidence."

"Go right ahead, Ms. Castellano."

David Hale slipped a disk into a computer, and as faces turned toward two large TVs in the front of the courtroom, the amateur film began.

The first of two segments showed a happy afternoon on the bay—the long pan of the landmarks, the camera eye coming to rest on a grinning Jack Rooney and his wife, just by happenstance catching an out-of-focus Alfred Brinkley sitting behind them, staring out over the water, plucking at the hairs on his arm.

The second segment was a scene of bloody horror.

Yuki watched the faces of the jurors as the gunshots and the terrified screams ricocheted around the small courtroom.

The pictures on the two screens slewed sideways, catching the shock on the little boy's face at the moment he was shot, captured his small frame blowing back against the hull before falling across his mother's body.

Yuki had seen the film many times, and still the shots were like punches to her own gut.

Red Dog was wrong. The jurors were anything but bored as they witnessed the slaughter, because this viewing of the Rooney tape was different from seeing it at home.

This time the killer sat only yards away.

Some jurors covered their mouths or averted their eyes, and over the course of the two segments, every one of them peered with dismay at Alfred Brinkley.

Brinkley didn't look back. He sat motionless in his chair, watching himself mow all those innocent people down.

"I have no questions," said Mickey Sherman, turning

to whisper into Alfred Brinkley's ear, the judge saying, "Thank you, Mr. Rooney. You may step down."

Yuki waited for Rooney to make his long, hip-swinging return trip up the aisle before saying, "The People call Dr. Claire Washburn."

Chapter 75

CLAIRE FELT ALL THE EYES in the room following her as she made her way to the witness stand. Yesterday at this time, she'd been in bed, and she hoped to God that two hours from now, she'd be there again.

Then she saw Yuki, cute little thing all of twenty-eight years old, all that passion in her face, scared half to death but not wanting to show it. So Claire smiled at her as she dragged her butt through the gate and walked to the witness stand.

Claire put her hand on the Bible as the bailiff took her through the "do you swears," and then she arranged the folds of her dress that now hung loosely around her from having lost fifteen pounds in just under three weeks. *The gunshot diet,* she thought as she settled into the chair.

"Thank you for coming today, Dr. Washburn. You just got out of the hospital a couple of days ago?"

"Yes, that's right."

"And can you tell the jury why you were in the hospital?"

"I was shot in the chest."

"Is the person who shot you sitting in court today?"

"Yes. That's the little shit-bird. Right there."

Sherman didn't bother to get out of his seat, simply said, "Your Honor, I object. I'm not really sure about the grounds, but I'm pretty sure the witness isn't allowed to call my client a shit-bird."

"Dr. Washburn, he's probably right about that."

"I'm sorry, Your Honor. It's just the pain talking." She looked down at Brinkley. "I'm terribly sorry," she said. "I shouldn't have called you a shit-bird."

The titters in the gallery flowed across the room and into the jury box, until the judge patiently banged his gavel, saying, "Everyone, and I do mean *everyone*" — he peered over his glasses at Claire — "there will be no more of this. This is not Comedy Central, and I will clear the courtroom if there are any more public outbursts. Ms. Castellano, please control your witnesses. That's part of your job."

"I'm sorry, Your Honor. I understand."

Yuki cleared her throat. "Dr. Washburn, what was the nature of your injuries?"

"I had a hole in my chest caused by a .38-caliber bullet that collapsed my left lung and nearly caused my death."

"That must have been very frightening and painful."

"Yes. More than I can say."

"The jury saw the film of the shooting," Yuki said, Claire reading her sympathetic look. "Can you tell us what you said to the defendant before he shot you?"

"I said, 'Okay, son, that's enough, now. Give me the gun.'"

"And then what happened?"

"He said something about *this* being *my* fault, that I

should have stopped him. Next thing I knew, I was being carted off the ferry by paramedics."

"You tried to stop him from shooting anyone else."

"Yes."

"You saw other people try to stop him."

"Yes. But he took aim and shot us all. Shot Mr. Ng's brains right onto the deck."

"Thank you, Doctor. Your witness," Yuki said.

Chapter 76

MICKEY SHERMAN HAD KNOWN CLAIRE Washburn for many years, liked her very much, and was glad she'd survived her ordeal on the *Del Norte.*

But she was a dangerous threat to his client.

"Dr. Washburn, what's your profession?"

"I'm the chief medical examiner of San Francisco."

"Unlike the coroner, you're a medical doctor, isn't that right?"

"Yes."

"When you were doing your internship, did you do rotations at a teaching hospital?"

"I did."

"And you rotated through the psychiatric ward?"

"Yes."

"Ever see any patients walking around with a blank stare in the psych ward?"

"Objection. Relevance, Your Honor," Yuki said.

"Overruled. The witness may answer the question."

"I really don't remember any of my psych patients, Mr. Sherman. All the patients I have *now* have blank stares."

"All right," Sherman said, smiling, hands in pockets, pacing a little bit in front of the jury box, turning back to Claire, saying, "Well, Doctor, you've had a chance to observe Mr. Brinkley, isn't that right?"

"Big stretch of the word 'observe.'"

"Yes or no, Dr. Washburn?"

"Yes. I 'observed' him on the ferry, and I see him right now."

"Let's just talk about what happened on the ferry. You just testified that my client said something like, 'This is your fault.' And 'You should have stopped me.'"

"That's right."

"*Were* the shootings your fault?"

"No."

"What did you think Fred Brinkley meant?"

"I have no idea."

"Did Mr. Brinkley appear to be of sound mind at that time? Did he appear to know right from wrong?"

"I really can't say. I'm not a psychiatrist."

"Well, did he deliberately try to kill you?"

"I'd say yes."

"Did he know you?"

"No, sirree."

"Did you provoke Mr. Brinkley into shooting you?"

"Just the opposite."

"So you'd have to say that the shooting was basically a random act based upon no foundation whatsoever?"

"I guess so."

"You guess so? You'd never met him before, and he was saying things to you that just didn't make sense. You *saw* him shoot four people before he aimed his gun at you, didn't you? Isn't there a simple word that describes someone who acts this way? Wouldn't that word be 'insane'?"

"Objection, Your Honor—argumentative, and that's a legal question for the jury."

"Sustained."

Yuki sat down, slumped back in her seat. Mickey saw her eyes dart from him to the jury to the witness and back to him. *Good. She was rattled.*

"Did Mr. Brinkley seem *sane* to you, Dr. Washburn?"

"No."

"Thank you. I have no further questions."

"Ms. Castellano, redirect?" the judge asked.

"Yes, Your Honor."

Yuki got out of her chair and approached her witness, Mickey noting Yuki's furrowed brow, her fingers knit together. He knew that Yuki was big with hand gestures and was probably training herself to keep her hands still.

"Dr. Washburn," she said, "do you know what Alfred Brinkley was thinking when he shot you?"

"No. I absolutely do *not,"* Claire said emphatically.

"In your *opinion,* Doctor, when Mr. Brinkley shot you, isn't it likely that he knew the wrongfulness of his acts, *that he knew what he was doing was wrong?"*

"Yes."

"Thank you, Dr. Washburn. I have nothing else for this witness, Your Honor."

As the judge dismissed Claire Washburn, Mickey Sherman spoke softly to his client, using his hand as a shield, as though what he was saying was deeply private.

"That went pretty well, Fred, don't you think?"

Brinkley nodded like a bobblehead doll, poor guy steeped in medication, Mickey hearing Yuki Castellano say, "Please call Sergeant Lindsay Boxer to the stand."

Chapter 77

I'D JUST SPENT a rocky night on Cindy's couch, waking up at odd hours to patrol the halls of the Blakely Arms. I'd checked the emergency exits, the stairwells, the roof, and the basement, finding no prowler, only a lone elderly woman doing her laundry at two a.m. When the sun came up, I made a quick pit stop at home to change my clothes, and now, sitting outside the courtroom, a trickle of adrenaline entered my bloodstream as the bailiff called my name.

I walked inside through the double doors and the vestibule, and down the well-worn oak floorboards to the witness stand, where I was sworn in.

Yuki greeted me formally and questioned me to establish my credentials.

Then she said, "Do you recognize the man who confessed to the ferry shootings?"

I said "yes" and pointed out the cleaned-up sack of shit sitting next to Mickey Sherman.

In truth, Alfred Brinkley looked very different than he had when I'd seen him last. His face had filled out, his darting eyes were still. Shaved and sheared, he looked six years younger than when he'd confessed to the *Del Norte* killings.

Scarily, he looked harmless now, like everyone's cousin Freddy, just an average joe.

Yuki spun toward me, pivoting on her pointy heels, asking, "Were you surprised when the defendant rang your doorbell?"

"I was kind of *stunned,* actually, but when he called up to my window and asked me to come downstairs and arrest him, I was ready to go."

"And what did you do?"

"I disarmed him, cuffed him, then called for backup. Lieutenant Warren Jacobi and I brought him to the police station, where Mr. Brinkley was booked and interrogated."

"Did you read Mr. Brinkley his rights?"

"Yes, outside my doorway and again at the station."

"Did he seem to comprehend what you were saying?"

"Yes. I gave him a mental-status test to make sure he knew his name, where he was, and what he had done. He waived his rights in writing and told me again that he'd shot and killed those people on the *Del Norte.*"

"Did he seem sane to you, Sergeant?"

"He did. He was agitated. He was unkempt. But Lieutenant Jacobi and I found him to be lucid and aware, which is what I call sane."

"Thank you, Sergeant Boxer," Yuki said. "Your witness."

The eyes of the jurors swung toward the dapper man sitting beside Alfred Brinkley. Mickey Sherman stood, fastened the middle button of his smart charcoal-gray suit jacket, gave me a dazzling smile.

"Hi, Lindsay," he said.

Chapter 78

I'D LEANED ON MICKEY some months ago when I was accused of police brutality and wrongful death, took his advice on how to testify, even what to wear on the stand and what tone of voice to use. And he hadn't let me down.

If it hadn't been for Mickey, I don't know what I'd be doing now, but it wouldn't be police work, of that I was sure.

I felt a wave of affection for the man who'd once been my champion, but I put up a mental shield against his wicked charm and focused on the pictures that had never left my mind: Alfred Brinkley's victims. The little boy who had died in the hospital. Claire, gripping my hand, thinking she was dying as she asked after her son.

And Sherman's client was guilty of all of it.

"Sergeant Boxer," Sherman said, "it's rare for a killer to turn himself in to a police officer at home, isn't it?"

"I'd say so."

"And Fred Brinkley specifically wanted to turn himself in to you, isn't that true?"

"That's what he told me."

"Did you know Mr. Brinkley?"

"No, I did not."

"So why did Mr. Brinkley ask you to arrest him?"

"He told me that he'd seen me on TV, asking for information about the ferry shooter. He said he took that to mean that he should come to my home."

"How did he find out where you live?"

"He said that he'd gone to a library and used a computer. Got my address off the Internet."

"You've testified that you disarmed Mr. Brinkley. You took away his gun, isn't that right?"

"Yes."

"Same gun he used to do the shootings?"

"Yes."

"And he'd brought a written confession with him to your doorstep, didn't he?"

"Yes."

"So to get this all perfectly straight," Mickey said, "my client heard your appeal to the public on television and interpreted that as an appeal to him *personally.* He Googled your name in a library and went to your front door *as if you'd ordered takeout.* And he was still carrying the handgun he used to kill four people."

"Objection, Your Honor. Argumentative," Yuki said.

"I'll allow it, but please get to the point, Mr. Sherman."

"Yes, Your Honor." Mickey walked over to me, gave me his full-bore, brown-eyed "you can trust me" look.

"Here's what I'm getting at, Sergeant. Wouldn't you agree that for a killer to keep the murder weapon and bring it to the home of a homicide inspector is not only unusual but *off the wall?*"

"It's unusual, I'll give you that."

"Sergeant, did you ask Mr. Brinkley why he shot those people?"

"Yes."

"And what did he say?"

I wanted to dig in, refuse to answer Mickey Sherman's question, but of course I didn't have that option. "He said he did it because voices told him to do it."

"Voices in his head?"

"That's how I interpreted his statement."

Mickey smiled at me as if to say, *Oh, yes. The defense is having a very good day.* "That's all I have. Thanks very much, Lindsay."

Chapter 79

YUKI SAT ACROSS FROM ME at a table by the door at MacBain's. She looked more than just worried. She looked as if she were beating herself up horribly.

"I should have done a redirect," Yuki said to me after we'd ordered. The place was absolutely jammed with lawyers and their clients, cops, and Hall of Justice workers of all kinds. Yuki had to raise her voice to be heard over the din. "I should have asked you what you *thought* when Brinkley told you about the voices."

"Who cares what I thought? It's no big deal."

"Oh, it's a big deal, all right." Yuki raked her hair back with her hands. "Sergeant Boxer, what did you think when Mr. Brinkley said he was hearing voices directing him to kill?"

I shrugged.

"Come on, Lindsay. You would have said that you thought he was already staging his insanity defense."

"Yuki, you can't nail everything down. You're doing a first-class job. I mean, *really*."

Yuki snorted. "Mickey is successfully flipping every

negative into a positive. 'My client killed people for no reason? That means he's insane, right?' "

"That's all he's got. Look, Brinkley seemed rational, and I said so. The jury's not going to take Brinkley's *word* that he was hearing voices."

"Yeah." Yuki shredded her paper napkin. "I wonder what Marcia Clark's best friend said to her just before the jury found O. J. Simpson 'not guilty.' 'Don't worry, Marcia. Nobody's going to care about that glove.' "

I sat back in my seat as Syd brought our burgers and piles of fries. "Hey," I said, "I saw Mickey on the steps of the courthouse, mobbed by reporters. Funny how much we loved his magic act with the press last summer. Now I think, *You media hog*."

Yuki didn't laugh.

"Yuki," I said, circling her wrist with my fingers, "you're coming off smart, on top of your case, and most of all you sound *right*."

"Okay, okay," she said, "I'm done whining. Thanks for your testimony. Thanks for your support."

"Do something for me, girlfriend."

"Hmmm?"

"Put some calories inside your body and have a little faith in yourself."

Yuki lifted her hamburger, then put it back down on the plate without biting into it. "You know what's going on with me, Linds? I made a mistake. In a case like this one, you don't make mistakes. *Not even one*. And for the first time, I really see that I could lose."

Chapter 80

"MACKLIN JUST CALLED," Jacobi said the minute I returned to the squad room after lunch. Conklin and I walked Jacobi to his office, Jacobi saying, "A kid was snatched off the street in Los Angeles three hours ago. A little boy. Described as some kind of math genius."

I didn't even sit down.

I fired a flurry of questions at Jacobi: Had the child been abducted by someone in a black van? Was there any evidence at the scene? A tag number, a description—anything? Had the parents of the child been checked out? Had they heard from the kidnapper? In short, did this abduction resemble the kidnapping of Madison Tyler?

"Boxer, curb your enthusiasm, will ya?" Jacobi said, chucking the remains of his cheeseburger into the trash can. "I'll give you everything I've got, every single detail."

"Well, make it snappy." I laughed. I sat down and leaned forward, putting my elbows on the desk as Jacobi filled us in.

"The parents were inside their house, and the kid was

playing in the backyard," Jacobi told us. "Mother heard a squeal of brakes. She was on the phone, looked out the window onto the street, and saw a black van speeding around the corner. She didn't think too much about it. A couple of minutes later, she looked into the backyard, realized the boy was gone."

"The kid wandered out to the front yard?" Conklin asked.

"Possibly. The gate was open. Kid could've opened it—he's smart, right?—or maybe someone else did it. The LAPD put out an Amber Alert, but the father, not taking any chances, called the Feds."

Jacobi pushed a fax toward me, headed with the logo of the FBI. The second page was a photocopy of an adorable little boy—big round eyes, dimples, looked to be a perfect little sweetheart.

"The boy's name is Charles Ray, age six. The LAPD did an analysis of the tire marks outside the Ray house, and they match the type that comes standard with a late-model Honda minivan. That said, there's no proof that the vehicle was involved in the abduction. They haven't pulled any useful prints off the gate."

"Did the child have a nanny?" I asked.

"Yes. Briana Kearny. She was at the dentist when Charlie was taken. Her alibi checks out. It's a long shot, Boxer. Maybe the same party who kidnapped Madison Tyler is involved, maybe not."

"We should interview the parents," Conklin said.

"Like I could stop the two of you if I wanted to," said Jacobi. "Pair of freakin' attack dogs."

Jacobi pushed two more sheets of paper over to our side of his desk—electronic airline tickets in my name and Conklin's, San Francisco to LAX, round-trip.

"Listen," Jacobi said, "until we learn otherwise, we're treating this boy's abduction as part of the Tyler case, so report back to Lieutenant Macklin. And *keep me in the loop*." Jacobi looked at his watch. "It's two fifteen. You could be in LA by four or so."

Chapter 81

SQUAD CARS WERE PARKED on the one-lane street outside the Rays' wood-frame cottage. It was one of several dozen similar houses butting up against one another, lining both sides of the street.

Cops were talking on the sidewalk. They greeted us when we flashed our badges. "The mother's home," a uniform told us.

Eileen Ray came to the door. She was white, early thirties, five nine, looked to be about eight months pregnant and terribly, terribly vulnerable. Her dark hair was banded up in a ponytail, and her face was raw and red from crying.

I introduced Conklin and myself, and Mrs. Ray invited us inside, where an FBI tech was wiring up the phone. "The police have been...wonderful, and we're so grateful," Mrs. Ray said, indicating a sofa and chair for us to sit on.

The living room was crammed with stenciled cabinets, baskets, birdhouses, and dried flowers, and folded-down cardboard boxes were stacked on the floor near the kitchen table. The pervasive fragrance of lavender added to the gift-shop effect of the Ray abode.

"We work at home," Mrs. Ray said, answering my unasked question. "EBay."

"Where is your husband now?" Conklin asked.

"Scotty and an FBI agent are driving around with Briana," she told us. "My husband is hoping to God that he might see Charlie wandering out there, lost.

"Charlie must be *terrified!*" Eileen Ray cried out. "Oh, my God, what he must be going through! Who would take him?" she asked, her voice breaking. *"And why?"*

Conklin and I had no answers, but we lobbed questions at Mrs. Ray—about her movements, her relationship with her husband, and why the gate to the yard was open.

And we asked if anyone—family, friend, or stranger—had shown excessive or inappropriate attention to Charlie.

Nothing she told us lit up the board.

Eileen Ray was twisting a handkerchief in her hands when Scott Ray came home with the FBI agent and the nanny, a baby-faced young woman who was still in her teens.

Conklin and I split up, Conklin interviewing Scott in the child's bedroom while I talked to Briana in the kitchen. Unlike the Westwood Registry's European imports, Briana Kearny was a second-generation American, a local girl who lived three blocks away and looked after Charlie on a per-hour basis.

In other words, Briana was a babysitter.

Briana cried deep, heart-wrenching sobs as I pressed her, asking about her friendships, about her boyfriend, and if anyone had questioned her about the Rays and their habits.

Conklin and I finally closed our notebooks and said

our good-byes, leaving the homey little cottage right as the electric candles in the windows came on.

"That girl had nothing to do with the child being snatched," I said.

"I didn't get anything bad off the husband, either," my partner told me. "This feels like a 'pedophile lures the kid into a van' thing."

"Yeah. It's just too fricking easy to steal a child. Perv says, 'Want to see my puppy?' Kid toddles over. Perv drags the kid inside and takes off. No witness. No evidence. And now," I said, "the long wait for a phone call...that never comes."

Chapter 82

SIX-YEAR-OLD CHARLIE RAY had been abducted more than seven hours before, and the kidnappers had not called his parents. The Rays, unlike the Tylers, were in a socioeconomic bracket that wouldn't normally indicate a kidnapping for ransom.

And that was a bad thing.

We sat in Captain Jimenez's office while FBI agent David Stanford briefed us. Stanford was a blue-eyed man with a graying ponytail who'd been working undercover on another case before being pulled into this one.

I took a flyer from the stack on the captain's desk, studied Charlie Ray's perfectly round eyes, baby teeth, and short-cropped dark curls.

Would his body be found weeks or months from now in a dump, or in a shallow grave, or washed up on the beach after a storm?

When the meeting broke up, I called Macklin and filled him in. And then Agent Stanford gave me and Conklin a lift to the airport. As we took the freeway exit, Stanford suggested we stop for a drink at the Marriott LAX before our flight. He wanted to hear everything we knew about Madison Tyler and her abduction.

Speaking for myself, I was ready for a drink. Possibly two.

The Latitude 33 lounge had a full bar and restaurant. Over beer and peanuts, we discussed Madison, then Stanford told us about a hideous child-abduction case he'd worked months before.

A ten-year-old girl had been snatched off the street as she walked home from school. She'd been found twenty-four hours later, raped and strangled, left on the altar of a church, her hands folded as if in prayer. The killer still hadn't been found.

"How often do these kidnappings end in a rescue?" I asked.

"The majority of the time, child abductions are done by family members. In those cases, the child is usually returned unharmed. When the kidnapper is a stranger, the recovery rate is about fifty-fifty." Stanford's voice was strained as he said, "Call it passion or maybe obsession, but I believe that the more child predators I can take down, the safer the world is for my three kids."

Chapter 83

"HOW ABOUT KEEPING ME COMPANY over dinner?" Stanford suggested.

Our waiter brought menus to the table, and as the eight o'clock flight to SFO had just departed without us, we took Stanford up on his offer.

The agent ordered a bottle of pinot grigio, and Conklin and I filled him in on what we knew about Paola Ricci's abduction and murder.

"Honestly, we're stuck," I told Stanford. "Our dead ends are turning up even more dead ends. We're in about the fifth generation of dead ends."

Our steaks arrived, and Stanford ordered another bottle of wine. And for the first time that long day, I finally relaxed, glad for the company and the chance to brainstorm while listening to the country-and-western music floating in from the live band in the lounge.

I was also becoming aware of Conklin's long legs next to mine under the table, his brown suede jacket brushing up against my arm, the now familiar cadence of his voice, and the wine slipping smoothly down my throat as the evening flowed into night.

At around 9:15, Dave Stanford picked up the tab, told us that he'd keep us posted after the Rays' phone records were dumped and that he'd alert us of anything that could help us with the Ricci/Tyler case.

We'd missed another flight back to San Francisco, and as Rich and I said good-bye to Stanford, we prepared ourselves for an hour's wait outside the United Airlines gate.

We were almost out the door when the band kicked up something from the Kenny Chesney collection, and the girl singer began exhorting the patrons into a line dance.

The bar crowd was made up of smashed young road warriors and airline personnel, and they started getting into the dance — a new spin on the Electric Slide.

Rich smiled and said, "You wanna get stupid out there?" and I grinned back, saying, "Sure. Why the heck not?"

I followed Rich's lead onto the dance floor and into a good time, hustling to the music, bumping into giddy strangers, and best of all laughing.

It had been a while since I'd doubled over with belly laughs, and it felt great.

When the song ended, the crooner unhooked the mic from the stand, licked her lips, and sang along with the guy at the electric piano as he played "Lyin' Eyes."

Couples paired up. When Rich stretched out his arms, I stepped in close. My God, my God, it felt so good to have Richie Conklin's arms around me.

The room was spinning a little, so I closed my eyes and held on to him, the space between us closing because there was just no room to move on that little dance floor. I even stretched up onto my toes to rest my head on his shoulder—and he gripped me more tightly.

When the music stopped, Rich said, "Man, I really don't want to go to the airport, do you?"

I remember saying that a case could be made that at that late hour, after the long workday and, by the way, having drunk a whole lot of wine, we had several bona fide, expense-reportable reasons to spend the night in LA.

Still, I was torn as I handed my credit card to the desk clerk at the Marriott LAX, telling myself this didn't mean a thing. I wasn't going to do anything but go to my room and sleep. *That was all.*

Rich and I stood at opposite sides of the elevator, a weary couple between us, as the mirrored car climbed ten silent flights. I hated to admit it, but I missed being in his arms.

When we stepped out of the elevator, I said, "Good night, Rich." Then I turned my back on him as I slipped the key card into the slot, aware that he was now doing the same in a door across the hall.

"See you in the morning, Lindsay."

"Sure thing. Sleep tight, Richie."

The tiny green light went on, and the door handle opened under my hand.

Chapter 84

I CLOSED AND BOLTED the door to my room, my mind reeling with longing and desire, relief and regret. I stripped off my clothes, and a minute later, the blood was pounding in my temples as I stood under the hot spray of the shower.

Clean and glowing pink, I buffed my body with warm terry-cloth towels and blew my hair dry. I toweled the steam off the mirror over the sink and assessed my naked self. I still looked young and good and desirable. My breasts were firm, my tummy flat, and my sandy blond hair cascaded in waves to below my shoulders.

Why hadn't Joe called me?

I wrapped myself in a white hotel robe, went to the bedroom, checked the empty voice mail on my cell phone, much like my stubborn answering machine at home.

It had been six days since I'd seen Joe.

Was it really, truly over between us?

Would I never see him again? Why hadn't he come after me?

I pulled the drapes shut, folded the gold-quilted spread,

and fluffed the pillows. Dizzy from the wine and the heat of the shower, I lay down.

Eyes closed, I found that the fading images of Joe were replaced by more urgent fantasies.

I was drawn back to only a half hour earlier, when Rich had held me. I relived the moment when dancing with him had gone from good to *too* good, when I'd felt him hard against me, when I'd put my arms around his neck and pressed my body against his.

It was okay to have these feelings, I told myself. I was only human, and so was he, and both of us were having a completely natural response to being alone together—.

A tapping at the door startled me.

My heart jumped as the knock came again.

Chapter 85

I CINCHED THE SASH OF MY ROBE and padded barefoot to the door. I saw Rich Conklin through the peephole. *He was wearing a flimsy clear-plastic shower cap on his head!*

I was laughing as I undid the bolt, my hand shaking as I pulled open the door. Conklin was wearing his trousers, his blue cotton shirt unbuttoned to about his third rib. And he was gripping a Marriott toothbrush with the stem in his fist, like it was a small white flag.

"I was wondering if you have any mouthwash, Lindsay. I got a lot of moisturizer in the complimentary toiletry basket, but no mouthwash."

His serious expression, combined with the wacky request and the shower cap, cracked me up. I swung the door open wide, said, "I didn't get mouthwash either, but I think I have something in my handbag."

The door closed behind me, and as I stooped for the handbag I'd dropped on the floor, I stumbled over one of my shoes.

Rich grabbed my elbow to steady me, *and there we*

were. Eye-to-eye. Woozy. Alone in LA in a hotel room. I reached up and pulled off the shower cap. His forelock of light-brown hair fell across his gorgeous face, and he dropped the toothbrush onto the floor. Then Rich put both arms around my waist and pulled me to him.

"I have only one problem with this working arrangement," he said. "And it's a *big* one."

Rich bent to kiss me, and I wanted him to. My arms went around his neck again, and his mouth found mine. Our first kiss set off a chemical explosion.

I clung to Rich as he lowered me to the bed in the dimly lit room. I remember lying beneath him, our fingers interlaced, his hands pressing my hands against the bed, saying my name softly, oh so gently.

"I've wanted to be with you like this, Lindsay, before you even knew my name."

"I've always known your name."

I *ached* for him, and I had a right to give myself over to this. But when my young, handsome *partner* opened my robe and put his lips to my breast, a bolt of pure reasoned panic pulled the emergency brake in my brain.

This had been a bad idea. *Really* bad.

I heard myself whisper, *"Richie, no."*

I clasped the edges of my robe together as Rich rolled onto his side, panting and flushed, looking into my eyes.

"I'm sorry," he said.

"No, don't be." I took his hand and held it to my cheek, covered his hand with mine. "I want this as much as you do. But we're partners, Rich. We have to take care of each other. Just…*not in this way.*"

He groaned as I said, "We can never do this again."

Chapter 86

I DROPPED THE KNOCKER on the door of the West-wood Registry that sunless morning after our return from LA. Conklin stood beside me as a round-faced man cracked the door open. He was in his fifties, with blond-going-gray hair and clear gray eyes that peered at me through frameless lenses perched over a sharp beak of a nose.

Did he have something to do with Madison Tyler's abduction?

Did he know where she was?

I showed him my badge, introduced my partner and myself.

"Yes, I'm Paul Renfrew," said the man at the door. "You're the detectives who were here a few days ago?"

I told him that we were, that we had some questions about Paola Ricci.

Renfrew invited us inside, and we followed the natty man down the narrow hallway, through the green door that had been padlocked when we'd last seen it.

"Please. Please sit," Renfrew said, so Conklin and I

each sat on one of the small sofas at right angles in a corner of the cozy office as Renfrew pulled up a chair.

"I suppose you want to know where I was when Paola was abducted," Renfrew said to us.

"That'd be a start," Conklin said. He looked tired. I suppose we both did.

Renfrew took a narrow notebook from his breast pocket, a thin daybook of the type that preceded handheld computers. Without prompting, he gave us a short verbal report of his meetings north of San Francisco in the days before, during, and after Paola's death, along with the names of the potential clients he'd met with.

"I can make you a photocopy of this," he offered. On a one-to-ten scale, ten being a three-alarm fire, the gauge in my gut was calling out a seven. Renfrew seemed too prepared and well rehearsed.

I accepted Renfrew's photocopy of his schedule and asked him about his wife's whereabouts during the same period.

"She's taking a slow tour through Germany and France," Renfrew told me. "I don't have a precise itinerary because she makes it up as she goes along, but I do expect her home next week."

I asked, "Do you have any thoughts about anyone who would have wanted to hurt Paola or Madison?"

"None at all," Renfrew told us. "Every time I turn on the television, I see another news story about a kidnapping. It's a virtual epidemic," he said. "Paola was a lovely girl, and I'm deeply distressed that she's dead. Everyone loved her.

"I met Madison only once," Renfrew continued. "Why would anyone do anything to such a precious child? I just don't know. Her death is a terrible, terrible tragedy."

"What makes you think Madison is dead?" I snapped at Renfrew.

"She's not? I just assumed...I'm sorry, I misspoke. I certainly hope you find her alive."

We were leaving the Westwood Registry when Renfrew's administrator, Mary Jordan, left her desk and followed us to the door.

Once outside in the dank morning air that was saturated with the smell of fish coming from the nearby market, Jordan put her hand on my arm.

"Please," she said urgently, "take me somewhere we can talk. I have something to tell you."

Chapter 87

WE WERE BACK AT THE HALL fifteen minutes later. Conklin and I sat with Mary Jordan in our cramped and grungy lunchroom. She clutched her container of coffee without sipping from it.

"After you left a few days ago, before Mr. Renfrew got back from his trip, I decided to poke around. And I found this," she told us, taking a photocopy of a lined ledger sheet out of her handbag. "It's from the Register. That's what they call it."

"Where did you find this, Mary?" Conklin asked.

"I found the key to the Renfrews' private office. They keep the Register in there."

I phoned the DA's office, got ADA Kathy Valoy on the phone. I filled her in, and she said she'd be down in a minute.

Valoy was one of those people who actually *meant* it when she said "a minute." She came into the lunchroom, and I introduced her to Mary Jordan.

"Did Sergeant Boxer or Officer Conklin ask you to retrieve these materials?"

"No, of course not."

"If you were asked by anyone to provide these materials," Valoy said, "that makes you an agent of the police, and we have to exclude the book this came from as evidence if there's a trial in the future."

"I did this all on my own," Jordan told the ADA. "So help me, God."

Valoy smiled, said, "Lindsay, we have to have lunch sometime." She waggled her fingers and left the lunchroom.

I asked Mary if I could see the paper, and she handed over a spreadsheet with headings across the top line — PLACEMENTS, CLIENTS, FEES — all entries dated this current calendar year.

The list of placements was made up of female names, most of them foreign. The clients' names, for the most part, had a "Mr. and Mrs." prefix, and the fees ran into the low five figures.

"All these girls were placed with these families this year?" I said.

Mary nodded, said, "Remember, I told you that a girl named Helga, one of the registry's nannies, disappeared about eight months ago when the registry was in Boston?"

"I remember."

"Well, I looked her up in the Register. Here she is," she said, stabbing at the page with a forefinger. "Helga Schmidt. And the people she was working for are here, too. Penelope and William Whitten."

"Go on," Conklin said.

"The records show that the Whittens have a child named Erica. She's a math prodigy, solving grade-school problems at only four. I looked up the Whittens on the Internet, and I found this interview in the *Boston Globe*."

Another piece of paper came out of Mary Jordan's handbag. She put a printout of a newspaper article on the table, turned it so we could read it, then summarized it for us as we read.

"This story appeared in the Lifestyle section last May. Mr. Whitten is a wine critic, and he and his wife were interviewed at home. Right here," Jordan said, pointing out a paragraph toward the end of the article, "is where Mr. and Mrs. Whitten told the reporter that their daughter Erica had gone to live with Mrs. Whitten's sister in England. That she was being privately schooled.

"And that seems sooooo *weird* to me," Jordan told us. "Like, unbelievable. The Whittens hired a nanny. The nanny left suddenly, and the Whittens sent their daughter to Europe? Erica is only four! The Whittens can afford any kind of tutors and governesses right here. Why would they send their little girl away?"

Rich and I exchanged looks as Jordan continued.

"Maybe I wouldn't have thought anything of it if it hadn't been for Paola's murder and Maddy having been kidnapped," Jordan said. "I just don't believe Erica Whitten is living in England. You think I'm crazy?"

"You know what I think, Mary?" I said. "You have the instincts of a good cop."

Chapter 88

JACOBI COUGHED SPASMODICALLY beside me. The air was blue with smoke from Tracchio's vile cigar, and the speakerphone crackled on his desk.

The line was open to the Whittens' home in Boston, and FBI agent Dave Stanford came back on the line.

"The Whittens are clearly rattled," he said, "but I got the story out of them. Their youngest daughter, Erica, was kidnapped along with her nanny, Helga Schmidt, eight months ago."

Was this *it?* Finally, a string that connected to the Ricci/Tyler case?

But if Erica had been kidnapped eight months ago, *why in hell hadn't the Whittens reported it to the police?*

"No one saw the kidnapping," Stanford continued, "but the Whittens found a note under their door about an hour after the time Erica and Helga were expected home from Erica's school. A half-dozen photos came along with the note."

"It was a *ransom note?*" Macklin asked, his voice a muted explosion.

"Not exactly. You got a fax machine over there?"

Tracchio gave Stanford the fax number. Voices inside the Whitten house could be heard in the background—a man and a woman quarreling softly but urgently. The woman's voice said, "Go on, Bill. Tell them."

Stanford said, "Everyone, this is Bill Whitten."

Bill Whitten said hello, and Tracchio introduced himself and the rest of us in a general way. Whitten's fear and anger had tightened his throat so that his voice was a strangled croak.

"You have to understand what you're doing to us," he said. "They said if we called the police, they'd kill our little girl. Our house could be bugged! They could be watching us *now. Do you understand?*"

The fax machine behind Tracchio's desk burped, and a sheet of paper clattered into the tray.

"Hang on a second," Tracchio said, lifting the fax out of the machine. He put the paper on his desk for us to read.

WE HAVE ERICA. CALL LAW ENFORCEMENT,
AND SHE DIES.
IF WE FEEL ANY HEAT, SHE DIES.
AND THEN WE'LL TAKE *RYAN*.
OR *KAYLA*. OR *PATTY*.
KEEP QUIET, AND ERICA WILL STAY HEALTHY.
YOU WILL RECEIVE A NEW PICTURE OF HER
EVERY YEAR. YOU MAY EVEN GET A PHONE
CALL. SHE MAY EVEN COME HOME.
BE SMART. BE QUIET.
ALL YOUR CHILDREN WILL LIVE TO THANK
YOU.

The note was eight months old, but the cruel language made the horror jump off the page. It felt as fresh as if the crime had just happened.

All the faces around the desk registered shock, but it was Macklin who grabbed the paper, gripping it as if he could wring the kidnapper's throat by proxy.

Tracchio retrieved a second page from the fax machine.

"I can't make out the pictures," Tracchio said to Stanford.

"Erica was photographed against a blank white background in the clothes she was wearing when she was taken. The other photos are snapshots of the Whittens' older kids at school. And there's one of Kayla shot through her bedroom window. We'll have the whole package analyzed."

I was thinking, *Sure, they'll try to collect prints and traces from the envelope and its contents, but what Stanford isn't saying in front of the Whittens is that every dead Jane Doe in the country will be compared to the stats and DNA of both Helga Schmidt and Erica Whitten.*

There was no doubt in my mind that the letter and the photos were a ruse to buy time.

Erica Whitten and Helga Schmidt were both dead.

But what had the kidnappers gained?

What did they want?

I was reeling with violent images featuring small girls and their equally helpless nannies when my cell phone rang. It was Inspector Paul Chi saying, "An emergency call just came in to the squad, Lindsay. Someone was attacked at the Blakely Arms."

Chapter 89

CONKLIN AND I STEPPED out of the Blakely Arms elevator onto a carpeted hallway on the sixth floor and saw two cops halfway down the hall outside the door to apartment 6G. I recognized Officer Patrick Noonan, who was bucking to move into homicide.

"What happened here, Noonan?"

"A bloody mess, that's what, Sergeant. The victim's name is Ben Wyatt. He's been living in the building for about a year."

Conklin held up the police tape and I ducked under it, Noonan still talking. "The assailant came through the door," Noonan told me. "Either the door was open, the vic let him in, *or the perp had a key*."

"Who called it in?"

"Woman next door. 6F. Virginia Howsam. H-o-w-s-a-m."

Conklin and I entered the victim's sparely furnished apartment. A halo of blood pooled around the man's head, a dark puddle on the polished oak floors.

He was a black male, early thirties, fit, wearing shorts,

a thin gray T-shirt, and running shoes. He was lying on his left side next to a treadmill.

I bent to get a better look. His eyes were closed and his breathing was labored — but he was still alive.

Paramedics clattered through the door, crowded around the victim, and on the count of three lifted him into a stretcher.

The paramedic standing closest to me said, "He's unconscious. We're taking him to San Francisco General. Could you step aside, Sergeant? Thanks."

The sirens were wailing up Townsend as Charlie Clapper and a couple of his crime-scene investigators entered Wyatt's living room, then crossed the floor to the treadmill.

"The cord to this thing's been cut," Clapper said, showing me where the clean separation had been made, as if with a sharp knife. "You saw the victim?" he said to me.

"Yes. He's alive, Charlie. At least he is now. Looks like he was really clobbered from behind."

As with Irene Wolkowski, whatever instrument had been used to bash Ben Wyatt's skull had been removed from the apartment. And also similar to the Wolkowski crime scene, very little else had been disturbed.

No doubt there was a connection between the attacks that were making terror an almost daily thing at the Blakely Arms.

What was that connection? What the hell was going on?

Chapter 90

BEN WYATT'S NEXT-DOOR NEIGHBOR Virginia Howsam was a woman in her late twenties who worked nights at a club downtown. She told us that Wyatt was a day trader and a really nice guy whom no one in his right mind would want to hurt.

We thanked Ms. Howsam for her help and took to the fire stairs, thinking maybe the people under Wyatt's apartment might have heard sounds that could help us pinpoint the time of the attack.

Conklin was right behind me on the stairs when the phone at my hip rang. I reached for it, saw Dave Stanford's name on the caller ID.

"This is Boxer."

"I've got good news for you."

I signaled to Conklin to put his ear next to the phone so we could both hear.

"You've got news on Erica Whitten?"

"No, but I thought you'd like to know that Charlie Ray has had his hot chocolate with extra whipped cream and is now sleeping in his own bed." Stanford chuckled.

"Fantastic, Dave! What happened?"

Stanford told me that the husband of a depressed woman had come forward. Their child had died of crib death weeks before.

"This woman who took Charlie was strung out on grief," Stanford said. "She was driving down the street, saw Charlie peeking over the fence. She stopped and grabbed him."

"She's in custody?"

"Yeah, but she's not the person we're looking for, Lindsay. She has nothing to do with Erica Whitten or Madison Tyler. She's on antidepressants, under a doctor's care, and yesterday was the first time she left home since her baby died."

I thanked Stanford and closed the cell phone. Conklin was right there. I was looking into his eyes, feeling the heat.

"So we've got nothing," Rich said.

"We've got *something*," I said, starting down the stairs again. "We've got a killer at large in this goddamned building. As for Madison Tyler, we've got another dead end."

Chapter 91

MICKEY SHERMAN SAT beside Alfred Brinkley at the defense table, trying to get his client to understand him through the haze of whatever meds he was on. The poor sap had all the energy of a parsnip.

"Fred. *Fred.*" Sherman shook his client's shoulder. "Fred, we start your defense today, you understand? So I'll be putting people on the stand to vouch for your character."

Brinkley nodded his head. "You're putting my doctor on the stand."

"Right. Dr. Friedman is going to talk about your mental condition, so don't get upset. He's on our side."

"I want a chance to tell my side of the story."

"We'll see. I don't know yet if we need to put you on the stand."

Mickey's assistant passed him a note saying that his witnesses were all accounted for. Then the bailiff called out, "All rise," and the judge entered the courtroom through the door behind the bench. The jurors filed in and were seated.

It was day four of Alfred Brinkley's trial, and court was in session.

"Mr. Sherman," Judge Moore said, "are you ready with your first witness?"

"The defense calls Mr. Isaac Quintana."

Quintana was wearing several layers of odd clothing, but his eyes were clear, and he smiled as he took the stand.

"Mr. Quintana," Sherman began.

"Call me Ike," the witness said. "Everyone does."

"I'll call you Ike, then," Mickey said good-naturedly. "How do you know Mr. Brinkley?"

"We were at Napa State together."

"That's not a college, is it?" Sherman said, smiling at his witness, jingling the coins in his pocket.

"Naw, it's a nuthouse," Ike said, grinning.

"It's a state mental institution, isn't that right?"

"Sure."

"Do you know why Fred was at Napa State?"

"Sure. He was depressed. Wouldn't eat. Wouldn't get out of bed. Had very bad dreams. His sister had died, you know, and when he checked into Napa, it was because he didn't want to live."

"Ike, how did you know that Fred was depressed and suicidal?"

"He told me. And I knew he was on antidepressants."

"And how long did you know Fred?"

"For about two years."

"Did you get along with him pretty well?"

"Oh, sure. He was a very sweet guy. That's why I know he didn't mean to kill those people on the ferry—"

"Objection! Your Honor, unresponsive," Yuki barked.

"I move that the witness's last statement be stricken from the record."

"Sustained. So ordered."

"Ike," Sherman asked reassuringly, "was Fred Brinkley ever violent when you knew him?"

"Gosh, no. Who told you that? He was very laid-back. Drugs'll do that to a person. Take a pill and you're not really crazy anymore."

Chapter 92

YUKI STOOD UP from the prosecution table and smoothed out the creases in her pin-striped skirt, thinking that Quintana was like a Muppet, with his wacky smile and outfit that made him appear to be wearing an entire tag sale.

It all seemed to work for him. The jurors were smiling, loving him, loving Brinkley by association.

She said, "Mr. Quintana, why were *you* at Napa State?"

"I have OCD. It's not dangerous or anything. It just takes up all my time, 'cause I'm always collecting things and checking all the time—"

"Thank you, Mr. Quintana. And are you also a psychiatrist?"

"No. But I know a few, that's for sure."

Yuki smiled as the jury tittered. It would be tricky to dismantle Quintana's testimony without turning the jury against her.

"What kind of work do you do, Mr. Quintana?"

"I'm a dishwasher at the Jade Café on Bryant. If you

want clean, you can't do better than having someone with OCD doing the dishes."

"I see your point," Yuki said as laughter rolled up from the gallery. "Do you have any medical training?"

"No."

"And apart from today, when did you last see Mr. Brinkley?"

"About fifteen years ago. He was checked out of Napa, like, in 1988 or so."

"You've had no contact with him between now and then?"

"No."

"So you wouldn't know if he's had two lobotomies and a heart transplant since you saw him last?"

"Ha-ha, that's funny. Um, is that true?"

"My point, Mr. Quintana, is that the sixteen-year-old you called 'a very sweet guy' may have changed. Are you the same person you were fifteen years ago?"

"Well, I have a lot more *stuff*."

Guffaws sprang up from the gallery; even the jurors were chortling. Yuki smiled to show she didn't, God forbid, lack a sense of humor.

When quiet resumed, she said, "Ike, when you said that Mr. Brinkley was crazy, that was your opinion as a friend, wasn't it? You weren't trying to say that he met the *legal* definition of insanity? That he didn't know right from wrong?"

"No. I don't know anything about that."

"Thank you, Mr. Quintana. I have no further questions."

Chapter 93

SHERMAN'S NEXT WITNESS, Dr. Sandy Friedman, walked up the aisle toward the witness stand. He was a good shrink, educated at Harvard, even looked the part of a psychiatrist, with his designer glasses and Brooks Brothers bow tie, a hint of Liam Neeson in his facial features.

"Dr. Friedman," Sherman said after the witness was sworn in and had cited his credentials, "have you had a chance to interview Mr. Brinkley?"

"Yes, three times since he's been incarcerated, pending trial."

"Have you diagnosed his illness?"

"Yes. In my opinion, Mr. Brinkley has schizoaffective disorder."

"Could you tell us what that means?"

Friedman leaned back in his chair as he organized his response. Then he said, "Schizoaffective disorder is a thought, mood, and behavioral disorder that involves elements of paranoid schizophrenia. One can think of it as a kind of bipolar disorder."

" 'Bipolar' meaning 'manic-depressive'?" Sherman asked.

" 'Bipolar' in the sense that people with schizoaffective disorder have ups and downs, despair and depression—and hyperactivity or mania, but they can often manage their illness for a long time and more or less fit in on the fringes of society."

"Would they hear *voices,* Dr. Friedman?"

"Yes, many do. That would be one of the schizoid aspects of this disease."

"Threatening voices?"

"Yes." Friedman smiled. "That would be the paranoia."

"Did Mr. Brinkley tell you that he thought people on television were talking to him?"

"Yes. That's also a fairly common symptom of schizoaffective disorder—an example of a break from reality. And the paranoia makes him think that the voices are aimed at him."

"Could you explain what you mean when you refer to a 'break from reality'?"

"Certainly. From the onset of Mr. Brinkley's disease in his teens, there has always been a distortion in the way he thinks and acts, in how he expresses his emotions. Most important, in how he perceives reality. That's the psychotic element—his inability to tell what is real from what is imagined."

"Thank you, Dr. Friedman," Sherman said. "Now bringing us up to the recent events that brought Mr. Brinkley to trial. What can you tell us about that?"

"With schizoaffective disorder, there is generally a precipitate that causes an increase in crazy behavior. In my judgment, that precipitate for Mr. Brinkley would have been when he got fired from his job. The loss of his routine, the subsequent eviction from his apartment, all of that would have exacerbated his illness."

"I see. Dr. Friedman, did Mr. Brinkley tell you about the ferry shooting?"

"Yes. I learned in our sessions that Mr. Brinkley hadn't been on a boat since his sister died in a sailing accident when he was sixteen. On the day of the ferry incident, there was an additional precipitate. Mr. Brinkley saw a sailboat. And that triggered the event. In layman's terms, that *sent him over the edge.* He couldn't distinguish between illusion and reality."

"Did Mr. Brinkley tell you that he was hearing voices on the ferry?"

"Yes. He said that they were telling him to kill. You have to understand that Fred has a fierce underlying anger about his sister's death, and that manifested itself in this explosive rage.

"The people on the ferry weren't real to him. They were only a backdrop to his delusions. The voices were his reality, and the only way he could stop them was to obey."

"Dr. Friedman," Sherman said, touching his upper lip with the tip of his forefinger, "can you state with a reasonable degree of medical certainty that when Mr. Brinkley obeyed those voices and shot the passengers on the ferry, he did not appreciate the difference between right and wrong?"

"Yes. Based on my interviews with Mr. Brinkley and my twenty years of experience working with the severely mentally impaired, it is my opinion that at the time of the shooting, Alfred Brinkley suffered from a mental disease or defect that prevented him from knowing right from wrong. I am absolutely convinced of it."

Chapter 94

DAVID HALE PUSHED A NOTE over to Yuki—a cartoon drawing of a large bulldog with a spiked collar and drool dripping from its jowls. The voice balloon said, "Go get 'em."

Yuki smiled, thought about Len Parisi taking a wide-legged stance in the middle of this oaken courtroom and shredding Mickey Sherman's hired shrink to ribbons.

She drew a circle around the cartoon, underscored it. Then she stood, speaking before she reached the podium.

"Dr. Friedman, you're quite well known as an expert witness, isn't that right?"

Friedman said that he was and that he'd testified for both prosecution and defense teams over the past nine years.

"In this case, the defense hired you?"

"Yes. That's right."

"And how much were you paid?"

Friedman looked up at Judge Moore, who peered down at him. "Please answer the question, Dr. Friedman."

"I was paid about eight thousand dollars."

"Eight thousand dollars. Okay. And how long were you treating Mr. Brinkley?"

"Mr. Brinkley wasn't technically my patient."

"Oh," said Yuki. "Then let me ask you, can you diagnose someone that you've never treated?"

"I've had three sessions with Mr. Brinkley, during which time I also gave him a battery of psychological tests. And yes, I can *assess* Mr. Brinkley without treating him," Friedman sniffed.

"So based on three interviews and these tests, you believe that the defendant was unable to understand right from wrong at the time of the killings?"

"That's correct."

"You didn't give him an X-ray and find a tumor pressing against a lobe of his brain, did you?"

"No, of course not."

"So how do we know that Mr. Brinkley wasn't lying and skewing the test results so he wouldn't be found guilty of murder?"

"He couldn't do that," Friedman said. "You see, the test questions are like a built-in lie detector. They're repeated in many different ways, and if the answers are consistent, then the patient is telling the truth."

"Doctor, you use those tests because you can't really know what's in the patient's mind, can you?"

"Well, you also make a judgment based on behavior."

"I see. Dr. Friedman, are you aware of the legal term 'consciousness of guilt'?"

"Yes. It refers to actions a person may take that show the person is aware what he or she did was wrong."

"Well put, Doctor," Yuki said. "Now, if someone

shoots five people and then runs away, as Alfred Brinkley did, doesn't that show consciousness of guilt? Doesn't it show that Mr. Brinkley knew what he'd done was *wrong?*"

"Look, Ms. Castellano, not everything a person does when he's in a psychotic state is illogical. People on that ferry were screaming, coming at him with intent to harm him. He ran. Most people finding themselves in that situation would have run."

Yuki stole a look at David, who gave her an encouraging nod. She wished he'd beam her something to nail Friedman with because she didn't have it.

And then she did.

"Dr. Friedman, does gut instinct play any part in your assessment?"

"Well, sure. Gut instinct, or intuition, is made up of many layers of experience. So, yes, I used gut instinct as well as formal psychological protocol in my assessment."

"And did you determine whether or not Mr. Brinkley is dangerous?"

"I interviewed Mr. Brinkley both before and after he was put on Risperdal, and it is my opinion that, properly medicated, Mr. Brinkley is not dangerous."

Yuki put both her hands on the witness box, looked Friedman in the eye, ignored everything and everyone in the courtroom, and spoke from the fear she felt every time she looked at that freak sitting next to Mickey Sherman.

"Dr. Friedman, you interviewed Mr. Brinkley behind bars. Check your gut instinct on this: Would you feel comfortable riding home in a cab with Mr. Brinkley? Would you feel safe having dinner with him in his home? Riding alone with him in an elevator?"

Mickey Sherman leaped to his feet. "Your Honor, I object. Those questions should be taken out and shot."

"Sustained," the judge grumbled.

"I'm done with this witness, Your Honor," Yuki said.

Chapter 95

AT 8:30 THAT MONDAY MORNING, Miriam Devine took the bundles of mail from the hallway console and brought them into the breakfast nook.

She and her husband had just returned home to Pacific Heights last night after their cruise, ten fabulous days in the Mediterranean, where they were mercifully cut off from phones and television and newspapers and bills.

She wanted to keep the real world at bay for at least a couple of days, keep that vacation feeling a little longer. If only she could.

Miriam made drip coffee, defrosted and toasted two cinnamon buns, and began her attack on the mail, stacking catalogs on the right side of the kitchen table, bills on the left, and miscellaneous items across from her coffee mug.

When she found the plain white envelope addressed to the Tylers, she shuffled it to the bottom of the "miscellaneous" pile and continued working, writing checks and tossing junk mail until Jim came into the kitchen.

Her husband drank his coffee standing up, said,

"Christ. I don't want to go to the office. It's going to be hell even if no one knows I'm there."

"I'll make meat loaf for dinner, sweetie. Your favorite."

"Okay. Something to look forward to anyway."

Jim Devine left the house and closed the front door behind him. Miriam finished dealing with mail, rinsed the dishes, and phoned her daughter before calling her next-door neighbor Elizabeth Tyler.

"Liz, honey! Jim and I just got back last night. I have some mail for you that was delivered here by mistake. Why don't I drop over so we can catch each other up?"

Chapter 96

I STOOD WITH CONKLIN in the Tylers' living room. It was only fifteen minutes since their neighbor Miriam Devine had dropped off the handwritten note from the kidnappers.

It had had the effect of an emotional nuclear *bomb* on Elizabeth Tyler and was having a similar effect on me.

I remembered canvassing the Devines' house the day of the abduction. It was a cream-colored clapboard Victorian almost identical to the Tylers' house, right next door. I'd spoken to the Devines' housekeeper, Guadalupe Perez. She'd told us in broken English that the Devines were away.

Nine days ago, I couldn't have imagined that Guadalupe Perez would have picked up an envelope that had been slid under the door and that she would have stacked it with the rest of the Devines' mail.

No one could have known, but I felt heartsick and responsible anyway.

"How well do you know the Devines?" Conklin asked Henry Tyler, who was furiously pacing the perimeter of the room. There were pictures of Madison on every wall and surface—baby pictures, family portraits, holiday snapshots.

"It's not *them*, okay? The Devines didn't do it!" Tyler shouted. "Madison is *gone!*" he yelled, holding his head with both hands as he paced. "It's too *late*."

I dropped my eyes back to the sideboard and the block letters on the plain white bond that I could read from five feet away:

WE HAVE YOUR DAUGHTER.
IF YOU CALL LAW ENFORCEMENT, SHE DIES.
IF WE FEEL ANY HEAT, SHE DIES.
RIGHT NOW, MADISON IS HEALTHY AND SAFE,
AND WILL STAY THAT WAY AS LONG AS YOU
KEEP QUIET.
THIS PHOTO IS THE FIRST. YOU WILL RECEIVE A
NEW PICTURE OF MADISON EVERY YEAR. YOU
MAY RECEIVE A PHONE CALL. SHE MAY EVEN
COME HOME.
BE SMART. BE QUIET.
ONE DAY MADISON WILL THANK YOU.

The photo of Madison that came with the note had been printed out on a home-style printer within an hour of the time she was abducted. The girl seemed clean and unharmed, wearing the blue coat, the red shoes.

"Could he *know* that we didn't get the note? Could he *know* that we didn't mean to defy him?"

"I just don't know, Mr. Tyler, and I can't really guess—"

Elizabeth Tyler interrupted me, the cords of her neck standing out as she strained to talk.

"Madison is the brightest, happiest little girl you can imagine. She sings. She plays music. She has the most wonderful laugh.

"Has she been raped? Is she chained to a bed in a basement? Is she hungry and cold? Is she hurt? Is she terrified? Is she calling out for us? Does she wonder why we don't come for her? Or is she past all that now and is safe in God's hands?

"This is all we think about, Officers.

"We have to know what has happened to our daughter. You have to do more than you ever thought you could do," Elizabeth Tyler told me. "You must bring Madison home."

Chapter 97

A PLASTIC BAG with the kidnapper's note inside was positioned on my desk so that Conklin and I could both read it.

IF YOU CALL LAW ENFORCEMENT, SHE DIES.
IF WE FEEL ANY HEAT, SHE DIES.

We were still rocked by those words, unable to shake the sickening feeling that by actually working the Ricci/Tyler case, we might have brought about Madison's death.

When Dave Stanford arrived at noon, we turned the kidnapper's note over to the FBI. Jacobi ordered a pie from Presto Pizza. Conklin pulled up a chair for Stanford, and we opened our files to him.

An hour later, it still all came down to one lead: *the Whittens in Boston and the Tylers in Pacific Heights had the Westwood Registry in common.*

We divvied up the client names that Mary Jordan had copied from the Register and started making phone calls. By the time the square box was in the round file, we were ready to go.

Conklin and Macklin went in Stanford's car. And Jacobi and I paired up, partners again for the day.

It was good seeing Jacobi's homely mug beside me, his expanding heft in the driver's seat.

"Pardon me for noticing, but you look like you've been keelhauled," he said.

"This goddamned case is making me *sick*. But since you mention it, Jacobi, I'm wondering about something. Did it ever occur to you to lie to me when I look like hell?"

"I don't think so, no."

"I guess that's one of the things I love about you."

"Ah, don't get mushy on me now." He grinned, took a hard right onto Lombard, and parked the car.

Over the next five hours, we tracked down and interviewed four Westwood Registry clients and their nannies. By the time the sun was lighting up a swath of pink cotton-candy clouds across the western sky, we had joined Macklin and the others back at the Hall.

It was a short meeting because our combined twenty-five man-hours had yielded nothing but praise for the Westwood Registry and their imported five-star nannies.

At around seven p.m. we told one another we'd pick it up again in the morning. I crossed Bryant, got my car out of the lot, and headed toward Potrero Hill.

Streetlights were winking on all across the city as I parked outside my home sweet home.

My hand was on the car-door handle when something eclipsed the light coming in from the passenger-side window, throwing me into shadow.

My heart hammered as I swung my head around and a dark figure came into view. It took a few seconds for my brain to put it all together. Even then, I doubted my eyes.

It was Joe.

Chapter 98

IT WAS JOE. It was *Joe.*

There was no one in the world I wanted to see more.

"How many times have I told you..." I said, heart racing, getting out of my car on the street side, slamming the door.

"Don't sneak up on an armed police officer?"

"Right. You've got something against telephones? Some kind of phobia?"

Joe grinned sheepishly at me from where he stood on the sidewalk. "Not even a hello? You're tough, Blondie."

"Ya think?"

I didn't feel tough, though. I felt depleted, vulnerable, close to tears, but I was determined not to show any of that. I scowled as I drummed my fingers on the hood of my car, but I couldn't help noticing how great Joe looked.

"I'm sorry. I took a chance," he said, his smile absolutely winning. "I just hoped to see you. So anyway, how have you been?"

"Never better," I lied. "You know. Busy."

"Sure, I know. You're all over the newspapers, Wonder Woman."

"More like, wonder if I'm ever going to solve a case," I said, laughing in spite of myself. "And you?" I said, warming up to Joe through and through. I stopped drumming my fingers and leaned a little bit toward him. "How's it going with you?"

"I've been busy, too."

"Well, I guess we're both keeping out of trouble." I locked the car, but I still didn't take a step toward him. I liked having that big hunk of metal between us. My Explorer as chaperone. Giving me a chance to think through what to do with Joe.

Joe grinned, said, "Yeah, sure, but what I *meant* was I've been busy trying to get a new life."

What was that? What had he just said?

My heart lurched and my knees started to give. I had a flash of insight—Joe looked and sounded great because he'd fallen in love with someone else. He'd dropped by because he couldn't tell me the news on the phone.

"I haven't wanted to call you until it was final," he said, his words dragging me back to the moment, "but I can't move the damned request through the system fast enough."

"What are you talking about?"

"I put in for a transfer to San Francisco, Lindsay."

Relief overwhelmed me. Tears filled my eyes to the brim as I stared at Joe. Images flashed, nothing I could help or stop, snatches of our months of high-flying romance, but it wasn't the romantic part that I remembered most. It was those homey moments, with Joe singing in the shower, me sneaking a peek in the mirror at his receding hairline when he didn't know I was looking. And the way he crouched over his cereal bowl as if someone might take it from him because he'd grown up in a house with six brothers and sisters, and none of them had the exclusive rights to anything. I thought about how Joe was the only person in my life who would just let me talk myself out and didn't expect me to be the strong one all the time. And okay, yeah, I flashed on the way he handled my body when we made love, making me seem small and weightless, and how safe I used to feel when I fell asleep in his arms.

"I've been given assurances but nothing definite..." His voice trailed off as he stared at me. "God, Lindsay," he said, "you have no idea how much I've missed you."

The wind coming off the bay blew the tears off my cheeks, and I was filled with gratitude for the unexpected gift of his visit and the night ahead. I still had an unopened bottle of Courvoisier in the liquor cabinet. And massage oil in the nightstand.... I thought about the delicious coolness of the air and how much heat Joe and I could turn up just lying together, before even reaching out our hands to touch.

"Why don't you come upstairs?" I finally said. "We don't have to talk on the street."

Something dark crossed his features as he came toward me and gently, deliberately, encircled my shoulders with his large hands.

"I want to come in," he said, "but I'll miss my flight. I just had to tell you, don't give up on me. Please."

Joe put his arms around me and pulled me to him. Instinctively, I stiffened, folded my arms over my chest, dropped my chin.

I didn't want to look up into his face. Didn't want to be charmed or swayed, because inside of three minutes, I'd ridden the entire Joe Molinari roller coaster.

Just over a week ago I'd steeled myself to break away from him because of this damned magic trick of his — now he's *here,* now he's *not.*

Nothing had changed!

I was furious. And I couldn't let Joe open me up only to let me down again. I looked at his face for the last time, and I pushed away from him.

"I'm sorry. Really. For a moment I thought you were someone else. You'd better go now," I sputtered. "Have a safe flight."

He was calling my name as I ran as fast as I could up the front steps of my building. I put my key in the lock and turned the knob in one movement. Then I slammed the door behind me and continued to run up the stairs. When I walked into my apartment, I had to go to the window, though.

I parted the curtain — just in time to see Joe's car drive away.

Chapter 99

MY PHONE STARTED RINGING before I dropped the curtain back across the glass. I knew Joe was calling from the car, and I had nothing to say to him.

I showered for a good long time, fifteen or twenty minutes under the spray. When I got out of the shower, the phone was still ringing. I ignored this call, too. Ditto the furiously blinking light on my answering machine and the tinny chime of my cell phone paging me from my jacket pocket.

I tossed my dinner in the microwave. I opened the Courvoisier and had poured out a tumblerful when my cell phone started up its damned ringing again.

I grabbed it out of my jacket pocket, growled, "Boxer," fully prepared to say, "Joe, leave me alone, okay?" I felt an inexplicable letdown when the voice in my ear was my partner's.

Rich said, "What's it take to get you to answer the phone, Lindsay?" He was annoyed with me and I didn't care.

"I was in the *shower*," I said. "As far as I know, that's still allowed. What's up?"

"There was another attack at the Blakely Arms."

The air went out of me.

"A homicide?"

"I'll let you know when I get there. I'm a couple of blocks away."

"Lock down the building. Every exit," I said. "No one leaves."

"I'm on it, Sergeant."

That's when I remembered the treadmill victim. *How could I have forgotten about him?*

"Rich, we forgot to check on Ben Wyatt."

"No, we didn't."

"You called the hospital?"

"Yeah."

"Is Wyatt awake?"

"He died two hours ago."

I told Rich I'd see him shortly and called Cindy — no answer. I snapped my phone closed, slapped it down on the kitchen counter so that I wouldn't throw it through a window. The microwave binged five times, telling me that dinner was ready.

"I'm going to lose my *mind!*" I shouted at the timer. "Going to fricking *lose* it."

Screw everything! I left the brandy untouched on the counter and my dinner in the microwave. I dressed quickly, buckled my shoulder holster, and threw on my blazer. I called Cindy and got her, told her what was happening.

Then I headed out to Townsend and Third.

By the time I strode into the lobby of the Blakely Arms, I was imagining my next conversation with Cindy. I wasn't going to take any guff from her, either.

She was going to move in with me until she had somewhere safe to live.

Chapter 100

CINDY WAS WAITING at the entrance to the Blakely Arms, her streaky blond curls blown every which way. Her lipstick looked *chewed* off.

"Jesus," she said. "Again? Is this really happening again?"

"Cindy," I said as we entered the lobby, "has there been any talk in the building? Any gossip? Any fingers pointed toward anyone?"

"Only thing I've heard is the nasty sound of people's nerves snapping."

We took the elevator together, and once again I was standing outside an apartment in the Freaky Arms that was bristling with uniformed cops.

Conklin nodded to Cindy, then introduced me to Aiden Blaustein. He was a tall white kid, about twenty-two, wearing black-on-black-on-black—torn jeans, Myst T-shirt, vest, a patched leather jacket, and choppy black hair that was short in back, falling across panicky brown eyes.

Conklin said, "Mr. Blaustein is the victim."

I heard Cindy say, "Cindy Thomas, the *Chronicle*. Would you spell your name for me?"

I exhaled. The kid was alive and unhurt but obviously scared half out of his mind.

"Can you tell me what happened?" I asked Blaustein.

"Fuck if I know! I went out for a six-pack around five," he said. "Ran into an old girlfriend and we got a bite. When I came home, my place had been totally *trashed*."

Conklin pushed open Blaustein's front door, and I walked inside the studio apartment, Cindy trailing behind me.

"Stay close—" I said.

"And don't touch anything," she finished.

The apartment looked like an electronics shop that had been trampled by a rhino on crack. I took a quick count of a desktop computer, three monitors, a stereo, and a forty-two-inch plasma-screen television that had been reduced to shards. Not stolen—destroyed! The desk was banged up, probably collateral damage.

Blaustein said, "It took me years to get all this together just the way I like it."

"What kind of work do you do?" Cindy asked.

"I design Web sites and games. This stuff cost probably twenty-five."

"Mr. Blaustein," I said, "when you went out, did you leave your door open?"

"I never leave my door open."

"Mr. Blaustein left the music on when he left the apartment," Rich said. His voice was matter-of-fact, but he didn't look at me.

"Did anyone complain to you about the music?" I asked.

"Today?"

"Ever," I said.

"I've gotten nasty phone calls from *one* person," Blaustein said.

"And who was that?"

"You mean, did he tell me his name? He didn't even say hello. His opening line was 'If you don't turn off that shit, I'm gonna kill you.' That was the first time. We've had these shouting matches a couple of times a week for a while now. All the time, cursing me. Cursing my children."

"You have kids?" I asked, unable to imagine it.

"No. He cursed any future children I might have."

"So what did you do?"

"Me? I know swearwords this dude never heard before. Thing is, I would've recognized the guy's voice if I'd heard it before. My ears are, like, good enough to be insured by Lloyd's of London. But I don't know him. And I know everyone who lives here. I even know *her*," he said, pointing to Cindy. "Third floor, right?"

"And you're saying no one else in the building complained about your sound system?"

"No, because *A,* I only work during the day, and *B,* we're allowed to play music until eleven p.m. Besides which, *C,* I don't play the music loud."

I sighed, unclipped my cell phone, and called the crime lab. I got the night-shift supervisor on the line and told him we needed him.

"You have someone you can stay with tonight?" Rich was asking Blaustein.

"Maybe."

"Well, you can't stay here. Your apartment's a crime scene for a while."

Blaustein looked around the wreck of his apartment, his young face sagging as he cataloged the destruction. "I wouldn't stay here tonight if you paid me."

Chapter 101

CINDY, RICH, AND I CONNECTED THE DOTS during the elevator ride down to the lobby.

"The dogs, the piano, the treadmill..." Rich was saying.

"The Web-meister's apartment..." Cindy added.

"It's all the same thing," I said. *"It's the noise."*

"Yep," Rich agreed. "Whoever this maniac is, noise makes him a little bit violent."

I said, "Rich, I'm sorry I snapped at you before. I had a bad day."

"Forget it, Lindsay. We close this case, we'll both feel better."

The elevator doors slid open, and we stepped out again into the lobby. At the moment, the space was packed with about two hundred freaked-out tenants, standing room only.

Cindy had her notepad out and moved toward the board president as Conklin used his body as a plow. I drafted behind him until we reached the reception desk.

Someone yelled, *"Quiet!"* and when the rumble died, I said, "I'm Sergeant Boxer. I don't have to tell you that there have been a series of disturbing incidents in this building—"

I waited out the heckling about the police not doing their jobs, then pushed on, saying that we were going to reinterview everyone and that no one was permitted to leave until we said it was okay.

A gray-haired man in his late sixties raised his hand, introducing himself as Andy Durbridge.

"Sergeant, I may have some useful information. I saw a man in the laundry room this afternoon whom I'd never seen before. He had what looked like a dog's bite marks on his arms."

"Can you describe this man?" I asked. I felt a new kind of tension in my gut. The good kind.

"He was about five six, muscular, brown hair going bald, in his thirties, I think. I looked around already, and I don't see him here."

"Thanks, Mr. Durbridge," I said. "Can anyone here pin *a name* on that description?"

A petite young woman with caramel-colored bedspring curls waded through the crowd until she reached me.

Her eyes were huge, and her skin was unnaturally pale—something was frightening her half to death.

"I'm Portia Fox," she said, her voice quavering. "Sergeant, may I speak with you privately?"

Chapter 102

I STEPPED OUTSIDE the Blakely Arms with Portia Fox.

"I think I know that man that Mr. Durbridge was refer-ring to," Ms. Fox told me. "He sounds like the guy who lives in my apartment during the daytime."

"Your roommate?"

"Not officially," the woman said, casting her eyes around. "He rents my *dining room*. I work during the day. He works at night. We're like ships crossing, you know?"

"It's *your* apartment, and this man is a sublet, is that what you're saying?"

She bobbed her head.

"What's his name?"

"Garry, two Rs, Tenning. That's what's printed on his checks."

"And where is Mr. Tenning now?" I asked.

"He's at his job with a construction company."

"He works in construction—at night?" I asked. "You have a cell phone number for him?"

"No. I used to see him every day for about a year in the Starbucks across the street. Sometimes we'd say hello, share a newspaper. He seemed nice, and when he asked if I knew of a place he could rent cheap . . . well, I needed the money."

This *child* had let a stranger move into her apartment. I wanted to shake her. I wanted to report her to her mother. Instead I asked, "When do you expect Mr. Tenning home?"

"Around eight thirty in the morning. Like I said, I've always left for work by the time he comes in, and now that I've got a coffeemaker at work, I don't go to Starbucks anymore."

"We're going to want to search your apartment."

"Absolutely," she said, pulling her key out of her handbag and offering it to me. "I really want you to. My God, what if I'm sharing my place with a murderer?"

Chapter 103

"JUST LIKE MINE," Cindy said as we walked into Portia Fox's apartment. The front door opened into a large living room facing the street—roomy, sunny, furnished in office-girl modern.

There was a galley-style kitchen off the living room, but where Cindy's dining room was open, Ms. Fox's had been boxed in with plasterboard walls and a hollow-core door.

"He stays in there," Ms. Fox told me.

"Any windows in his room?" I asked.

"No. He likes that. That's what sealed the deal."

It was too bad that the dining room had been walled off, because now we'd need either permission from Tenning to enter it or a search warrant. Even though Tenning wasn't on Fox's lease, he paid rent to her, and that gave him legal standing.

I put my hand on the doorknob to Tenning's room on the off chance that it would turn, but no surprise—the door was locked.

"You have a friend you can stay with tonight?" I asked Ms. Fox.

I put a patrolman outside the apartment door while Portia gathered up some things.

I gave Cindy my keys and told her to go to my place. She didn't even fight me.

Then Rich and I spent another two hours questioning the tenants of the Blakely Arms. We returned to the Hall at ten p.m.

As grim as the squad room was during the day, it was worse at night, the overhead lighting giving off a deadening white illumination. The place smelled of whatever food had been dumped into the trash cans during the day.

I threw a container of cold coffee into the garbage and turned on my computer as Rich followed suit. I called up a database, and although I was prepared for a long search for Garry Tenning's life story, everything we needed flashed onto my computer screen in minutes.

There was an outstanding warrant for Tenning's arrest. It was a small-potatoes charge of failure to appear in court for a traffic violation, but any arrest warrant was good enough to bring him in.

And there was more.

"Garry Tenning is employed by Conco Construction," Rich said. "Tenning could be patrolling any of a hundred job sites. We won't be able to locate him until Conco's office opens in the morning."

"He have a license to carry?" I asked.

Rich's fingers padded across his keyboard.

"Yep. Current and up-to-date."

Garry Tenning owned a gun.

Chapter 104

THE NEXT MORNING a heavy gray torrent came down on San Francisco like one of the forty days of the flood.

Conklin parked our squad car in a vacant construction zone on Townsend in front of Tower 2 of the Beacon, a residential high-rise with retail shops on the ground floor, including the Starbucks where Tenning and Fox had met.

On a clear day, we would have had a good view of both the front doors of the six-story redbrick Blakely Arms and the narrow footpath that ran from Townsend along the east side of the building, leading back to the courtyard and rear entrance.

But today's rain nearly obliterated our view through the windshield.

Inspectors Chi and McNeil were in the car behind us, also peering through the downpour. We were scanning the locale for a white man, five six with thinning brown hair, possibly wearing a uniform and probably packing a Colt revolver.

Unless he changed his pattern, Tenning would stop at

the Starbucks, then cross Townsend, arriving "home" sometime between 8:30 and 9:00.

We were guessing that Tenning would take the footpath to the rear entrance of the building, use a key to the back door, and take the fire stairs, avoiding tenants.

I watched through the blurred windows as pedestrians in trench coats, their faces shielded by black umbrellas, stopped at the Walgreens, dropped off laundry at Fanta dry cleaners, scurried for the Caltrain.

Rich and I were both dangerously sleep deprived, so when a man matching Tenning's description crossed Townsend, no coffee in hand, I couldn't be sure if he was our guy — or if I just wanted him to be our guy. *Really, really badly.*

"In the gray Windbreaker, black umbrella," I said.

A light changed to green, and the stream of traffic obscured our view long enough for the suspect to disappear in the crush of pedestrians on the far side of the street. I thought maybe he'd slipped down the Blakely Arms' back alley.

"Yeah. Yeah. I think so," Conklin said.

I called Chi, told him we were about to make our move. We let a couple of minutes pass — then Conklin and I put up our collars and made for the front entrance of the Blakely Arms.

We rode an elevator to the fifth floor. Then I used Portia Fox's key to unlock her front door without opening it.

I drew my gun.

When Chi and McNeil arrived, Conklin breached the door to Fox's apartment. The four of us stepped inside and checked each of the outer rooms before approaching Tenning's private space.

I put my ear to the flimsy door, heard a drawer closing,

shoes falling one after the other onto the uncarpeted floor.

I nodded to Conklin, and he knocked on Tenning's door.

"SFPD, Mr. Tenning. We have a warrant for your arrest."

"Get the hell out of here," an angry voice called back. "You don't have a warrant. I know my rights."

"Mr. Tenning, you parked your car in a fire zone, remember? August fifteenth of last year. You failed to appear in court."

"You want to arrest me for *that?*"

"Open up, Mr. Tenning."

The doorknob turned, and the door whined open. Tenning's look of annoyance changed to anger as he saw our guns pointed at his chest.

He slammed the door in our faces.

"Kick it in," I said.

Conklin kicked twice beside the knob assembly, and the door splintered, swung wide open.

We took cover on both sides of the door frame, but not before I saw Tenning standing ten feet away, bracing his back against the wall.

He was holding his Colt .38 in both hands, pointing it at us.

"You're not taking me in," he said. "I'm too tired, and I'm just not up for it."

Chapter 105

MY HEART RATE ROCKETED. Sweat ran down the inside of my shirt. I pivoted on my right foot so that I was standing square in the doorway.

I held my stance, legs apart, my Glock trained on Tenning. Even though I was wearing a vest, he could cap me with a head shot. And the paper-thin plasterboard walls wouldn't protect my team.

"Drop your weapon, asshole!" I shouted. "I'm one second away from drilling a hole through your heart."

"Four armed cops on a traffic warrant? That's a laugh! You think I'm stupid?"

"*You* are *stupid, Tenning,* if you want to die over a fifty-dollar ticket."

Tenning's eyes flicked from my weapon to the three other muzzles that were aimed at him. He muttered, "What a pain in the ass."

Then his gun thudded to the floor.

Instantly we swarmed into the small room. A chair tipped over, and a desktop crashed to the ground.

I kicked Tenning's gun toward the door as Conklin

spun him around. He threw him against the wall and cuffed him.

"You're under arrest for failure to appear," Conklin said, panting, "and for interfering with a police officer."

I read Tenning his rights. My voice was hoarse from the stress and the realization of what I'd just done.

"Good work, everyone," I said, feeling almost faint.

"You okay, Lindsay?" McNeil asked, putting a beefy hand on my shoulder.

"Yeah. Thanks, Cappy," I said, thinking how this arrest could have turned into a bloodbath—and still all we had on Tenning was a traffic violation.

I looked around his rented room, a ten-by-twelve box with a single bed, small pine dresser, two file cabinets that had once formed the base of his desk. The wide plank that had served as the desktop was on the floor, along with a computer and sheaves of scattered paper.

Something else had been dislodged during the fracas. A pipe had rolled out from under the bed.

It was about an inch and a half in diameter, eighteen inches long, with a ball joint screwed onto one end.

A two-part construction that looked like a club.

I stooped down to examine it closely.

There was a fine brown stain in the threads where the ball joint screwed onto the pipe. I drew Conklin's attention, and he stooped down beside me. Our eyes met for a second.

"Looks like this was used as a bludgeon," Conklin said.

Chapter 106

WE WERE IN INTERVIEW ROOM NUMBER TWO, the smaller of the interrogation rooms at the squad. Tenning sat at the table, facing the mirrored window. I sat across from him.

He was wearing a white T-shirt and jeans. He had his elbows on the table. His face was turned down so that the overhead light made a starburst pattern on his balding scalp.

He wasn't talking because he'd asked for a lawyer.

It would take about fifteen minutes for his request to filter down to the public defender's office. Then another fifteen minutes before some attorney would come up and find his or her client in our interrogation room.

Meanwhile, nothing Tenning said could be used against him.

"We got our warrant to search your premises," I told him. "That pipe contraption you used to kill Irene Wolkowski and Ben Wyatt? It's at the lab now. We'll have results before your PD shows up."

Tenning smirked. "So leave me the hell alone until he gets here, okay? Leave me alone with my thoughts."

"But I'm *interested* in your thoughts," I said to Tenning. "All those statistics on the papers I saw in your apartment. What's that about?"

"I'm writing a book, and I'd like to get back to it, actually."

Conklin came into the room carrying a battery-operated radio. Richie slammed the door hard, then turned on the radio. Loud static came through the speakers. He fiddled with the dials, turned the volume up.

He said to Tenning, "It's tough getting reception in here. I'd really like to know when the rain's going to let up."

I saw the alarm in Tenning's eyes as the static climbed to an electronic squeal. He watched Conklin thumb the radio dial, starting to sweat now.

"Hey," Tenning finally said, "could you turn that thing off?"

"In a minute, in a minute," Conklin said. He dialed up the volume, set the radio down on the table. "Can I get you some coffee, Garry? It's not Starbucks, but it's got all the caffeine you could ask for."

"Look," Tenning said, staring at the radio, his eyes jitterbugging inside his head, "you're not supposed to question me without my lawyer. You should put me in a holding cell."

"We're *not* questioning you, buddy," Conklin said. He picked up a metal chair, set it down with a loud bang right next to Tenning, and sat beside him.

"We're trying to *help* you. You want a lawyer—that's *fine*," Conklin said directly into Tenning's ear. "But you're giving up your opportunity to *confess* and cut yourself a *deal*. And that's okay with us, isn't it, Sergeant?"

"Fine with me," I said over the radio static. I fiddled

with the dial, found some '80s heavy metal, turned it up so that the discordant electronic twang almost vibrated the table.

"We're going to exhume the dogs you killed, Garry," I said over the music. "Match the teeth up with those wounds in your arm. And we're going to match the DNA from the blood on your club to your victims.

"And then Inspector Conklin and I are going to sign up for front-row seats for your execution in twenty years or so, unless of course you want to have me call the DA. See if we can get the death penalty off the table."

I looked at my watch. "I figure you've got about ten minutes to decide."

A band called Gross Receipts launched into its jarring rendition of "Brain Buster." Tenning shrank into a ball, wrapped his arms over his ears.

"*Stop. Stop.* Call off the lawyer. I'll tell you what happened. Just please, *shut that thing off.*"

Chapter 107

IT WAS STILL POURING when I parked behind Claire's SUV.

I cut across the street in the lashing rain, ran fifty yards to the front door of Susie's. I opened it to the ringing beat of steel drums and the smell of curried chicken.

I hung my coat on the rack inside the door, saw that Susie was coaxing her regulars into a limbo competition as the band tuned up.

Susie called to me, "Lind-say, get out of your wet shoes. You can do this, girl."

"No way, Suz." I laughed. "Don't forget, I've seen this before." I showed myself into the back room. I button-holed Lorraine and ordered a Corona.

Yuki waved to me from the back booth. Then Cindy looked up and grinned. I slid onto the banquette next to my best friend, Claire. It had been a while since we'd been out together as a group. *Way too long.*

When my beer came, Cindy proposed a toast to me for the takedown of Garry Tenning.

I laughed off the toast, saying, "I was extremely motivated, Cindy. I didn't want a roommate, and you were going to have to move in with me permanently if we didn't catch that bastard." Yuki and Claire hadn't heard the details, so I filled them in.

"He's 'writing' this book called *The Accounting,*" I told them. "It's subtitled *A Statistical Compendium of the Twentieth Century.*"

"Come on! He's writing about *everything* that happened in the last hundred years?" Yuki asked.

"Yeah, if you can call page after page of statistics 'writing'! Like, how much milk and grain were produced in each state in each year, how many kids went through grade school, the number of accidents involving kitchen appliances—"

"Jeez, you can Google that stuff," Yuki said.

"But Garry Tenning thinks *The Accounting* is his calling," I said as Lorraine dropped off beer and menus. "His paycheck came from being a night watchman at a construction site. Gave him 'time to think big thoughts,' he told us."

"How'd he even hear all those people and their noises in his closed-off little room?" asked Claire.

"Sound travels through the plumbing and the vents," Cindy said. "Comes out in weird places. Like, I can hear people singing through my bathroom air duct. Who are they? Where do they live? I don't know."

"I'm wondering if he doesn't have hyperacusis," said Claire.

"Come again?" I said.

"It's when the auditory processing center of the brain has a problem with noise perception," Claire told us over the racket in the back room and the clanking of dishware from the kitchen. "Sounds that others can barely hear are intolerable to the person who has hyperacusis."

"To what effect?" I asked.

"It would make the person feel isolated. You stir all that up with explosive-anger disorder and sociopathology, well, you get Garry Tenning."

"The Phantom of the Blakely Arms," Cindy said. "Just tell me there's no chance he's going to get out on bail."

"None," I said. "He confessed. We have the murder weapon. He's in and he's done."

"Well, if he really has this auditory disorder, Garry Tenning is going to go absolutely bug-nuts in prison," Yuki said as Lorraine brought our dinners.

"Hear! Hear!" said Cindy, pointing at her ears.

We dug in, swapped stories and worries, Claire telling us that her workload had doubled and that "We're having a farewell pour for Dr. G. tonight. He got a job offer he couldn't refuse. Somewhere in Ohio."

We toasted Dr. Germaniuk, and then Claire asked Yuki how she was feeling these days.

"I'm feeling a little bipolar," Yuki said, laughing. "Some days I think Fred-a-lito-lindo is going to convince the jury he's a legitimate psycho. The next morning I wake up absolutely sure I'm going to beat Mickey Sherman's pants off."

We got into a good-natured competition to name Claire's unborn baby, Cindy calling out, "Margarita, if she's a girl," and winning the next round for free.

Way too soon, dinner had been reduced to bones, coffee had been served, and hungry would-be diners were backed up in the doorway.

We tossed money at the check on the table and dared one another to rush into the rain. I was last out the door.

I drove toward Potrero Hill, absorbed by the rhythm of the wiper blades and the halos around oncoming headlights, finding that the vacuum of silence in the wake of the tumultuous day and the camaraderie with my friends was bringing me back down.

Joe wouldn't be sitting on my front steps when I got home.

Even Martha was still on vacation.

Thunder rumbled as I ran up the steps to my apartment. It was still raining when I went to bed alone.

Chapter 108

RICH AND I FRETTED at our desks the next morning, waiting for Mary Jordan to come through the gate. She arrived ten minutes late, looking rattled.

I invited the Westwood Registry's office manager to join us in the windowless cell we call the lunchroom. Rich pulled out a chair, and I made coffee—black, two sugars, the way she'd taken it when we'd seen her last.

"I've been praying for Madison," Jordan said, twisting her hands in her lap. There were prune-colored smudges under her eyes. "I feel in my heart that I've done what God would want me to do."

Her words stirred up a little eddy of apprehension in the pit of my stomach. "What did you do, Mary?"

"When Mr. Renfrew went out this morning, I opened the door to his office again. I did some more digging in there."

She hefted a large leatherlike handbag onto the table and removed a slate-blue, clothbound, old-fashioned accountant's ledger. It was labeled QUEENSBURY REGISTER.

"This is in Mr. Renfrew's handwriting," Jordan said,

pointing out the neat block letters and numerals. "It's a record of a business the Renfrews had in Montreal two years ago."

She opened the ledger to where a stiff rectangle of paper was wedged between two pages. Jordan took it out and flipped it over.

It was a photograph of a blond-haired boy of about four, with incredible blue-green eyes.

"Got a few minutes?" I asked Jordan.

She nodded her head.

I'd ridden up in the elevator with ADA Kathy Valoy, so I knew she was at her desk. I called her and explained about the Queensbury Register and the photo of the boy.

I said, "The Renfrews are hopscotching around the continent, opening and closing these registries. Kathy, I'm guessing *we're looking at a picture of another victim.*"

Kathy must have taken the stairs two at a time, because she appeared in the lunchroom doorway almost before I'd hung up the phone.

She asked Mary Jordan again if she'd dug up this information on her own, and again Jordan swore that she was not acting as our agent.

"I'll put in a call to Judge Murphy," Valoy said, staring at the photo, running both hands through her short black hair. "Let's see what I can do."

Minutes after we'd escorted Jordan out to the elevator, Kathy Valoy was back on the line. "I'm faxing you the search warrant right now."

Chapter 109

PAUL RENFREW ANSWERED our knock and swung open the door to the Westwood Registry. He was looking smart in a gray herringbone suit, crisp shirt, bow tie, and well-cut wheat-colored hair. His flyaway eyebrows lifted over his frameless lenses, and his smile broadened.

He seemed completely delighted to see us.

"Is it good news? Have you found Madison?" he asked.

Then the four uniformed officers climbing out of the property van caught his eye.

"We have a search warrant, Mr. Renfrew," I said.

Conklin signaled to the uniforms, and they clomped up the stairs with empty cartons in hand. They followed us down the long hallway to the Renfrews' office.

The workplace was orderly—a mug of tea was on the desk, a plate of half-eaten muffins resting beside a sheaf of open files.

"Why don't you tell us all about the Queensbury Register?" I asked Renfrew.

"Sit down, sit down," he said, indicating one of the two small sofas at right angles in the corner of the room. I took a seat, and Renfrew wheeled over his desk chair, all the while shooting concerned looks as Conklin directed the cops. They dropped file folders into boxes.

"Queensbury isn't a *secret*," Renfrew said. "I surely would have told you, but we closed that business because it failed."

He showed me his palms as if to say there was nothing up his sleeves.

"I'm just a terrible businessman in a lot of ways," Renfrew said.

"We need to talk to your wife," I said.

"Of course, of course, and she wants to talk to you. She's flying out from Zurich this evening."

Renfrew's open manner was so winning, I let him think he'd won. I smiled, then asked, "Do you know this child?"

Renfrew took the photo of the blond-haired, blue-green-eyed boy and scrutinized it.

"I don't recognize him. Should I?"

Conklin came over with a cop in tow and several blue-covered ledgers under his arm.

"Mr. Renfrew, you're prohibited from doing business for seventy-two hours, and that includes using your business phone. This is Officer Pat Noonan. His job is to make *sure* your business is closed until the warrant expires."

"He's staying here?"

"Until his relief comes in about eight hours. You know anything about football? Pat is a big fan of the Fighting Irish. Can talk your ear off if you let him."

Noonan smiled, but Renfrew's face went blank.

"And, Mr. Renfrew, don't try to leave town. That would look really bad."

Chapter 110

THE TENSION IN TRACCHIO'S OFFICE was almost unbearable. The insatiable media beast had been roaring at us nonstop for more than a week—on air, in the legit papers, and in supermarket tabloids. And we had no rebuttal.

A nineteen-year-old girl had been murdered. The child of a prominent family was missing and presumed dead.

It was a horrible feeling, and everyone in Tracchio's office took it personally.

"Boxer, lay it out for the chief," Jacobi instructed.

I gave Jacobi a look that said, *I know what to do, Lieutenant.*

I described what I had as I slapped each of our exhibits down on the desk. First, the copies of the kidnappers' notes. Next, the photos of three children—Erica Whitten, Madison Tyler, and the unknown boy with the blue-green eyes.

I said, "We don't know the identity of this little boy. Renfrew says he doesn't know him, but the child's picture was inside this ledger of his."

Rich placed the Queensbury Register on the desk next to two of the Westwood Registers.

I said, "We know the Renfrews ran three consecutive nanny businesses—one in Boston, the one they're running here, and an earlier service, the Queensbury Registry in Montreal.

"The Montreal police have a cold case," I continued. "A little boy named André Devereaux was taken from a playground near his home two years ago. *He had a nanny.*"

"She came from the Queensbury Registry?"

"Yes, sir," said Conklin. "I went over these ledgers. Between the rent, the cost of recruiting and importing girls from overseas, and the office and legal expenses—even with hefty placement fees—the Renfrews are *hemorrhaging money.*"

"And yet they keep working at it," I said. "And you have to wonder why. *Where's the payoff?*"

Lieutenant Macklin slid a photo printout over to Tracchio.

"This is André Devereaux," he said of the abducted Canadian child. "He looks to be the same boy as the one whose picture was found inside the Queensbury Register.

"André's nanny was Britt Osterman, a Swedish citizen. She was employed by the Queensbury Registry. A week after the abduction of André Devereaux, Britt Osterman was found dead in a ditch off a secondary road. Bullet to the head.

"The Queensbury Registry was owned by two Americans, called themselves John and Tina Langer," Macklin continued. "The Langers disappeared after the Devereaux/ Osterman abductions. The Canadian police e-mailed this photo of the Langers."

Macklin put another laser-print photo on Tracchio's desk, a man and a woman, white, late forties.

It was an informal snapshot taken at a holiday party. Beautiful room. Carved paneling. Men in dinner suits. Women in cocktail dresses.

Macklin's finger was pressed against the photo, nailing a brunette woman in her late forties, wearing a low-cut bronze-colored dress. She was leaning against a smiling man, who had his arm around her.

I could only guess at the woman's identity, but I knew the man. His hair was black, combed straight back. He had a goatee, and he didn't wear glasses.

But I'd looked into that face only a short time ago, and I knew him.

John Langer was Paul Renfrew.

Chapter 111

AT JUST AFTER NOON that day, Conklin and I were at Uncle's Café in Chinatown. We'd both ordered the Wednesday special: pot roast, mashed potatoes, and green beans. Conklin had made inroads into his potatoes, but I had no appetite for food.

We had a straight-on view through the plate glass across the gloomy street to a row of brick houses and the Westwood Registry.

A pregnant Chinese woman in pigtails refilled our cups of tea. When I looked through the window a nanosecond later, Paul Renfrew, as he was calling himself, was stepping out of his doorway and heading down the front steps.

"Lookit," I said, tapping Conklin's plate with my fork. My cell phone rang. It was Pat Noonan.

"Mr. Renfrew said he's going out for lunch. Coming back in an hour."

I doubted it.

Renfrew was going to run.

And he had no idea how many eyes were watching him.

Conklin paid the check, and I made calls to Stanford and Jacobi, zipped my jacket over my vest, and watched Renfrew's peppy march past herbal shops and souvenir stores as he headed toward the corner of Waverly and Clay.

Conklin and I got into our Crown Vic just as Renfrew unlocked the door of his midnight-blue BMW sedan. He looked over his shoulder, then entered his car and headed south.

Dave Stanford and his partner, Heather Thomson, pulled in behind Renfrew when he reached Sacramento Street while Jacobi and Macklin took a northern route toward Broadway. Our walkie-talkies bleeped and chattered as our team members called in their locations and that of the BMW, following, dropping back, weaving into place, and picking up the trail.

My heart was thudding at a good steady rate as we followed Paul Renfrew's run to wherever the hell he was taking us.

We crossed the Bay Bridge and drove east on Highway 24, finally entering Contra Costa County.

Conklin and I were in the lead car as Renfrew turned off Altarinda Road onto one of the smaller roadways in Orinda—a quiet, upscale town almost hidden within the folds of the surrounding hills.

I heard Jacobi on the car radio, telling the local police we were conducting a surveillance in an ongoing homicide investigation. Macklin requested backup from the state police and then called the Oakland PD and asked for chopper surveillance. The next voice I heard was Stanford's. He called for the big guns, an FBI response team.

"The SFPD just lost control of the takedown," I said to

Conklin as Renfrew's BMW slowed, then turned into the driveway of a white multigabled house with blue shutters.

Conklin drove past the house, casual-like.

We made a U-turn at the junction at the end of the road, came back up the street, and nosed our car into a tree-shaded spot across from where Renfrew had parked his blue BMW next to a black Honda minivan.

It couldn't be a coincidence.

That had to be the van used to abduct Madison Tyler and Paola Ricci.

Chapter 112

I RAN THE VAN'S PLATES on the car computer. I was thinking ahead to a search warrant, impounding the van, fanning a flame of hope that a speck of Paola Ricci's blood could be found inside a seam in the van's upholstery — real evidence to link the Renfrews to the abduction of Paola Ricci and Madison Tyler.

During the next hour, two perimeters were set up: The inner perimeter encircled the gabled house. The outer perimeter sealed off a two-block area around it.

There'd been no activity from the house, making me wonder what was going on inside. *Was Renfrew packing? Destroying records?*

It was almost four in the afternoon when five black SUVs rolled up the road. They parked on the sidewalk, perpendicular to the front of the gabled house.

Dave Stanford walked up to my car window. He handed me a bullhorn. His ponytail had been clipped to FBI standards, and the humor in his blue eyes was gone. Dave wasn't working undercover anymore.

He said, "We're calling the shots, Lindsay. But since

Renfrew knows you, try getting him to come out of the house."

Conklin turned the key in the ignition and we rolled out, crossing the street, coming to a stop in front of the Renfrew driveway. We were blocking in both the van and the BMW.

I took the bullhorn and stood behind my open car door. I called out, "*Paul Renfrew,* this is Sergeant Boxer. We have a warrant for your arrest on suspicion of homicide. Please come out slowly with your hands in the air."

My voice boomed out over the quiet suburban block. Birds took flight, drowning out the flutter of the chopper blades.

Conklin said, "Movement on the second floor."

Every muscle in my body tensed. My eyes flicked across the face of the house. I saw nothing, but my skin prickled. I could feel a gun pointed at me.

I lifted the bullhorn again—pressed the button.

"Mr. Renfrew, this is your last and best chance. There's enough artillery aimed at your house to reduce it to rubble. Don't make us use it."

The front door cracked open. Renfrew appeared in the shadows. He called out, *"I'm coming out. Don't shoot! Please, don't shoot!"*

I cut a look to my left to see how the FBI response team was reacting. A dozen or more M16 rifles were still aimed at the front door. I knew that on a roof somewhere, maybe a hundred feet away, a sniper had a Remington Model 700 with a high-powered scope trained on Renfrew's forehead.

"Step outside where we can see you," I called to the man in the doorway. "Good decision, Mr. Renfrew," I said. "Now, turn around and *back up* toward the sound of my voice."

Renfrew was standing under the pediment that defined the entryway to the house. Thirty feet of clipped green lawn stretched between us.

"I can't do that," Renfrew said in a weak, almost pleading voice. "If I go out there, she'll shoot me."

Chapter 113

RENFREW LOOKED FRIGHTENED, and he had reason to be. If he made a wrong move, his life expectancy was something under two seconds.

But he wasn't afraid of us.

"*Who* wants to shoot you?" I called out.

"My wife, Laura. She's upstairs with a semiautomatic. I can't get her to come out. I think she's going to try to stop me from surrendering."

This was a bad turn. If we wanted to learn what happened to Madison Tyler, we had to keep Paul Renfrew alive.

"Do *exactly* what I tell you!" I shouted. "Take off your jacket and toss it away from you.... Okay. Good. Now turn out your pants pockets."

The mic on my radio was open so that everyone on our channel could hear me.

"Unbuckle your belt, Mr. Renfrew. And drop your trousers."

Renfrew shot me a look, but he obeyed. The pants went down, his shirt covering him to the tops of his thighs.

"Now turn around slowly. Three hundred sixty degrees. Hold up your shirt so I can see your waist," I said as he struggled to comply. "Okay, you can pull up your pants."

He hurried to do so.

"Now I want you to hoist up your pants legs all the way to your knees."

"Nice legs for a guy," Conklin said to me over the roof of the car. "Now let's get him outta here."

I nodded, thinking that if the wife charged downstairs, she could blow Renfrew away through the open door.

I told Renfrew to release his pants legs, come out, and hug the wall of the house.

"If you do what I say, she can't get a bead on you," I said. "Keep both hands on the walls. Make your way around the south corner of the house. Then lie down. Interlace your hands behind your neck."

When Renfrew was on the ground, a black Suburban rolled up onto the lawn. Two FBI agents jumped out and cuffed him, patted him down.

They were folding him into the backseat of their vehicle when I heard glass breaking from the second floor of the gabled house. *Oh, shit.*

A woman's face appeared at the window.

She had a gun in her hand, and it was pressed against the temple of a little girl whose expression was frozen into a slack-mouthed stare.

The little girl was Madison Tyler.

The woman who held her captive was Tina Langer, aka Laura Renfrew, and she looked like a killer. Her face was furrowed with anger, but I didn't see a trace of fear.

She called out through the window, "The end of the

game is the most interesting part, isn't it, Sergeant Boxer? I want safe passage. Oh, I mean safe passage for me *and* Madison. That helicopter is a good place to start. Someone better give the pilot a ring. Get him to land on the lawn. Do it now. Right now.

"Oh, by the way... if anyone makes a move toward me, I'll shoot this little—"

I saw the black hole appear in her forehead before I heard the echoing crack of the Remington's report from the rooftop across the street.

Madison screamed as the woman calling herself Laura Renfrew stood framed in the window.

She released the little girl as she fell.

Chapter 114

WAS MADISON TYLER ALL RIGHT? That's all I was thinking as Conklin and I burst into the front bedroom, second floor. We didn't see the girl anywhere, though.

"Madison?" I called out, my voice high.

A single unmade bed was against the wall adjacent to the door. An open suitcase was on the bed, with girls' clothing tossed inside.

"Where are you, honey?" Rich Conklin called out as we approached the closet. "We're the police."

We reached the closet at the same time. "Madison, it's okay, sweetie," I said, turning the knob. "Nobody's going to hurt you."

I opened the door, saw a pile of clothing on the floor of the closet, moving in time with someone's breathing.

I stooped down, still afraid of what I might see. "Maddy," I said, "my name is Lindsay and I'm a police-woman. I'm here to take you home."

I nudged aside the pile of clothing on the closet floor until I finally saw the little girl. She was whimpering softly, hugging herself, rocking with her eyes closed.

Oh, God, thank you. It was Madison.

"It's okay, sweetheart," I said, my voice quavering. "Everything is going to be okay."

Madison opened her eyes, and I reached out my arms to her. She flung herself against me, and I held her tightly, putting my cheek to her hair.

I unclipped my cell phone and dialed a number I'd committed to memory. My hands were shaking so hard I had to try the number again.

My call was answered on the second ring.

"Mrs. Tyler, this is Lindsay Boxer. I'm with Inspector Conklin, and we have Madison." I put the phone up to Madison's face, and I whispered, "Say something to your mom."

Chapter 115

EARLY THAT EVENING, Conklin and I were at FBI headquarters on Golden Gate Avenue, thirteenth floor. We sat in a room with fifteen other agents and cops, watching on video monitors as Dave Stanford and his partner, Heather Thomson, interviewed Renfrew.

I sat beside Conklin, watching Stanford and Thomson dissecting the acts of terror committed by Paul Renfrew, aka John Langer, aka David Cornwall, aka *Josef Waller, the name he was given at birth.*

"He's lapping up the attention," I said to Conklin.

"It's a good thing I'm not in the box with him," Conklin said. "I couldn't handle this."

"This" was Waller's smugness and affability. Instead of smart-mouthing or showing defiance, Waller talked to Stanford and Thomson as if they were colleagues, as if he expected to have an ongoing relationship with them after he'd finished the clever telling of his story.

Macklin, Conklin, and I sat riveted to our chairs as Waller caressed their names: André Devereaux, Erica

Whitten, Madison Tyler, and a little girl named Dorothea Alvarez from Mexico City.

A child we hadn't known about.

A child who might still be alive.

While he sipped his coffee, Waller told Stanford and Thomson where the three missing children were living as sex toys in rich men's homes around the globe.

Waller said, "It was my wife's idea to import pretty European girls, place them as nannies with good families. Then find buyers for the children. I worked with the nannies. That was my job. My girls were proudest of the kids who were the most beautiful, intelligent, and gifted. And I encouraged the girls to tell me all about them."

"So the nannies fingered the children, but they never knew what you planned to do with them," Thomson said.

Renfrew smiled.

"How did you find your buyers?" Stanford asked.

"Word of mouth," Renfrew said. "Our clients were all men of wealth and quality, and I always felt the children were in good hands."

I wanted to throw up, but I gripped the arms of my chair, kept my eyes on the screen in front of me.

"You kept Madison for almost two weeks," Thomson said. "Seems kind of risky."

"We were waiting for a money transfer," Waller said regretfully. "A million five had been pledged for Madison, but the deal stalled. We had another offer, not as good, and then the original buyer came back into play. Those few extra days cost us everything."

"About the abduction of Madison and Paola," Stanford said, "so many people were in the park that day. It was broad daylight. A very impressive snatch, I have to say. I'd really like to know how you pulled that off."

"Ah, yes, but I have to tell you, it almost went all to hell," Waller said, exhaling loudly at the memory, seeming to think through how he wanted to tell the story.

"We drove the van to the Alta Plaza playground," said the psychopath in the gray herringbone suit.

"I asked Paola and Madison to come with us. See, the children trusted the nannies, and the nannies trusted *us*."

"Brilliant," said Stanford.

Renfrew nodded, and having received so much encouragement, he wanted to go on. "We told Paola and Madison that there had been an emergency at the Tyler house, that Elizabeth Tyler had taken a fall.

"I knocked out Madison with chloroform in the backseat, the precise plan we'd used with three other abductions. But Paola tried to grab the steering wheel. We could have all been killed. I had to take her down fast. What would you have done?" Renfrew asked Dave Stanford.

"I would have smothered you at birth," Stanford said. "I wish to God I could have done that."

Part Five

FRED-A-LITO-LINDO

Chapter 116

THE GALLERY WAS JAM-PACKED with law clerks, crime reporters, families of the victims, and dozens of people who were on the *Del Norte* when Alfred Brinkley had fired his fatal shots. Hushed voices rose to a rumble as two guards escorted Brinkley into the courtroom.

There he was!

The ferry shooter.

Mickey Sherman stood as Brinkley's cuffs and waist chains were removed. He pulled out a chair for his client, who asked him, "Am I going to get my chance?"

"I'm thinking about it," Sherman said to his client. "You sure about this, Fred?"

Brinkley nodded. "Do I look okay?"

"Yep. You look fine."

Mickey sat back and took a good look at his pale, skin-and-bones client with the patchy haircut, razor rash, and shiny suit hanging from a scarecrow frame.

General rule is that you don't put your client on the stand unless you're sucking swamp water, and even then, only when your client is credible and sympathetic enough to actually sway the jury.

Fred Brinkley was nerdy and dull.

On the other hand, what did they have to lose? The prosecution had eyewitness testimony, videotape, and a *confession.* So Sherman was kicking the idea around. Avoiding big risk versus a chance that Fred-a-lito-lindo could convince the jurors that the noise in his head was so *crushing,* he was out of his mind when he fired on those poor people....

Fred had a right to testify in his own defense, but Sherman thought he could dissuade him. He was still undecided as the jurors settled into the jury box and the judge took the bench. The bailiff called the court into session, and a blanket of expectant silence fell over the wood-paneled courtroom.

Judge Moore looked over the black rims of his thick glasses and asked, "Are you ready, Mr. Sherman?"

"Yes, Your Honor," Sherman said, standing up, fastening the middle button of his suit jacket. He spoke to his client. "Fred..."

Chapter 117

"AND SO AFTER YOUR SISTER'S ACCIDENT, you went to Napa State Hospital?" Sherman asked, noting that Fred was very much at ease on the witness stand. Better than he'd expected.

"Yes. I had myself committed. I was cracking up."

"I see. And were you medicated at Napa?"

"Sure, I was. Being sixteen is bad enough without having your little sister die in front of your eyes."

"So you were depressed because when your sister was hit by the boom and went overboard, you couldn't save her?"

"Your Honor," Yuki said, coming to her feet, "we have no objection to Mr. Sherman's testifying, but I think he should at least be sworn in."

"I'll ask another question," Sherman said, smiling, cool, just talking to his client. "Fred, did you hear voices in your head before your sister's accident?"

"No. I started hearing *him* after that."

"Fred, can you tell the jury who you're talking about?"

Brinkley clasped his hands across the top of his head,

sighed deeply as if describing the voice would bring it into being.

"See, there's more than one voice," Brinkley explained. "There's a woman's voice, kind of singsongy and whiny, but forget about *her*. There's this other voice, and he's really *angry*. Out-of-control, screaming-reaming angry. And he *runs* me."

"This is the voice that told you to shoot that day on the ferry?"

Brinkley nodded miserably. "He was yelling, '*Kill, kill, kill,*' and nothing else *mattered*. All I could hear was *him*. All I could do was what he *told* me. It was just *him*, and everything else was a horrible dream."

"Fred, would it be fair to say that you would never, *ever* have shot anyone if it were not for the voices that 'ran you' for the fifteen years following your sister's accident?" Sherman asked.

Sherman noticed that he'd lost his client's attention, that Fred was staring out over the gallery.

"That's my *mother*," Brinkley said with wonder in his voice. "That's my *mom!*"

Heads swiveled toward an attractive, light-skinned African American woman in her early fifties as she edged along a row of seats, smiled stiffly at her son, and sat down.

"Fred," Sherman said.

"Mom! I'm going to tell," Brinkley called out, his voice warbling with emotion, his expression twisted up in pain.

"Are you listening, Mom? Get ready for the truth! Mr. Sherman, you've got it wrong. You keep calling it an *accident*. Lily's death was *no accident!*"

Sherman turned to the judge, said matter-of-factly, "Your Honor, this is probably a good time for a break—"

Brinkley interrupted his lawyer, saying sharply, "I don't need a *break*. And frankly, I don't need your help anymore, Mr. Sherman."

Chapter 118

"YOUR HONOR," SHERMAN SAID evenly, doing his best to act as though his client hadn't gone off road and wasn't about to go airborne over a cliff, "I'd ask that Mr. Brinkley's testimony be stricken."

"On what grounds, Mr. Sherman?"

"I was having *sex* with her, Mom!" Brinkley shouted across the room. "We'd done it *before*. She was taking off her *top* when the boom came around—"

Someone in the gallery moaned, "Oh, my God."

"Your Honor," Sherman said, "this testimony is unresponsive."

Yuki jumped to her feet. "Your Honor, Mr. Sherman opened the door to his witness—*who is also his client!*"

Brinkley turned away from his mother, pinned the jurors to their seats with his intense, shifting stare.

"I swore to tell the truth," he said as chaos swamped the courtroom. Even the judge's gavel, banging hard enough to split the striker plate, was drowned out by the commotion. "And the truth is that I didn't lift a finger to save my sister," Brinkley said, spittle flying from his lips. "And I killed those people on the ferry because *he* told me, I'm a *very danger-ous man*."

Sherman sat down in his seat behind the defense table and calmly put folders into an accordion file.

Brinkley shouted, "That day on the ferry. I lined those people up in my gun sight and I pulled the trigger. *I could do it again.*"

The jurors were wide-eyed as Alfred Brinkley wiped tears from his sunken cheeks with the palms of his hands.

"*That's enough,* Mr. Brinkley," the judge barked.

"You people took an oath to do justice," Brinkley trumpeted, rhythmically gripping and slapping at his knees. "You have to execute me for what I did to those people. That's the only way to make sure that I'll never do it again. And if you don't give me the death penalty, I *promise* I'll be back."

Mickey Sherman put the accordion file into his shiny metal briefcase and snapped the locks. Closing up shop.

"Mr. Sherman," Judge Moore said, exasperation coloring his face a rich salmon pink, "do you have any more questions for your witness?"

"None that I can think of, Your Honor."

"Ms. Castellano? Do you wish to cross?"

There was nothing Yuki could say that would top Brinkley's own words: *If you don't give me the death penalty, I promise I'll be back.*

"I have no further questions, Your Honor," Yuki said.

But as the judge told Brinkley to stand down, a little red light started blinking in Yuki's mind.

Had Brinkley really just nailed his own coffin shut?

Or had he done more to convince the jury that he was insane than anything Mickey Sherman could have said or done?

Chapter 119

FRED BRINKLEY SAT ON THE HARD BED in his ten-by-six-foot cell on the tenth floor of the Hall of Justice.

There was noise all around him, the voices of the other prisoners, the squealing of the wheels on the meal cart, the clang of doors shutting, echoing along the row.

Brinkley's dinner was on a tray on his lap, and he ate the dry chicken breast and watery mashed potatoes and the hard roll, same as they gave him last night, chewing the food thoroughly but without pleasure.

He wiped his mouth with the brown paper napkin, balled it up until it was as tight and as round as a marble, and then dropped it right in the center of the plate.

Then he arranged the plastic utensils neatly to the side, got up from the bed, walked two paces, and slid the tray under the door.

He returned to his bunk bed and leaned back against the wall, his legs hanging over the side. From this position, he could see the sink-commode contraption to his left and the whole of the blank cinder-block wall across from him.

The wall was painted gray, graffiti scratched into the concrete in places, phone numbers and slang and gang names and symbols he didn't understand.

He began to count the cinder blocks in the wall across from him, traced the grouting in his mind as if the cement that glued the blocks together was a maze and the solution lay in the lines between the blocks.

Outside his cell, a guard took the tray. His badge read OZZIE QUINN.

"Time for your pills, Fred-o," Ozzie said.

Brinkley walked to the barred door, reached out his hand, and took the small paper cup holding his pills. The guard watched as Brinkley upended the contents into his mouth.

"Here ya go," Ozzie said, handing another paper cup through the bars, this one filled with water. He watched as Brinkley swallowed the pills.

"Ten minutes until lights-out," Ozzie said to Fred.

"Don't let the bedbugs bite," Fred said.

He returned to his mattress, leaned back against the wall again. He tried singing under his breath, *Ay, ay, ay, ay, Mama-cita-lindo.*

And then he gripped the edge of the bunk and launched himself, running headfirst into the cement-block wall.

Then he did it again.

Chapter 120

WHEN YUKI REENTERED the courtroom, her boss, Leonard Parisi, was sitting beside David Hale at the defense table. Yuki had called Len as soon as she'd heard about Brinkley's suicide attempt. But she hadn't expected to see him in court.

"Leonard, good to see you," she said, thinking, *Shit! Is he going to take over the case? Can he do that to me?*

"The jurors seem okay?" Parisi asked.

"So they told the judge. No one wants a mistrial. Mickey didn't even ask for a continuance."

"Good. I love that cocky bastard," Parisi muttered.

Across the aisle, Sherman was talking to his client. Brinkley's eyes were black-and-blue. There was a large gauze bandage taped across his forehead, and he was wearing a pale-blue cotton hospital gown over striped pajama bottoms.

Brinkley stared down at the table, plucking at his arm hair as Sherman talked, not looking up when the bailiff called out, "All rise."

The judge sat down, poured a glass of water, then asked Yuki if she was ready to close.

Yuki said that she was.

She advanced to the lectern, hearing the soft *ka-dum, ka-dum* of her pulse pounding in her ears. She cleared the slight croak in her throat, then greeted the jurors and launched into her summation.

"We're not here to decide whether or not Mr. Brinkley has psychological problems," Yuki said. "We *all* have problems, and some of us handle them better than others. Mr. Brinkley said he heard an angry voice in his head, and maybe he did.

"We can't know, and it doesn't matter.

"*Mental illness is not a license to kill,* Ladies and Gentlemen, and hearing voices in his head doesn't change the fact that Alfred Brinkley knew what he was doing was *wrong* when he executed four innocent people, including the most innocent—a nine-year-old boy.

"How do we know that Mr. Brinkley knew what he was doing was wrong?" she asked the jury. "Because his behavior, his *actions,* gave him away."

Yuki paused for effect, looked around the room. She noted Len Parisi's hulk and pinched expression, Brinkley's crazy glower—and she saw that the jurors were all tuned in, waiting for her to continue....

"Let's look at Mr. Brinkley's behavior," she said. "First, he carried a loaded Smith & Wesson Model 10 handgun onto the ferry.

"Then he waited for the ferry to *dock* so he wouldn't be stuck in the middle of the bay with no way out.

"These acts show *forethought. These acts show premeditation.*

"While the *Del Norte* was docking," Yuki said, keeping her eyes on the jury, "Alfred Brinkley took careful aim and unloaded his gun into five human beings. Then he *fled*. He ran like hell," Yuki said. "That's consciousness of guilt. *He knew what he did was wrong*.

"Mr. Brinkley evaded capture for two days before he turned himself in and confessed to the crimes—because *he knew what he'd done was wrong*.

"We may never know precisely what was in Mr. Brinkley's head on November first, but we know what he *did*.

"And we know for certain what Mr. Brinkley told us in his own words yesterday afternoon.

"He lined up the gun sight on his victims," Yuki said, making her hand into a gun and slowly swinging it around in a semicircle, shoulder high, sweeping the gallery and the jury box.

"He pulled the trigger *six times*. And he warned us that he's a *dangerous man*.

"Frankly, the best evidence of Mr. Brinkley's sanity is that he agreed with us on both points.

"He's guilty.

"And he should be given the maximum punishment allowed by law. Please give Mr. Brinkley what he asked for so that we never have to worry about him carrying a loaded firearm ever again."

Yuki felt flushed and excited when she sat down beside Len Parisi. He whispered, "Great close, Yuki. First class."

Chapter 121

MICKEY SHERMAN STOOD immediately. He faced the jury and told them a simple and tragic story as if he were speaking to his mother or his girlfriend.

"I've gotta tell you, folks," he said, "Fred Brinkley *meant* to fire his gun on those people, and he *did* it. We never denied it and we never will.

"So what was his motive?

"Did he have a gripe with any of the victims? Was this a stickup or drug deal gone bad? Did he shoot people in self-defense?

"No, no, no, and no.

"The police failed to find any rational reason why Fred Brinkley would have shot those people because there *was* no motive. And when there's zero motive for a crime, you're still left with the question — why?

"Fred Brinkley has schizoaffective disorder, which is an *illness,* like leukemia or multiple sclerosis. He didn't do anything wrong in order to get this illness. *He didn't even know he had it.*

"When Fred shot those people, he didn't know that

shooting them was wrong or even that those people were *real*. He told you. All he knew was that a loud, punishing voice inside his head was telling him to *kill*. And the only way he could get the voice to stop was to obey.

"But you don't have to take our word for it that Fred Brinkley is legally insane.

"Fred Brinkley has a history of mental illness going back fifteen years to when he was a patient in a mental institution.

"Dozens of witnesses have testified that they've heard Mr. Brinkley talking to television sets and singing to himself and slapping his forehead so hard that his handprint remained visible long afterward—that's how much he wanted to knock the voices out of his head.

"You've also heard from Dr. Sandy Friedman, a highly regarded clinical and forensic psychiatrist who examined Mr. Brinkley three times and diagnosed him with schizoaffective disorder," Sherman said, pacing now as he talked.

"Dr. Friedman told us that at the time of the crime, Fred Brinkley was in a psychotic, delusional state. He was suffering from a mental disease or defect that prevented him from conforming his conduct to the laws of society. That's the *definition* of legal insanity.

"This is not a lawyer-created illness," Sherman said. He walked two paces to the defense table and picked up a heavy hardcover book.

"*This* is the DSM-IV, the diagnostic bible of the psychiatric profession. You'll have it with you in the deliberation room so that you can read that schizoaffective disorder is a psychosis—a severe mental illness that drives the actions of the person who has it.

"My client is not admirable," he said. "We're not trying to pin a medal on him. But Fred Brinkley is *not* a *criminal*, and nothing in his past suggests otherwise. His conduct yesterday demonstrated his illness. *What sane man asks the jury to have him put to death?*"

Sherman went back to the defense table, put down the book, and sipped from his water glass before returning to the lectern.

"The evidence of insanity is overwhelming in this case. Fred Brinkley did not kill for love or hate or money or thrills. He is not evil. He's *sick*. And I'm asking you today to do the only fair thing.

"Find Fred Brinkley 'not guilty' by reason of insanity.

"And trust the system to keep the citizens safe from this man."

Chapter 122

"IT'S TOO BAD you guys didn't catch Yuki's close," Cindy said, putting an affectionate arm around Yuki, beaming across the table at Claire and myself. *"It was killer."*

"This would be your impartial journalistic point of view?" Yuki asked, coloring a little but smiling as she tucked her hair behind her ears.

"Hell, *no*." Cindy laughed. "This is *me* speaking. Off the record."

We were at MacBain's, across from the Hall, all four of us with our cell phones on the table. Sydney MacBain, our waitress and the owner's daughter, brought four glasses and two tall bottles of mineral water.

"Water, water, everywhere," Syd said. "What's up, ladies? This is a *bar,* ya know what I mean?"

I answered by pointing at each of us. "It's like this, Syd. Working. Working. Working." I pointed to Claire and said, *"Pregnant* and working."

Sydney laughed, congratulated Claire, took our orders, and headed to the kitchen.

"So does he hear voices?" I asked Yuki.

"Maybe. But a lot of people hear voices. Five to ten thousand in San Francisco alone. Probably a couple of them here in this *bar*. Don't see any of them shooting the place up. Fred Brinkley might very well hear voices. But that day? He knew what he was doing was wrong."

"The bastard," said Claire. "That's *me,* speaking *on* the record as a very biased eyewitness and victim."

That day flooded back to me with sickening clarity— the blood-slicked deck and the screaming passengers and how scared I was that Claire might die. I remembered hugging Willie and thanking God that Brinkley's last shot had missed him.

I asked Yuki, "You think the jury will vote to convict?"

"I dunno. They damn well *should*. If anyone deserves the needle, it's him," Yuki said as she vigorously salted her french frics, her hair swinging freely in front of her face so that none of us could read her cyes.

Chapter 123

IT WAS AFTER TWO in the afternoon, day three since the jury had begun their deliberation, when Yuki got the call. A shock went through her.

This was it.

She sat rigid in her seat for a moment, just blinking. Then she snapped out of it.

She paged Leonard and speed-dialed Claire, Cindy, and Lindsay, all of whom were within minutes of the courtroom. She got up from her desk, crossed the hall, and leaned into David's cubicle.

"They're back!"

David put down his tuna sandwich and followed Yuki to the elevator, which they then rode to the ground floor.

They crossed the main lobby, went through the leather-studded double doors to the second lobby, cleared security outside the courtroom, and after going through the glassed-in vestibule, took their places behind the table.

The courtroom had filled up as word spread. Court TV set up their cameras. Reporters from the local papers and stringers from the tabloids, wire services and national news, filled the back row. Cindy was on the aisle.

Yuki saw Claire and Lindsay sitting in the midsection, but she didn't see the defendant's mother, Elena Brinkley, anywhere.

Mickey Sherman came through the gate wearing a flattering dark-blue suit. He put his metallic briefcase down in front of him, nodded to Yuki, and made a phone call.

Yuki's phone rang. "Len," she said, reading his name off the caller ID, *there's a verdict."*

"I'm at my fucking cardiologist," Len told her. "Keep me posted."

The side door to the left of the bench opened, and the bailiff entered with Alfred Brinkley.

Chapter 124

BRINKLEY'S BANDAGE HAD BEEN removed, exposing a line of stitches running vertically from the middle of his forehead up through his hairline. The bruises around his eyes had faded to an overboiled egg-yolk color, yellowish-green.

The bailiff unlocked Brinkley's waist chains and handcuffs, and the defendant sat down beside his lawyer.

The door to the right of the jury box opened, and the twelve jurors and two alternates walked into the courtroom, dressed up, hair sprayed and styled, a sprinkling of jewelry on the women's hands and around their necks. They didn't look at Yuki and they didn't look at the defendant. In fact, they looked tense, as though they may have been fighting over the verdict until an hour ago.

The door behind the bench opened, and Judge Moore entered his courtroom. He cleaned his glasses as court was called into session, then said, "Mr. Foreman, I understand that the jury has a verdict?"

"We do, Your Honor."

"Would you please hand your verdict to the bailiff."

The foreman was a carpenter, with shoulder-length blond hair and nicotine-stained fingers. He looked keyed up as he gave a folded form to the bailiff, who brought it to the bench.

Judge Moore unfolded the form and looked at it. He asked the people in the gallery to please respect the protocol of the court and to not react outwardly when the verdict was read.

Yuki clasped her hands on the table before her. She could hear David Hale's breathing beside her, and for a fraction of a moment, she loved him.

Judge Moore began to read. "In the charge of murder in the first degree of Andrea Canello, the jury finds the defendant, Alfred Brinkley, 'not guilty' by reason of mental disease or defect."

A wave of nausea hit Yuki.

She sat back hard in her chair, barely hearing the judge's voice as each name was read, each charge a finding of "not guilty" by reason of insanity.

Yuki stood up as Claire and Lindsay came forward to be with her. They were standing around her as Brinkley was shackled, and they all saw how he looked at Yuki.

It was an odd look, part stare, part secret smile. Yuki didn't know what Brinkley intended by it, but she felt a prickling of hairs rising at the nape of her neck.

And then Brinkley spoke to her. "Good try, Ms. Castellano. Very good try. But don't you know? Someone's got to pay."

One of the guards gave Brinkley a shove, and after a last look at Yuki, he shuffled up the aisle between his keepers.

Sick or sane, Alfred Brinkley was going to be off the streets for a long time. Yuki knew that.

And still—she felt afraid.

Chapter 125

A MONTH LATER, Conklin and I were back in Alta Plaza Park, where it all began.

This time, we watched Henry Tyler come down the path toward us, his coat whipping around him in the wind. He reached out a hand to Conklin, gripping it hard, and then stretched his hand out to me.

"You've given us back our lives. I can't find words to thank you enough."

Tyler called out to his wife and to the little girl playing on a hexagonal construction, some new kind of jungle gym. Face brightening in surprise, Madison dropped down from the bars and ran toward us.

Henry Tyler swung his daughter up into his arms. Madison leaned over her father's shoulder and put an arm around my neck and Rich's, gathering us into a three-way hug.

"You're my favorite people," she said.

I was still smiling when Henry Tyler put Madison down and said to us, his face radiant, "We're all so grateful. Me, Liz, Maddy — we're your friends for life."

My eyes watered up a bit.

It was an excellent day to be a cop.

As Richie and I took the path back toward the car, we talked about the hell we have to go through to solve a case — the drudgery, the up close contact with killers and druggies, the false leads.

"And then," I said, "a case turns out like this and it's such a high."

Rich stopped walking, put his hand on my arm. "Let's stop here for a minute," he said.

I sat on one of the broad steps that had been warmed by the sun, and Rich got down beside me. I could see that there was something on his mind.

"Lindsay, I know you think I have a crush on you," he said, "but it's more than that. Believe me."

For the first time it hurt to look into Rich Conklin's handsome face. Thoughts of our grappling in a hotel in LA still made me squirm with embarrassment.

"Will you give us a chance?" he said. "Let me take you out to dinner. I'm not going to put any moves on you, Lindsay. I just want us to . . . ah . . ."

Rich read the feelings on my face and stopped talking. He shook his head, finally saying, "I'm going to shut up now."

I reached out and covered his hand with mine.

"I'm sorry," I said.

"Don't be. . . . Forget it, Lindsay. Forget I said anything, okay?" He tried to smile, almost pulled it off. "I'll deal with this in therapy for a few years."

"You're in *therapy?*"

"Would that help? No." He laughed. "I'm just, look, you know how I feel about you. That's almost enough."

It was a tough ride back to the Hall. Conversation was strained until we got a call to respond to a report of a dead body in the Tenderloin. We worked the case together past quitting time and into the next shift. And it was good, as if we'd been partners for years.

At just after nine p.m., I told Rich I'd see him in the morning. I'd just unlocked my car door when my cell phone rang.

"What now?" I muttered.

There was a crackle of static, then a deep, resonant voice came out of that phone, turning night back into day.

"I know not to surprise an armed police officer on her doorstep, Blondie. So...fair warning. I'm going to be in town this weekend. I have news. And I really want to see you."

Chapter 126

MY DOORBELL RANG at home.

I stabbed the intercom button, said, "I'm coming," and jogged down my stairs. Martha's dog sitter, Karen Triebel, was outside the front door. I gave her a hug and bent to enfold Sweet Martha in my arms.

"She really missed you, Lindsay," Karen said.

"Ya think?" I said, laughing as Martha whimpered and barked and knocked me completely off my feet. I just sat there on the threshold as Martha pinned down my shoulders and soaked my face with kisses.

"I'll be going now. I see that you two need to be alone," Karen called out, walking down the steps toward her old Volvo.

"Wait, Karen, come upstairs. I have a check for you."

"It's okay! I'll catch you next time," she said, disappearing into her car, tying the door closed with a piece of clothesline, cranking up the engine.

"Thank you!" I called out as she drove past me and waved. I returned my attention to my best girl.

"Do you know how much I love you?" I said into one of Martha's silky ears.

Apparently, she did.

I ran upstairs with her, put on my hat and coat, and changed into running shoes. We took to the streets we love so much, running down Nineteenth toward the Rec Center Park, where I flopped onto a bench and watched Martha doing her border-collie thing. She ran great joyous circles, herding other dogs and having a heck of a good time.

After a while, she came back to the bench and sat beside me, rested her head on my thigh, and looked up at me with her big brown eyes.

"Glad to be home, Boo? All vacationed out?"

We jogged at a slower pace back to my apartment, climbed the stairs. I fed Martha a big bowl of chow with gravy and got into the shower. By the time I'd toweled off and dried my hair, Martha was asleep on my bed.

She was completely out—eyelids flickering, jowls fluttering, paws moving in some great doggy dream.

She didn't even cock an eyelid open as I got all dressed up for my date with Joe.

Chapter 127

THE BIG 4 RESTAURANT is at the top of Nob Hill, across from Grace Cathedral. It was named for the four Central Pacific Railroad barons, is elegantly paneled in dark wood, staged with sumptuous lighting and flowers. And according to a dozen of the glossiest upmarket magazines, the Big 4 has one of the best chefs in town.

Our starters had been served—Joe was having apple-glazed foie gras, and I'd been seduced by the French butter pears with prosciutto. But I wasn't so taken with the setting and the view that I didn't see the shyness in Joe's eyes and also that he couldn't stop looking at me.

"I had a bunch of corny ideas," he said. "And don't ask me what they were, okay, Linds?"

"No, of course not." I grinned. "Not me." I pushed a morsel of hazelnut-encrusted goat cheese onto a forkful of pear, let it melt in my mouth.

"And after a lot of deep thought—no, really, Blondie, *really* deep thought—I figured something out, and I'm going to tell you about it."

I put my fork down and let the waiter take my plate away. "I want to hear."

"Okay," said Joe. "You know about my six sibs and all of us growing up in a row house in Queens. And how my dad was always away."

"Traveling salesman."

"Right. Fabrics and notions. He traveled up and down the East Coast and was away six days out of seven. Sometimes more. We all missed him a lot. But my mother missed him the most.

"He was her real happiness, and then one time he went missing," Joe told me. "He always called at night before we went to bed, but this time he didn't. So my mother called the state troopers, who located him the next day sleeping in his car up on a rack in an auto-repair shop outside of some small town in Tennessee."

"His car had broken down?"

"Yeah, and they didn't have cell phones back then, of course, and Christ, until we heard from him, you can't imagine what we went through. Thinking that his car was in a ditch underwater. Thinking he'd been shot in a gas-station holdup. Thinking that maybe he had another life."

I nodded. "Ah, Joe. I understand."

Joe paused, fiddled with his silverware, then started again. "My dad saw how much my mom was suffering, all of us, and he said he was going to quit his job. But he couldn't do that and still provide for us the way he wanted to. And then one day, when I was a sophomore in high school, he did quit. He was home for good."

Joe refilled our wineglasses, and we each took a sip while the waiter placed our entrées in front of us, but from the catch in Joe's throat and a feeling that was growing in me, I'd lost all desire to eat.

"What happened, Joe?"

"He stayed home. We left, one by one. My parents got by on less, and they were happier for it. They're still happy now. And I saw that and I promised myself I would never do to my family what my dad had done to us by being away.

"And then I looked at your face when I showed up last time and told you that I had a plane to catch. And everything you've been saying finally got to me.

"I saw that without meaning to, I'd done just what my dad had done. And so, Lindsay, this is the news I wanted to tell you. I'm home for good."

Chapter 128

I HELD JOE'S HAND as he told me that he'd relocated to San Francisco. I was listening, and I was watching Joe's face—full of love for me. But the wheels in my mind were spinning.

Joe and I had talked about what it would be like to be in the same place at the same time, and I'd broken up with him because it seemed we'd fallen into a way of *talking* more than forming a plan to make that talk come true.

Now, sitting so close to this man, I wondered if the problem had really been Joe's job or if we had conspired together to keep a safe distance from a relationship that had all the potential to be lasting and real.

Joe picked up his coffee spoon and put it in his handkerchief pocket—I'm pretty sure he thought that the spoon was his pair of reading glasses.

Then he fumbled in his jacket pocket and took out a jeweler's box, black velvet, about two inches on all sides.

"Something I want you to have, Lindsay."

He put aside the vase of sweetheart roses that was between us on the table and handed the box to me.

"Open it. Please."

"I don't think I can," I said.

"Just lift up the lid. There's a hinge at the back."

I laughed at his joke, but I'm pretty sure I stopped breathing as I did what he said. Inside, nestled on velvet, was a platinum ring with three large diamonds and a small one on each side sparkling up at me.

I finally sucked in my breath. I had to. The ring was a "gasper." And then I looked across the table into Joe's eyes. It was almost like gazing into my own, that's how well I knew him.

"I love you, Lindsay. Will you marry me? Will you be my wife?"

The waiter came by and, without saying a word, sailed off. I closed the box. It made a dull little click, and I could swear that the light in the room dimmed.

I swallowed hard, because I didn't know what to say. The wheels inside my head were still spinning, and I was feeling the room spin, too.

Joe and I had both been married.

And we'd both been divorced.

Was I ready to take a chance again?

"Linds?"

I finally choked out, "I love you, too, Joe, and I'm ... I'm overwhelmed." My voice cracked as I struggled to speak.

"I need some time to do some deep thinking of my own. I *need* to be absolutely sure. Will you hold on to this, please?" I said, pushing the small box back across the table.

"Let's see how we do for a while. Just doing normal things," I said to Joe. "The laundry. The movies. Weekends that don't end with you getting into a car and heading to the airport."

Disappointment was written all over Joe's face, and it hurt me terribly to see it. He seemed lost for a moment, then turned my hand over, put the box in my palm, and closed my fingers around it.

"You keep this, Lindsay. I'm not changing my mind. I'm committed to you no matter how much laundry we have to do. No matter how many times we wash the car and take out the garbage and even fight about whose turn it is to do whatever. I'm really looking forward to all of that." He grinned.

Unbelievable how the room brightened again.

Joe was smiling, holding both my hands in his. He said, "When you're ready, let me know so I can put this ring on your finger. And tell my folks that we're going to have a big Italian wedding."

Chapter 129

IT WAS JUNE 6 when Jacobi called me and Rich into his office. He looked really pissed off, as bad as I'd ever seen him.

"I got some bad news. Alfred Brinkley escaped," he said.

My jaw dropped.

Nobody got out of Atascadero. It was a mental institution for the criminally insane, and that meant it was a maximum-security *prison* more than a hospital.

"How'd it happen?" Conklin asked.

"Bashed his head against the wall of his cell..."

"Wasn't he medicated? And under a suicide watch?"

Jacobi shrugged. "Dunno. Anyway, the doc usually comes to the cell block, but this doc named Carter insists that the prisoner be brought to his office. Under guard. In the minimum-security wing."

"Oh, no," I said, seeing it happen without being told. "The guard had a gun."

Jacobi explained to Conklin, "The guards wear their guns only when moving prisoners from one wing to another. So the doc says Brinkley has to be unshackled so he can give him the neuro test."

Jacobi went on to say that Brinkley had grabbed a scalpel, disarmed the guard, snatched the gun. That he'd put on the doctor's clothes, used the guard's keys to get out, and took the doctor's car.

"It happened two hours ago," said Jacobi. "There's an APB out on Dr. Carter's blue Subaru Outback. L.L.Bean edition."

"Probably dumped the car by now," Conklin said.

"Yeah," said Jacobi. "I don't know what this is worth," he added, "but according to the warden, Brinkley was all cranked up about this serial killer he read about, Edmund Kemper."

Conklin nodded. "Killed about six young women, lived with his mother."

"That's the guy," said Jacobi. "One night he comes home from a date, and his mother says something like, 'Now I suppose you're going to bore me with what you've been doing all night.'"

"His mother knew about the killings?" I asked.

"No, Boxer, she did not," Jacobi said. "She was just a ballbreaker. Look, I was on the way to the can when the call came in, so may I finish the story, please?"

I grinned at him. "Carry on, boss."

"So anyway, Mother Kemper says, 'You're going to bore me, right?' So Edmund Kemper waits until she goes to bed and then cuts off her head and puts it on the fireplace mantel. And then he tells his mother's *head* all about his night out. The long version, I'm sure."

"That psycho turned himself in, I seem to remember," Conklin said. He cracked his knuckles, which is what Rich does when he's agitated.

I was rattled, too, at the idea of Brinkley at large, armed and seriously psychotic. I remembered the look on Brinkley's face when he'd stared Yuki down after his trial. He'd leered at her and said, "Someone's got to pay."

"Yeah, Kemper turned himself in. Thing is, when he confessed to the cops, he said that he'd actually killed those girls *instead* of his mother. Get it?" Jacobi was talking to me now. "He'd finally killed the right person."

"And the warden said that Kemper meant something to Alfred Brinkley?"

"Right," Jacobi said, standing, hoisting up his pants by the belt, making his way around Conklin's long legs toward the door. "Brinkley was obsessed with Edmund Kemper."

Chapter 130

FRED BRINKLEY WALKED ALONG Scott Street, looking straight ahead under the brim of Dr. Carter's baseball cap. He was watching the small peaks of sails in the marina at the end of the street, smelling the air coming off the bay.

His head still hurt, but the meds had quieted the voices so that he could *think*. He felt strong and *ka-pow-pow* powerful. The way he'd felt when he and Bucky had wasted those pitiful assholes on the ferry.

As he walked, he replayed the scene in Dr. Carter's office, how he'd exploded into action when the cuffs came off like he was some kind of superhero.

Touch your nose.

Touch your toes.

Grab the scalpel.

Put it to the doctor's jugular and ask the guard for his *gun.* Fred was laughing now, thinking about that stupid guard snarling at him as he taped the guard and the doctor naked together, shoved gauze into their mouths, and locked them inside the closet.

"You'll be back, freak."

Fred touched the gun inside the doctor's jacket pocket, thinking, *I'll be back, all right.*

I'm planning on it.

But not just yet.

The small stucco houses on Scott Street were set back twenty feet from the road, butted up close to one another like dairy cows at the trough. The house Fred was looking for was tan with dark-brown shutters and a one-car garage under the second-floor living space.

And there it was, with its crisp lawn and lemon tree, looking just like he remembered. The car was in the garage, and the garage door was open.

This was excellent. *Perfect timing, too.*

Fred Brinkley walked the twenty feet of asphalt driveway, then slipped inside the garage. He edged alongside the baby-blue '95 BMW convertible and took the cordless nail gun off the tool bench. He slammed in a cartridge, fired into the wall to make sure the tool was working. *Tha-wack.*

Then he walked up the short flight of stairs, turned the doorknob, and stepped onto the hardwood floor of the living room. He stood for a moment in front of the *shrine.*

Then he took the leather-bound photo albums off the highboy, grabbed the watercolor from the easel, and carried the load of stuff to the kitchen.

She was at the table, paying the bills. A small under-the-cabinet TV was on — *Trial Heat.*

The dark-haired woman turned her head as he entered the kitchen, her eyes going huge as she tried to comprehend.

"Hola, Mamacita," he said cheerfully. "It's me. And it's time for the *Fred and Elena Brinkley Show.*"

Chapter 131

"YOU SHOULDN'T BE HERE, Alfred," his mother said.

Fred put the nail gun down on the counter, locked the kitchen door behind him. Then he flipped through the photo albums, showed his mother the pictures of Lily in her baby carriage, Lily with Mommy. Lily in her tiny bathing suit.

Fred watched Elena's eyes widen as he took the water-color portrait of Lily, broke the glass against the counter.

"No!"

"Yes, Mama. Yes, sirree. *These are dirty pictures.* Filthy dirty."

He opened the dishwasher and stacked the albums on the lower rack, put the watercolor in the top rack. Slammed the dishwasher door on the complete photographic collection of his sainted sister and dialed the timer to five minutes.

Heard the machine begin to tick.

"Alfred," said his mother, starting to stand, "this isn't *funny.*"

Fred pushed her back down in her seat.

"The water isn't going to come on for five minutes. All I want is your undivided attention for *four,* and then I'll set your precious picture albums free."

Fred pulled out a chair and sat down right next to his mother. She gave him her "you're revolting" look, showing him the disdain that had made him hate her for his entire life.

"I didn't *finish* what I was telling you that day in court," he said.

"That day when you lied, you mean?" she said, twisting her head toward the ticking dishwasher, shooting a look to the bolted kitchen door.

Fred removed the guard's Beretta from his jacket pocket. Took off the safety.

"I want to talk to you, Mama."

"That's not loaded."

Fred smiled, then put a shot through the floor. His mother's face went gray.

"Put your arms on the table. Do it, Mom. You want those pictures back, right?"

Fred wrenched one of his mother's arms away from her side, put it on the table, put the head of the nail gun to her sleeve, and pulled the trigger.

Tha-wack. Nailed the other side of the cuff. *Tha-wack, tha-wack.*

"See? What did you think, Mama? That I was going to hurt you? I'm not a *madman,* you know."

After he secured the first sleeve, he nailed down the second one, his mother flinching with each thwack, looking like she was going to cry.

The knob on the dishwasher timer advanced a notch as a minute went by.

Tick, tick, tick.

"Give me my pictures, Fred. They're all I have…"

Fred put his mouth near his mother's ear. Spoke in a loud stage whisper. "I did lie in court, Mom, because I wanted to hurt you. Let you know how I feel *all the time*."

"I don't have time to listen to you," Elena Brinkley said, pulling her arms against the nails, fabric straining.

"But you do have time. Today is all about me. See?" he said, shooting the three-quarter-inch framing nails up the sides of her sleeves to her elbows.

Tha-wack, tha-wack, tha-wack.

"And the truth is that I *wanted* to do the dirty with Lily, and that was *your fault*, Mom. Because you made Lily into a little fuck-doll, with her tiny skirts and painted nails and high heels—on a twelve-year-old! What were you thinking? That she could look like that and no one would want to do her?"

The telephone rang, and Elena Brinkley turned her head longingly toward it. Fred got up from his seat and pulled the cord out of the wall. Then he lifted the knife block from the counter and put it down hard on the table. BLAM.

"Forget the phone. There's no one you need to talk to. I'm the most important person in your world."

"What are you *doing*, Alfred?"

"What do you think?" he said, taking out one of the long knives. "You think I'm going to cut your *tongue* out? What kind of psycho do you think I am?"

He laughed at the horror on his mother's face.

"So the thing is, Mommy, I saw Lily going down on this guy, Peter Ballantine, who worked at the marina."

"She did no such thing."

Brinkley began to swipe the eight-inch-long blade against the sharpener—a long Carborundum rod. It made a satisfying *whicking* sound.

"You should leave now. The police are looking—"

"I'm not *finished* yet. You're going to listen to me for the first time in your spiteful, miserable..."

Ticketa, ticketa, tick.

Inside his head, *he* was saying, *Kill her. Kill her.*

Fred put down the blade and wiped the sweat from his palms onto the sides of Dr. Carter's khakis. Picked up the knife again.

"As I was saying, Lily had been teasing me, Mom. Flouncing around, half naked, and then she puts her mouth on Ballantine's dick. *Forget the pictures and listen to me!*

"Lily and I took the day-sailer out, and we anchored far out where no one could see us — and Lily took off her top."

Liar. Coward. Blaming her.

"And so I reached out to her. Touched her little titties, and she looked at me like you're looking at me. Like I was dog shit."

"I don't want to hear this."

"You *will* hear it," Brinkley said, touching the blade gently to the crepey skin of his mother's neck. "So there she was in her little bitty half of a bathing suit, saying that *I* was the freak, saying, 'I'm going to tell Mom.'

"*Those were her last words,* Mama. 'I'm going to tell Mom.'

"When she turned away from me, I pulled back on the boom and gave it a shove. It smacked her across the back of the head, and—"

There was the sound of breaking glass, followed by a deafening concussion and a blaze of light.

Fred Brinkley thought that the world had blown apart.

Chapter 132

I WATCHED THROUGH the small kitchen window, horrified, as Brinkley held a sharpened knife to the side of his mother's neck.

We were armed and ready, but what we needed was a clear line of fire, and Mrs. Brinkley was blocking our shot. Breaking in through either door would give him time enough to kill her.

Fear for the woman climbed up my spine like a lit fuse. I wanted to scream.

Instead, I turned toward Ray Quevas, head of our SWAT team. He shook his head—no—again telling me he couldn't take the shot. This situation could go south in an instant no matter what we did, so when he asked for a green light on the flashbang, I said go ahead.

We pulled on our masks and goggles, and Ray jabbed the window with the launcher barrel, breaking the glass—and then he fired.

The grenade bounced off the far wall of the kitchen and exploded in an ear-shattering, blinding concussion.

The SWAT team had the door down in a half second,

and we were inside the smoke-filled room, wanting only one thing: to incapacitate Brinkley before he could get his head together and grab his gun.

I found Brinkley on the floor, facedown, legs under the table. I straddled his back and bent his arms behind him.

I had the cuffs nearly closed when he flipped over and shoved me off his body. He was as strong as a freaking bull. As I struggled to right myself, Brinkley grabbed his gun, which had fallen onto the floor.

Conklin ripped off his mask and yelled, *"Keep your hands where I can see them."*

It was a standoff.

Chapter 133

LASERS WERE POINTED at Brinkley's head—but he had two hands on his gun grip, prone position, his military training kicking in. His Beretta was aimed at Conklin. And Rich's gun was on Brinkley.

I was right there.

I screwed my Glock into Brinkley's first vertebra hard enough so that he could really feel it, and I yelled through my mask, *"Don't move. Don't you move an inch, or you're dead."*

Richie kicked out at Brinkley's gun, sending it skittering across the floor.

Six weapons were trained on Brinkley as I cuffed him, exhilaration flowing through me—even as Brinkley laughed at us.

I pulled off my mask, gagging a little from the phosphorus still in the air. I didn't know what Brinkley found so funny.

We had him. We had him alive.

"He was going to *kill* me!" Elena Brinkley shouted at Jacobi. "Can't you keep him locked up?"

"What happened?" Brinkley said, looking over his shoulder into my face.

"Remember me?" I said.

"Oh, yeah," he said. "My friend, Lindsay Boxer."

"Good. You're under arrest for your prison break," I said. "And I think we've got a reckless endangerment charge to go with it. Maybe attempted murder, too."

Behind me, Jacobi was telling Elena Brinkley to hold still and he'd get her out of that chair.

"You have the right to remain silent," I said to Brinkley.

Elena freed herself—ripped the fabric loose on one sleeve and, tearing open her blouse, released the other arm. She walked over to her son.

"I hate you," she said. "I wish they'd *killed* you." Then she struck him hard across the face.

"Wow. What a *shock,*" he said slyly to me.

"Anything you say can and will be used against you," I continued.

"Who are you kidding?" Brinkley shouted at me, seeming oblivious to the roomful of pumped-up law enforcement officers who'd love nothing more than to kick the crap out of him.

"All you can do is take me back to Atascadero," Brinkley said. "Nothing you charge me with is going to stick."

"Shut up, asshole," I said. "Be glad we aren't zipping you into a body bag."

"No, *you* shut up!" Brinkley said, shouting me down, spit flying, a hellish brightness lighting his face. "I'm not guilty of anything. You know that. I'm legally *insane.*"

And suddenly I heard Elena Brinkley scream, *"No!"*—as the dishwasher started its run.

THE 6TH ROUND

Epilogue
THE 9TH ROUND

Chapter 134

I DIDN'T KNOW the poor man laid out in his birthday suit on Claire's table, only that his death might have been related to the *Del Norte* tragedy. Claire had peeled and folded the patient's scalp down over his face like the cuff of a sock, sawed off the top of his skull, and removed his brain.

She now held a shard of a bullet in the grip of her thumb and forefinger.

"It passed through something first, sugar," Claire told me. "Piece of wood, maybe. Whatever it was, it reduced the velocity and the impact but finally killed this guy anyway."

I called Jacobi, who said, "You know what to do, Boxer. Tell him your story, but keep it simple."

Then he patched me through to the chief.

I told Tracchio the cut-to-the-chase version—that Wei Fong, a thirty-two-year-old construction worker, had just died that morning. That he'd been in a persistent vegetative state for months at Laguna Honda Hospital long term care because of an inoperable gunshot wound to the head.

That he'd taken that bullet the day Alfred Brinkley shot up the passengers on the *Del Norte*.

"Brinkley's sixth round went wild," I said. "And it finally killed Wei Fong."

"You've got my cell phone number?" Tracchio asked.

Claire's normally steady hands shook as she put the fragment into a glassine envelope. Then we both signed the paperwork, and I called the crime lab.

I heard Claire say to the dead man on her table, "Mr. Fong, honey, I know you can't hear me, but I want to say thank you."

Claire's Pathfinder was just outside the ambulance bay. I moved her dry cleaning from the passenger seat and strapped myself in.

"Kind of like in the Manson killings," I said as we pulled out onto Harriet Street. "*Two sets* of murders — Tate and LaBianca. *Two sets* of cops working side by side for weeks before they realized that the same perps did the killings. And now this. Macklin's crew working Wei Fong's case, coming up with nothing."

"Until he died. You've got everything?" Claire asked.

"Yep. I do."

The bullet fragment was resting within my breast pocket. The gun was inside a sealed paper bag between my feet. We took the 280 to Cesar Chavez, and from there went to Hunters Point Naval Shipyard, where the crime lab was housed inside a blue-and-gray concrete building.

Claire parked in a spot under one of the three Phoenix palms standing sentry in the parking lot.

I was out of the car an instant before Claire set the hand brake.

Chapter 135

THE CRIME LAB'S DIRECTOR, Jim Mudge, was waiting inside his office. He greeted us, took the paper bag from me, and then removed Alfred Brinkley's lethal friend "Bucky."

We followed Mudge down the hall, second door to the right, and into the indoor range, where he handed the gun to the firearms inspector, who fired the Smith & Wesson Model 10 handgun into a long water-filled chamber. He retrieved the .38 slug and handed it back to me.

"Here you are, Sarge. Good luck with it. Bring that bastard down."

Mudge escorted Claire and me down to a room at the end of the hallway. It had a horseshoe arrangement of tables and workstations, and a long wall of comparison microscopes.

A young woman greeted us, saying, "I'm Petra. Let's see what we've got."

I handed her the .38 slug from Alfred Brinkley's gun and the fragment Claire had removed from Mr. Fong's brain.

I sucked in my breath and mentally crossed my fingers.

Claire and I crowded around the technician as she set each of the rounds on a stage under the microscope.

Petra was smiling when she stepped back and said, "Take a look for yourselves."

It was clear even to me as I peered through the double eyepieces and compared the two slugs.

The striations, the lands and grooves on the fragment, were a match to the bullet just fired from Alfred Brinkley's gun.

The fragment was from the sixth shot, which Alfred Brinkley had fired at Claire's son Willie—and missed.

That same bullet was going to put Alfred Brinkley on trial again.

I turned to Claire but didn't know whether to slap her a high five or hug her—so I did first one, then the other.

"Got him," Claire said as we held each other.

Chapter 136

AN HOUR LATER, Rich Conklin and I stood in a gray room full of small tables and chairs at Atascadero. Brinkley entered, looking rosy-cheeked and well-fed.

I thought he might ask me to dance, he looked so glad to see me. "Do you miss me, Lindsay? Because I sure think about the last time I saw you!"

"Don't bother to sit down, Fred," I told him. "We're here to arrest you. We're charging you with homicide."

"You're joking. Kidding me, right?"

I gave him a smile I couldn't contain due to the fireworks display that was exploding inside my head. I was that happy. "Your big day on the *Del Norte*?"

"What about it?"

"That last shot you fired missed Willie Washburn. But it found another target. We're here to arrest you for killing Mr. Wei Fong, Fred-o. Charge of murder, second degree."

"No way, Lindsay," Brinkley said and shrugged indifferently. "You're saying I shot someone I didn't even see?"

"Yeah. You're a hell of a great shot."

"You're dreaming, little lady. I've been cleared of the

Del Norte shootings. I'm legally insane, remember? What you're talking about is double jeopardy."

"You weren't charged for Mr. Fong's death in your trial, Fred. This is a new case. New evidence. New jury. And I'm guessing that your mother is going to be a witness for the prosecution this time."

Brinkley's smile faded as I told him to turn around. I cuffed him, and Conklin read him his rights.

Rich and I marched Alfred Brinkley out to our car. As soon as we arranged him in the backseat behind the mesh screen, his face changed, took on a pained expression that made me think perhaps he'd gone back to an earlier time—when he was a boy and bad things started happening to him.

But Fred was singing by the time we got back to the freeway. *"Ay, ay, ay, ay, canta y no llores / Porque cantando se allegran / Cielito lindo."*

"Your mother teach you that, Fred?" I asked him. I knew the words to the old song: "Sing, don't cry. Because by singing, the sky lightens and becomes beautiful."

I glanced into the rearview mirror and was startled to see that Brinkley was looking at the reflection of my eyes. He stopped singing and said in a loud stage whisper, "Hey, Lindsay, you really think you've got me?"

About the Authors

JAMES PATTERSON is one of the best-known and best-selling writers of all time. He is the author of the two top-selling new detective series of the past decade: the Alex Cross novels and the Women's Murder Club series. He has written many other #1 bestsellers, including *Suzanne's Diary for Nicholas, Lifeguard, Honeymoon, Beach Road,* and *Judge & Jury.* He lives in Florida.

MAXINE PAETRO is a novelist and journalist. She is the co-author for *4th of July, The 5th Horseman,* and *7th Heaven.* She lives with her husband in New York.

Other Books

Against Medical Advice: A True Story (Hal Friedman)
Sail (Howard Roughan)
Sundays at Tiffany's (Gabrielle Charbonnet)
You've Been Warned (Howard Roughan)
The Quickie (Michael Ledwidge)
Step on a Crack (Michael Ledwidge)
Judge & Jury (Andrew Gross)
Beach Road (Peter de Jonge)
Lifeguard (Andrew Gross)
Honeymoon (Howard Roughan)
santaKid
Sam's Letters to Jennifer
The Lake House
The Jester (Andrew Gross)
The Beach House (Peter de Jonge)
Suzanne's Diary for Nicholas
Cradle and All
When the Wind Blows
Miracle on the 17th Green (Peter de Jonge)
Hide & Seek
The Midnight Club
Black Friday
(originally published as *Black Market*)
See How They Run
(originally published as *The Jericho Commandment*)
Season of the Machete
The Thomas Berryman Number

For more information about James Patterson's novels, visit
www.jamespatterson.com.

What if your imaginary friend
was your one true love?

Please turn this page

for a preview of

*Sundays
at Tiffany's*

by James Patterson

Available now.

PART ONE

*Once Upon
a Time in
New York*

One

EVERY DETAIL of those Sunday afternoons is locked in my memory, but instead of explaining me and Michael right off, I'll start with the world's best, most luscious, and possibly most sinful ice cream sundae, as served at the St. Regis Hotel in New York City.

It was always the same: two fist-sized scoops of coffee ice cream, swirled with a river of hot fudge sauce, the kind that gets thicker, gooey and chewy, when it hits the ice cream. On top of that, *real* whipped cream. Even at eight years old, I could tell the difference between real whipped cream and the fake-o nondairy product you squirt from a can.

Across from me at my table in the Astor Court was Michael: hands down the handsomest man I knew, or have *ever* known, for that matter. Also, the nicest, the kindest, and probably the wisest.

That day his bright green eyes watched me gaze at the sundae with undisguised delight as the white-coated waiter set it in front of me with tantalizing slowness.

For Michael, a clear glass bowl of melon balls and

lemon sherbet. His ability to deny himself the pleasure of a sundae was something my child's brain couldn't wrap itself around.

"Thanks so much," Michael said, adding extreme politeness to his list of enviable qualities.

To which the waiter said — not a word.

The Astor Court was the place to go for a fancy dessert at the St. Regis Hotel. That afternoon it was filled with important-looking people having important-looking conversations. In the background, two symphony-worthy violinists fiddled away as if this were Lincoln Center.

"Okay," Michael said. "Time to play the Jane-and-Michael game."

I clapped my hands together, my eyes lighting up.

Here's how it worked: One of us pointed to a table, and the other had to make up stuff about the people sitting there. The loser paid for dessert.

"Go," he said, pointing. I looked at the three teenage girls dressed in nearly identical pale yellow linen dresses.

Without hesitation, I said, "Debutantes. First season. Just graduated from high school. Maybe in Connecticut. Possibly—probably — Greenwich."

Michael tilted his head back and laughed. "You're definitely spending too much time around adults. Very good, though, Jane. Point for you."

"Okay," I said, gesturing toward another table. "That couple over there. The ones who look like the Cleavers in *Leave It to Beaver*. What's their story?"

The man was wearing a gray-and-blue-checked suit; the woman, a bright pink jacket with a green pleated skirt.

"Husband and wife from North Carolina," Michael rattled off easily. "Wealthy. Own a chain of tobacco shops.

He's here on business. She came to do some shopping. Now he's telling her that he wants a divorce."

"Oh," I said, looking down at the table. I let out a deep breath, then took another spoonful of sundae and let the rich flavors unfold in my mouth. "Yeah, I guess everyone gets divorced."

Michael bit his lip. "Oh. Wait, Jane. I got it all wrong. He's *not* asking for a divorce. He's telling her that he has a surprise — he's made arrangements for them to go on a cruise. To Europe on the *QE2*. It's their second honeymoon."

"That's a much better story," I said, smiling. "You get a point. Excellent."

I looked down at my plate and saw that somehow my ice cream sundae had completely vanished. As it always did.

Michael looked around the room dramatically. "Here's one you won't get," he said.

He pointed to a man and a woman just two tables away.

I looked over.

The woman was about forty years old, well dressed, and stunningly pretty. You might have taken her for a movie actress. She wore a bright red designer dress and matching shoes and had a big black pocketbook. Everything about her said, *Look at me!*

The man she was with was younger, pale, and very thin. He was wearing a blue blazer and a patterned silk ascot, which I don't think anyone was wearing even back *then*. He waved his arms enthusiastically as he spoke.

"That's not funny," I said, but I couldn't help grinning and rolling my eyes.

Because, of course, the couple was my mother, Vivienne Margaux, the famous Broadway producer, and that year's celebrity hairdresser, Jason. Jason, the hothouse flower, who didn't have time for a last name.

I looked over at them again. One thing was for sure: My mom *was* beautiful enough to be an actress herself. Once, when I asked her why she hadn't become one, she said, "Honey, I don't want to *ride* the train. I want to *drive* the train."

Every Sunday afternoon when Michael and I had dessert at the St. Regis, my mother and a friend had dessert and coffee there too. That way she could gossip or complain or conduct business but still keep an eye on me, without actually having to be *with* me.

After the St. Regis, we would cap off our Sundays at Tiffany's. My mother loved diamonds, wore them everywhere, collected them the way other people collect crystal unicorns, or those weird ceramic Japanese cats with the one paw in the air.

Of course I was okay, those Sundays, because I had Michael for company. Michael, who was my best friend in the world, maybe my only friend, when I was eight years old.

My imaginary friend.

Two

I SNUGGLED CLOSER to Michael at our table. "Want to know something?" I asked. "It's kind of a bummer."

"What?" he asked.

"I think I know what my mother and Jason are talking about. It's Howard. I think Vivienne's tired of him Out with the old, in with the new."

Howard was my stepfather, my mother's *third* husband. The third one I knew about, anyway.

Her first husband had been a tennis pro from Palm Beach. He'd lasted only a year.

Then had come Kenneth, my father. He'd done better than the tennis pro, lasting three years. He was really sweet, and I loved him, but he traveled a lot for business. Sometimes I felt as if he forgot about me. I'd heard my mother tell Jason that he'd been "spineless." She didn't know I'd overheard.

She'd said, "He was a good-looking jellyfish of a man who will never amount to anything."

Howard had been around for two years now. He never traveled on business and didn't seem to have a job, other than helping Vivienne. He massaged her feet when she was tired, checked that her food was salt-free, and made sure that our car and driver were absolutely always on time.

"Why do you think that?" Michael asked.

"Little things," I said. "Like Vivienne used to buy him stuff all the time. Fancy loafers from Paul Stuart and ties from Bergdorf Goodman's. But she hasn't given him anything in ages. And, last night, she ate at home. Alone. With me. Howard wasn't even there."

"Where was he?" Michael asked. I could see the sympathy and concern in his eyes.

"I don't know. When I asked Vivienne, she just said, 'Who knows and who cares?' " I imitated my mother's voice, then shook my head. "Okay," I said. "New topic. Guess what day Tuesday is."

Michael tapped his chin a few times. "No idea."

"C'mon. You know perfectly well. You *know,* Michael. This isn't funny."

"Valentine's Day?"

"Stop it!" I told him, kicking him gently under the table. He grinned. "You know what Tuesday is. You have to. It's my birthday!"

"Oh, yeah. Wow, you're getting *old,* Jane."

I nodded. "I think my mother is having a party for me."

"Hmm," Michael said.

"Well, anyway, I don't care about a party, really. What I really want is a real, live puppy."

Michael nodded.

"Cat got your —" I started to say but then stopped in midsentence.

Out of the corner of my eye, I saw Vivienne signing the check. In a minute she and Jason would be standing over our table, hustling me off. This Sunday at the St. Regis was coming to a close. It had been another wonderful afternoon for me and Michael.

"Here she comes, Michael," I whispered. "Look invisible."